Praise for *Break Out*

"The dialo... the love scen
sizzling ... reading *Break Out*,
sequel, *De...*

—Joyce Lamb, *USA Today*

An exci...ng roller-coast...

—Julia Rachel Barrett,
award-winning author of *Captured*

"Absolutely hysterical! Rico—you had me at 'bring me my goddamn spaceship.'"

—Dawn McClure, author of *Heaven Sent*

D1013533

DEADLY PURSUIT

NINA CROFT

St. Martin's Paperbacks

This is a work of fiction. All of the characters, organizations, and events portrayed in this novel are either products of the author's imagination or are used fictitiously.

DEADLY PURSUIT

Copyright © 2011 by Nicola Cleasby.
Bonus Scenes copyright © 2014 by Nicola Cleasby.

All rights reserved.

For information address St. Martin's Press, 175 Fifth Avenue, New York, NY 10010.

ISBN: 978-1-250-05810-2

Printed in the United States of America

Entangled Publishing edition in 2011
St. Martin's Paperbacks edition / November 2014

St. Martin's Paperbacks are published by St. Martin's Press, 175 Fifth Avenue, New York, NY 10010.

10 9 8 7 6 5 4 3 2 1

To Rob – who puts up with me filling the house with vampires, werewolves, and aliens!

PROLOGUE

Twenty-four years ago . . .

A pair of sickle moons hung low in the sky, casting a sullen, bloodred glow insufficient to light the path. High Priest Hezrai Fischer swore under his breath as he tripped over a tree root and only just prevented himself from sprawling on the ground in an undignified heap.

"How much farther?" he snapped.

"Not far now, my Lord," the guide murmured soothingly. He'd been saying the same words for the last hour.

The procession wound its way up a steep track cut into the side of a mountain, on what had to be the most godforsaken planet in the known universe. Sweat soaked his robes, and every muscle ached from the unusual exercise. "Why here?" he asked the world in general. "Why couldn't she have been born on some nice, civilized planet?"

"God works in mysterious ways," Sister Martha spoke softly from beside him.

Sanctimonious bitch.

He gritted his teeth as the words hovered on his lips. Personally, he would have preferred a little less mystery and a little more common sense from God. Biting back the blasphemous thought, he peered sideways at his companion. She had no trouble maneuvering up the track, seeming to glide in her long, black robes. Her face was serene; only the subdued glow in her eyes hinted at her excitement.

Left to him, he would have chosen a different companion. Sister Martha always set his teeth on edge, but as the head of the Order of the Sisters of Everlasting Life, it would be her duty to take charge of the new priestess. He hadn't been able to think of a reasonable excuse to leave her behind.

The old High Priestess had died a month ago. They had immediately sent out seekers to all the inhabited planets to search for the new vessel; a baby girl born at the exact moment of the old priestess's death into whom the holy spark would have been transferred.

"We're here, my Lord."

"Here" appeared to be a tiny hovel. Dull orange light flickered from the single window. He smoothed his robes, raised his fist, and banged on the wooden door.

It was opened seconds later by one of the brothers. "My Lord."

Hezrai nodded brusquely. "They know we are coming? Have they agreed?"

"Yes, my Lord. For one thousand credits, they will hand over the child."

"They should hand her over for the glory of the Church," he snarled.

"They are not members, my Lord, but they are poor."

Hezrai detected a slight censure in the words; he'd ignore it for now, but made a mental note of the man's name. "Let's get this over with."

He followed the brother into the house, though "house" was an ambitious word for the single, dingy space he found himself in. The air held a sharp, sour smell, and he wrinkled his nose.

At the far side of the room, a man and a woman huddled together. The man held a baby in his arms.

"At last," Hezrai muttered. Perhaps now they could finish this and get back to civilization. He stepped closer and peered down at the baby. He didn't know much about babies, and wasn't sure what he'd been expecting, but some sense of holiness at the very least.

"Are we sure?" It was an ugly little thing with a squashed-up face, strange gray eyes rimmed with black, and a shock of dark red hair. Hezrai frowned. "Has there ever been a red-haired priestess?"

"Not that I remember." Sister Martha sounded dubious. "Can we see the sign?"

The father parted the robes. A purple birthmark showed clearly on her right thigh in the perfect shape of a cross.

Hezrai nodded. It was enough for him. "Make the transfer."

He waited, tapping his foot on the rough wood floor, trying to ignore the stench of the place. Finally, the transaction was complete. "Right then . . . Get the girl and let's go."

The parents hadn't said a word, but now the mother stepped forward. "Please, I don't—"

Her husband halted her with a hand on her arm. "Shut up, Lisa. There'll be other babies."

"But—"

"We discussed this. What sort of life will she have here? With the Church, she'll have a chance—a future."

Hezrai rolled his eyes. Yeah right, they were doing this for the infant, nothing to do with the thousand credits. He really hoped the woman wasn't going to be difficult. Before she could say another word, the man edged closer to Hezrai and shoved the baby into his arms.

Hezrai almost dropped her.

Now he knew where the disgusting smell was coming from. Staring down into her red face, he tried to feel some religious awe. This was the High Priestess returned to them. She blinked at him from intense gray eyes, screwed up her features, and screamed, nearly bursting his eardrums.

"Quiet, child." He made an effort to keep his voice even. If he gave in to his natural inclination and screamed back, he suspected it would do more harm than good.

She shrieked louder.

"Give her to me." Sister Martha held out her arms.

A second ago, he would have gladly handed her over; now that the sister had asked, he tightened his grip and gritted his teeth. "The child belongs to God now. She must learn obedience."

The baby quieted, her lips curving into a sweet smile.

"There, you see, she just needs discipline."

She opened her mouth and regurgitated vile-smelling, half-digested milk down his pristine black robe.

That was the moment Hezrai Fischer began to hate the brand new High Priestess of the Church of Everlasting Life.

CHAPTER ONE

Where the hell am I?

Jon's head throbbed, and his mouth tasted like shit. He shivered with the cold, and then a moment later sweat broke out on his forehead. Nausea roiled in his gut. He rolled off the bed, landed on all fours, and retched. There was nothing in his stomach, but he stayed, head hanging low while he attempted to piece together what was going on.

He was alive, and he wasn't sure how he felt about that.

Shaking his head, he tried to clear the haze from his mind. Cryo always did that to him—left his reactions slow, his brain sluggish, and the rest of him feeling like crap.

What the hell had happened?

The last thing he remembered was being captured, and his last thought had been that he was as good as dead.

Instead, he was here. Wherever *here* was.

It appeared to be a cabin—not a cell, and he wasn't restrained in any way, but his inner senses were screaming danger. Closing his eyes, he breathed in and caught the lingering scent of death in the air. Not the usual sort of death that vanished with time, but the evil, blood-sucking sort that refused to lie down and rot.

A sharp buzz shrilled through the cabin, and his muscles tightened. He forced himself to relax as he realized someone was outside. At least they were being polite. He stumbled to his feet, swayed, and supported himself with one hand flat against the wall until his legs steadied beneath him.

Goddamn cryo made him as weak as a puppy. He was also naked, so he grabbed a small towel from the bed and wrapped it around his hips.

At the door, he peered into the monitor. A boy stood in the corridor, skinny with a shock of dark red hair and big gray eyes. Shifting from foot to foot, the boy had a bundle of clothes tucked under one arm and a tray of food balanced on the other. Jon's stomach rumbled.

After locating the panel beside the entrance, he pressed his palm to it and then stood aside as the door slid open and the boy shuffled inside. Up close, the kid only came as high as Jon's shoulder—he must have been fourteen, fifteen at the most. At the sight of Jon, his eyes widened and his gaze flicked down over Jon's body before fixing somewhere to the left of him.

"Yes?" he snapped when the boy said nothing.

His gaze shot back to Jon's face then settled on his chest. "I'm Al, the cabin boy."

"So?"

"I brought you some clothes. And we've had supper, but earlier you said you wouldn't eat with a piece of Collective . . ."

"I did?"

Christ, he couldn't remember, though it sounded like the sort of thing he would say. He hated the Collective. Not as much as he hated the Church, which wasn't really saying much. Forcing his mind to concentrate, he struggled to remember where he was and how he'd gotten here. A vague memory of the boy showing him to the cabin earlier flickered through his mind. There had been some talk about the Collective, but Jon had only just come around from the cryo, and he hadn't been paying attention.

Al nodded. "Anyway . . . I brought you some food. Though the captain says you're not a prisoner, and if you stay on this ship, you eat with her crew."

Jon had no intention of staying on this ship or eating with the crew. At the first opportunity, he was away. He had a bloody double-crossing bastard to hunt down and exterminate.

"If I'm not a prisoner, I presume I'm free to leave."

"I suppose so. Though you don't have a ship, and we're in deep space, and . . ." Al shrugged a shoulder. "There's a meeting tomorrow to decide what we should do. Skylar says the Collective will come after you."

"Skylar?"

"She's Collective, but she said she was your sister—that's why we broke you out of prison."

Well, that was really sweet, except he didn't have any family. So what the fuck was going on? "I don't have a sister."

Al shrugged again. "Anyway, you should stay here. The captain will keep you safe."

Jon didn't want anyone keeping him safe. He worked alone, and he liked it that way. But it occurred to him he should find out a little about where he was, who had gotten him out of prison, and what they wanted in return.

"Where is here?" he asked. "What is this ship?"

"It's the *El Cazador. El Cazador de la Sangre.*"

The name sounded vaguely familiar, but he couldn't place it. "What sort of shit name is that?"

"It's old Earth talk. It means The Blood Hunter."

Jon breathed in deep and caught again the lingering scent of death. "Well, that figures. Who's the captain?"

When he didn't get an answer, he frowned. "Well?"

Jon belatedly realized Al was still juggling the clothes and the tray and looked about to drop both.

"Sorry, I . . . here." The boy held out the tray, and the bundle tucked under his arm tumbled to the floor. Jon took the food and put it down on the small table by the bed, his stomach rumbling again as the smell drifted up. Then he picked up the clothes. Black pants and a black shirt. After dropping the towel, he pulled on the pants. They fit—just.

He glanced up. Al stood frozen in place, staring as though he'd never seen a man before. Jon ignored him and shrugged into the shirt. It was tight across the shoulders, but it would have to do. He'd chucked his own clothes down the recycling shoot to rid the cabin of the stench of prison.

Al was still gawking at him. Jon opened his mouth to tell the boy to piss off when a loud crash rang in his ears, and the ship jolted sideways. Jon reached instinctively for the kid, wrapping his arms around his skinny frame as the force hurled them both to the floor. He crashed, and Al landed on top of him.

Swearing, Jon gripped the boy's shoulders, intending to toss him away—he wasn't in the business of protecting anyone these days—but another shock hit the ship, flinging them across the room. This time they came to rest with Al beneath him.

Jon stayed still, waiting. Al wriggled, but he ignored the movement. If the ship was hit again, the floor was the best place to be.

"I can't breathe." Al's voice sounded weak, and a small hand pushed between them and shoved at Jon's chest.

After a minute when nothing else happened, Jon levered himself up slightly. For the first time he really studied the face beneath him. The gray eyes, the irises circled in black, thick dark lashes, creamy skin, the small nose, and the wide mouth. Something wasn't right. Closing his eyes, he breathed in and allowed his other senses to take over.

When he looked again, the new knowledge must have shown because Al's eyes widened with panic. He wriggled again, but Jon held him still, his hands curved around a narrow waist, then slowly he pressed his hips down. Shock held him immobile.

Al shoved hard. This time, Jon didn't try to hold on. Instead, he watched through narrowed eyes as Al twisted from beneath him and scrambled to his feet.

"I have to go find out what happened," he said, his tone breathless, and then he whirled around and vanished through the door.

Jon sat on the floor, his back against the wall and watched as the "boy" disappeared. Though one thing was for sure—Al was no boy. He remembered the curve of her waist, the feminine cradle of her hips. She was also older than the fourteen or fifteen years he'd first guessed. He shifted in the too tight pants, frowning at the unfamiliar ache in his groin. How long since he'd allowed a woman to affect him that way? Too many years to remember.

Jon dismissed the thought. It was none of his business what or who Al was. He just wanted off this ship. Preferably before someone blew it into tiny pieces. At least the attack appeared to have stopped. He pushed himself to his feet and glanced around the room.

"Shit." His dinner was on the floor.

Alex hurried down the narrow corridor, but when no more blasts hit the ship, she slowed her pace and finally came to a halt.

Holy Everlasting Life.

Her heart hammered against her rib cage, but she was aware it had nothing to do with the attack. This wasn't fear racing through her blood. Her body tingled where he had touched her, and the imprint of his fingers burned at her waist.

Closing her eyes, she pictured Jon as he'd appeared when she opened the door. His huge body hardly covered with that tiny little towel. She swallowed and wiped her clammy hands down her pants. Her breasts ached where she'd bound them tight beneath her shirt, and she had to resist the urge to run her hands across them. What would it feel like if Jon . . .

She was a sick woman. There was no doubt, and she should probably fall down to her knees and pray. But she didn't want to pray.

He'd been so big and bulky with massive sloping shoulders; a lean, ridged belly; and long, muscular legs. His shaggy hair had hung down to his shoulders, a blend of dark brown and gold, the colors repeated in the stubble on his chin and the smattering of dark hair over his chest.

And when he'd fallen on top of her he'd felt hard. Everywhere.

Had he known?

He'd certainly spotted something he hadn't been expecting, and she'd seen the shock in his eyes. They were beautiful eyes—amber with thick lashes. Skylar had told her Jon was an assassin, but nobody with eyes like that could be really bad.

Alex forced herself to move on. She needed to get to the bridge and find out who'd shot at them. Was it the Collective? Had they found Jon already?

When she reached the bridge, the rest of the crew was already there. Only the Trog was missing, but then he never left his engine rooms unless the captain gave him a direct order. No one paid Alex any attention as she edged into the room.

As usual, Janey was busy on her console, tapping away with her perfectly manicured fingernails, ignoring the rest of the crew. Daisy sat in the copilot's seat, watching the others and twirling a strand of long green hair that had come free of her ponytail.

Rico's long, lean, black-clad figure lounged in the pilot's chair. Skylar stood beside him, matching in her black jumpsuit and knee-high boots. One hand rested possessively on Rico's shoulder, the deep purple ring he had given her sparkling on her finger. They scanned the monitors while Tannis, the captain, paced the floor, her hands jammed in the pockets of her tight black pants.

"Great, just great," Tannis muttered, not quite under her breath.

Rico rolled his eyes. "Get over it."

Tannis scowled and jabbed a finger at Skylar. "You do know this is all your fault, don't you?"

"Yes," Skylar snapped. "And you know how I know? Because you already told me. Lots of times."

They glared at each other; both were tall women and they stood eye to eye. A quick stab of jealousy poked at Alex, and she tried to stretch a little taller. Not that it would do much good.

"Well, do something about it," Tannis growled.

"Like what?"

"Like do that mind-reading thing with your Collective friends and persuade them to hold off blowing us into pieces."

"I have."

"And?"

"And whoever that ship is out there"—Skylar waved a hand at the monitor—"they're not Collective."

Rico swiveled around in his chair. "What? Are you sure?"

"Believe me, if it was Collective, I'd know."

Alex believed her. Although they hadn't known it until earlier that day, Skylar was a member of the Collective.

Five hundred years ago, Meridian, a rare radioactive element, had been discovered on Trakis Seven. Meridian had the ability to bestow immortality on those lucky enough to afford its exorbitantly high price, and a new class had evolved—the Collective. Ultra-rich and powerful, they now controlled most of the civilized universe.

That Skylar was one of them still filled Alex with awe.

Tannis frowned. "If it's not the Collective, who the hell is it?"

"I have no clue." Skylar smiled sweetly. "But hey, you know what? It's just possible that everything is not my fault, after all. It's possible that maybe you've managed to piss off quite a few people all on your own."

Tannis pursed her lips but didn't answer. "Rico, you got any ideas?"

Rico grinned, revealing the tips of his sharp white fangs. "Could be one of thousands."

"Well, they seem to have gone quiet. Have we lost them?"

"No. There they are." Rico swung his chair back around and pointed at the monitor. Alex inched closer to peer around Skylar. The screen showed a ship, getting bigger by the second as it closed the distance between them.

"And it looks like they're coming back for another go at us. Hold on, everyone." Rico grabbed Skylar and pulled her onto his knee. "If we're going to die, we might as well die happy."

Alex spotted an empty seat, threw herself into it, and fastened the harness. Adrenaline surged through her bloodstream as she waited for the shot to hit them. They might all be going to die in a few seconds, and she had never felt so alive in her entire life.

The ship rocked as the blast struck *El Cazador*'s stern. For a few seconds, the lights flashed, and Alex's small hands gripped the armrests tightly, her muscles locked solid. Then the ship righted herself, the lights returned to normal, and Alex released her breath.

"Any damage?" Tannis asked.

"None." Rico studied the console in front of him. "At a guess, they're warning shots . . . so far."

"Yeah—but warning us of what?"

"They're trying to comm us," Janey said. "You want to hear what they have to say?"

Tannis shrugged. "Why not?"

"Just a moment—I'll put it on speaker."

"This is High Priest Hezrai Fischer."

As the familiar voice boomed around the bridge, Alex jumped and her breath caught in her throat. She would have fallen out of her chair if she hadn't been strapped in. After the initial shock, she froze in her seat and peeked surreptitiously around, sure everyone must be able to see her guilty secret. No one was paying her the slightest attention, and she forced her muscles to relax. Maybe it was nothing to do with her. Maybe it was a huge coincidence. She chewed on a fingernail.

Should she sneak away now? But she needed to know, and besides, she was on a space cruiser heading through deep space; where was she supposed to hide?

"*Dios*," Rico muttered, "it's the goddamn Church. Have I mentioned how much I hate the Church?"

"Frequently," Skylar said drily.

Five hundred years ago, the old religions had almost died out, but that had all changed with the discovery of Meridian. While not everyone could afford that route to immortality, everyone wanted to live forever, and the old beliefs had gained a new popularity. The Church of Everlasting Life offered the masses a cheaper, if less reliable, alternative with its promise of an afterlife in paradise. They had quickly grown until they were now the second most powerful faction in the civilized universe.

Tannis opened her comm link. "So, you're a High Priest. Big deal. Whatever it is you're selling, we don't want any."

Hezrai ignored the comment. He'd always been excellent at ignoring what he didn't want to hear. Which included most of what Alex had ever said. She and Hezrai had existed in a state of mutual animosity for as long as Alex remembered. Longer than that even, according to Sister Martha. Apparently, Alex had thrown up all over him at their first meeting and things had only gone downhill from there.

"We believe you have something that belongs to us," Hezrai said. "We want it back."

It?

Wasn't it just like him to refer to her as an *it*? He'd never seen her as a person.

Rico glanced around the room. "Anyone got a clue what he's talking about?"

"No idea," Tannis said.

Alex shrank into her chair and tried to make herself very, very small.

All her life, except for the last three months, she had done her duty, and it had been hard—every single day a struggle against the stultifying boredom of ritual and routine. Even so, this time away was only ever meant to be temporary. She'd always known she had to go back sometime. There were people who believed in her, had given up their lives for her. But was it so wrong to want to see a tiny bit of the world before she returned? To live a little?

Yes, she'd go back. But just not yet. There were things she had to do. An image of Jon's nearly naked body flashed across her mind—important things.

Tannis ran a hand through her short, dark hair. "They've obviously fucked up and confused us with someone else. We have shit that belongs to them." She was silent for a moment as she considered their options. "As far as I'm aware, at the present time we're not holding any illegal contraband on the ship. Why not let them board, check things out, and maybe they'll piss off and leave us alone."

Alex sneaked another peek around the room and found Skylar watching her, her inhuman violet eyes speculative as she studied Alex. Skylar raised one eyebrow, and Alex sank lower into her chair and tried to keep her expression blank.

Skylar swung around to face Tannis. "You really think that's a good idea?"

"You have a better one?"

"Well, it would be hard to come up with a worse one. You've a couple of GMs on board—including yourself, by the way—as well as someone the Church believes is a close relation to the antichrist."

Rico grinned. "Hey, sweetheart, you referring to me? Because I've got to tell you—me and the antichrist—we're not actually related."

"Tell that to the Church," Skylar suggested sweetly.

GMs stood for genetically modifieds. Captain Tannis and Daisy were both GMs—or abominations as the Church referred to anyone with less than a hundred percent human DNA. The Church had exterminated most of them in the Purge—one of the Church's policies Alex had never believed in. Unlike Hezrai, who pursued it with maniacal zeal.

Daisy was a plant hybrid—she was green and could photosynthesize, which Alex thought was amazingly cool. *El Cazador* had picked up her damaged escape pod in deep space after the experimental station where she'd lived had been attacked and her family exterminated by the Church.

Tannis's mixed heritage was a little less obvious but still clear in her skin—luminous ivory run through with shimmering iridescent lights—and her yellow reptilian eyes. No one knew where Tannis came from, except maybe Rico, and she never spoke of her past, but she also never made any attempt to hide her genetic modifications, which was unusual given the genocidal climate fostered by the Church.

As for Rico, well, the Church didn't have an official stance on vampires. In fact, Alex had never even believed they existed until she'd met Rico. It had been a shock—one she hadn't yet fully recovered from.

"We could make ourselves scarce," Tannis said, gesturing to Daisy and herself. "Janey can deal with this High Priest. They can poke around a bit, satisfy themselves we don't have whatever it is they think we have, and hopefully that will finish it."

Skylar glanced briefly at Alex. "No."

She knew.

She had to know. But how?

"No?" Tannis asked, her eyes narrowing so the pupils were no more than black slits.

Skylar stood her ground. "You made me security officer. This is a security issue, and I say no one from the Church is coming on board this ship."

Tannis released an exaggerated sigh. "So what *do* you suggest?"

Skylar turned back to Rico. "Get us out of here."

He grinned. "You know, I love it when you're bossy."

She rolled her eyes. "Just go."

CHAPTER TWO

After a few quick maneuvers, including one that still had Alex's pulse thrumming, they left the cruiser far behind. Alex loosened her grip on the arms of her seat and breathed again.

"Piece of cake," Rico murmured. "The Church hasn't a clue about evasive tactics."

Would that be the end of it?

Alex didn't know, mainly because she was still reeling with shock from the idea that Hezrai appeared to be making a genuine effort to find her. That was unexpected. Oh, she was important in the Church's hierarchy, and no doubt, it was embarrassing for them to have mislaid her. But she'd thought they'd keep quiet, and later she'd be able to slip back as though nothing had happened.

As usual, nobody was taking any notice of her, and she stood slowly and edged out of the room. But as she turned at the entrance, she sensed someone watching her. She was sure it was Skylar but kept her gaze fixed on the floor. Only when the door shut behind her did she break into a run and head for her cabin.

Once inside, she activated the lock, scooped up Mogg,

and sank onto the bed. She stroked the soft black fur of his head. Mogg was a cat, like they used to have on Earth. Well, sort of. They'd become friends on Trakis Twelve, and Alex had smuggled him aboard *El Cazador*—she wasn't sure how Rico would feel about animals on his ship. For all she knew, vampires might like cat blood—it wasn't a risk Alex was willing to take.

The buzzer sounded.

Glancing at the viewer by the bed, she wasn't surprised to see Skylar standing outside. Alex bit her lip, trying to decide whether to ignore her, but she couldn't stay locked in here forever.

She had to face this. The buzzer came again, and she sighed.

After tucking Mogg under the bed, she rose to her feet and placed her palm to the panel until the door opened.

When Alex had first met Skylar, she'd thought her the most beautiful woman ever, with her long blond hair and silver tube dress. Now without the wig and wearing a fitted black jumpsuit and a laser pistol strapped to her waist, she still looked beautiful, but strong and tough as well. She was everything Alex longed to be, and a familiar shaft of jealousy prodded her in the gut.

"Hey, kid," Skylar said. "You want to talk to me about anything?"

For a brief moment, she thought maybe Skylar didn't know, hadn't seen beneath her disguise. But the hope faded quickly under Skylar's pointed gaze.

"Well?" Skylar prompted.

Alex stepped aside and allowed her to enter, but Skylar stood just inside the room and glanced around the small space. "Shit, this place is a mess."

The room was a little untidy; Alex usually didn't notice. She loved her cabin the way it was—she'd never had her own private space before. Back at the Abbey, privacy had been an unknown concept. She'd had people to pick up after her, to clean her room, bring her food—her every need catered to. Everything kept perfect. It had driven her mad. Now she preferred a little chaos.

Shoving her hands in her pockets, she stuck out her lower lip in her favorite "cabin boy" expression. "I like it like this."

Skylar shrugged and opened her mouth to speak, but Mogg took that moment to stroll out from under the bed.

"Hey, you've got a cat." Skylar stretched out a hand. Mogg hissed and leaped lightly onto the bed, where he sat watching them, his tail twitching.

Skylar cleared the clothes off the single chair and sat. "Come on, Al. Talk to me."

Alex sighed and sank down onto the bed, stroking Mogg as she thought of what to say. "How did you know?"

"I knew you were a girl almost from the moment we met. I think you've only fooled the others because you've perfected the art of being invisible."

She thought about what Skylar had said and a faint glimmer of hope awoke inside her. "So you don't actually know *who* I am."

"Sorry, kid. You're Alexia, High Priestess of the Church of Everlasting Life."

The glimmer evaporated.

"It came to me tonight," Skylar continued. "I knew you looked familiar. I'd seen the comms—they're all over the waves."

"The comms?"

"Apparently you went missing, and they want you back. The comms hinted that you'd been kidnapped though. Anyway, there's a picture—which doesn't look a lot like you— and they're offering a big reward. Tonight, it clicked. Rico said something about your reasons for hiding being your own—"

Shock tightened her gut, and her gaze flew to Skylar's face. "Rico knows?"

"Not who you are, but what you are."

"Has he known all along?"

"No. You might be a good actor, but you slip occasionally—he got interested."

"Oh."

It was over. Skylar was her friend. She might have been willing to keep her secret, but not the vampire. "Are you going to tell him?"

"Look, kid—"

Annoyance flicked her nerve endings. "I'm not a kid. I don't think I've ever been a kid."

Skylar ran her gaze over Alex, who managed to hold herself from squirming under the intense scrutiny. When she reached Alex's eyes, her brows drew together. "No. I can see that when I look—you have old eyes. Just how old are you?"

"Twenty-four."

"Holy Meridian. Really? I placed you no more than fourteen—maybe fifteen."

She gritted her teeth. "Yes, really."

Skylar was still staring as though she didn't believe her. "I'm little, okay. It makes me look younger."

"It certainly does. You must be a *very* good actor."

"I've had to be." Alex didn't try to hide the bitterness in her voice. All her life she'd been acting, pretending to be the dutiful priestess while everything screamed in denial. Now she was heading back, and it was the end of her dreams.

It wasn't fair.

She bit the words back, kept them inside—that was a child's view of life, and she wasn't a child.

"Don't worry—I was always planning to go back. Now you can take me and get the reward. At least the captain will be happy." Everyone knew Tannis was obsessed with getting enough credits together to pay for the Meridian treatment. Alex attempted a mirthless grin. It was nice to know she would be of some use. Not.

"Do you want to go back?" Skylar asked.

She shrugged. "I told you, I'd always planned to. I just wanted a little more time."

"So what happened? I take it you ran away—but why?"

Alex leaped to her feet and paced the room. "One day, it all got to be too much. I couldn't stand it anymore. The boring routines, the endless rituals, the people. They were all so pompous and good and boring. And I'd never seen anything of the world, and I never would." She halted in front of Skylar. "Have you ever felt like you'd explode if you didn't do something . . . anything?"

Skylar nodded slowly. "Yeah, I've felt like that." They sat in silence for a minute. "You know, we're not so different—I've run away as well."

Alex realized she meant from the Collective. Maybe Skylar did understand. "So what are you going to do?"

"It's not up to me. I won't make you go back—it's your decision. You want more time—take as much as you like."

Hope blossomed inside her, and her lips tugged up at the corners.

"But—"

Alex's smile faded. "But?"

"Chances are, your friends *will* come after us again. They must want you back badly."

Alex chewed on her fingernails. "I don't understand that bit. Honestly."

"Perhaps because you're their High Priestess," Skylar said gently. "They love you."

"Some of them maybe. Sister Martha. But Hezrai hates me."

"The High Priest we spoke to?"

"Yeah, he's a pompous old goat."

"Well, he cares enough to come after you. All I'm saying is you need to come clean. Tell Tannis and Rico who you are, so they can keep away from the Church."

"They'll send me back."

"They won't."

"The captain will want the reward."

"Tannis likes money, but once you're crew she won't give you up. You know she'd die keeping her crew safe."

"Maybe." Alex felt a small resurgence of hope. Skylar was right—the captain took care of her people. But while Tannis might be the captain, Rico actually owned *El Cazador*. "What about the vampire?"

"Rico?" A small smile curved Skylar's lips, and she stroked the purple stone on her finger. "He won't be a problem."

Alex knew Rico had given Skylar the ring. They thought they were in love. Well, as much in love as a vampire and a member of the Collective could be. Alex could see the attraction—sort of. Rico was gorgeous, with his long, lean body and midnight dark hair, but he was also a blood-sucking monster.

Still, Alex wasn't sure she believed in love. She'd seen no evidence of its existence during her short life. Her own family had sold her to the Church for a measly thousand credits, and while the Church preached incessantly about love, the inner council was actually riddled with political intrigue and petty power squabbles. No, she didn't believe in love. But she was glad Skylar did if it meant Alex could stay on *El Cazador*.

And it would be good to stop acting for a while. Her mind flashed back to Jon. Maybe he'd like her if she appeared more womanly. She could stop wrapping up her breasts, which was becoming increasingly irksome. And maybe Janey would help her. Janey knew how to dress and wear makeup . . .

"What's going through your mind?"

Alex jumped a little at Skylar's question and gave a casual shrug. "Nothing."

"Hmm. So will you tell them?"

"I suppose so." She took a deep breath. "When?"

"What's wrong with now?"

Alex could have given her a load of reasons why now was not a good time. Why she needed about a year to prepare herself for the confrontation. Instead, she shoved her hands in her pockets. "Let's go."

Rico and the captain were still on the bridge when they got back. Alex's stomach churned with nausea. What if Skylar was wrong? What if the captain hated Alex for lying to them? For bringing the Church after them?

She might even throw Alex out the airlock.

Tannis raised an eyebrow in query. "What is it?"

"Al has something to tell you both."

Rico rose smoothly to his feet. He reminded Alex of some sleek predator when he moved, and she had to keep her feet glued to the floor to stop herself retreating. She watched, fascinated, as he came to a halt in front of them and leaned in close to Skylar.

"Can't it wait?" he murmured. "The ship's on autopilot, Daisy's got the next watch, and I had plans for this evening." He kissed Skylar's neck. "Interesting plans."

Alex shivered at the dark promise in his voice—glad it wasn't aimed at her.

Skylar stepped away. "Later. First . . ." Turning around, she gestured to Alex. "Al?"

Alex shuffled her feet and cleared her throat as three sets of eyes focused on her. She opened her mouth to speak when everyone's gaze swung away to stare over her left shoulder.

"Shit," a deep, gravelly voice said. "I thought I could smell something rotten on this ship. And here it is."

"Holy crap," Tannis said. "If it isn't 'little' Jonny come to visit."

A low rumble vibrated the air. Alex realized the sound was coming from Rico, and a primeval terror stirred deep inside her. This was what she had feared all along. Darkness glittered in the vampire's eyes, and his lips curled back to reveal razor-sharp white fangs.

Tension spiraled until it was a tangible force, and Alex was sure it would snap.

Skylar reached out a hand and rested it on Rico's arm. For a moment, it made no difference, and then the tension drained from him. His muscles relaxed, and a lazy smile replaced the snarl.

"Christ," he drawled. "Who let the fucking dog on board?"

Alex turned slowly. Jon lounged in the open doorway, arms folded across his chest. He wore the black pants and shirt she had given him. The shirt was open. From the look of it, it wasn't a fashion statement, he was just too broad across the shoulders for the sides to meet. The opening revealed a vast expanse of golden skin over the smooth swell of muscle, and a slow-burning heat started in the pit of her stomach. She forced herself to look away.

Rico was dressed identically, but his clothes fit, which wasn't surprising as both sets belonged to him. He was a sleek black jungle cat to Jon's powerful predator.

Tannis frowned. "Dog?"

"He's a goddamn stinking werewolf," Rico said. "And he's wearing my clothes."

"A werewolf? No freaking way." Tannis looked from Rico to Jon and back again. "Really? Do they actually exist?"

"Yeah, they exist." Rico raised his head and sniffed the air. "Can't you smell him?"

Alex breathed in deeply, but could detect nothing untoward, just a faint musky scent that was far from unpleasant. Jon didn't appear in the least perturbed by the accusation though, nor was he denying it.

Could he really be a werewolf? Did they even exist? Of course she hadn't believed vampires existed before she met Rico. Why not werewolves as well?

Jon pushed himself upright from where he leaned against the doorway and stepped into the room. The bridge was suddenly smaller.

He exuded an almost palpable sense of danger, and Alex couldn't take her eyes off him as he strolled across the bridge and halted only a foot away from Rico. They stared at each other for long moments while Alex held her breath. They were pretty much the same height, though Jon was broader, bulkier. Alex had never seen Rico fight, but she had heard Tannis talk about it in almost reverent tones. And Jon was bound to still be weak from the cryo. What if he got hurt? The vampire might even kill him. She inched closer to Skylar. Skylar would be able to stop this.

"Get back," Rico snarled.

For a moment, Alex thought he was speaking to Jon, but it was the rest of them he was referring to. Shaking off Skylar's hand, he took a step forward.

"Rico—"

He patted her arm. "Sweetheart—me and the dog have a couple of things to sort out between us. Like why the hell's he wearing *my* clothes? So why don't you sit down, and I'll be with you in a moment."

Skylar's eyes narrowed, then she shrugged. "Beat the shit out of each other if you want to. But he's bigger than you, darling."

Rico grinned, flashing his fangs. "Yeah, but I have bigger teeth."

Skylar glanced across at Jon. "I wouldn't bet on it." She stepped back. "Come on, Al. Let's give the . . . *men* some room."

Alex couldn't believe Skylar was so calm, and it didn't look as though the captain was going to be any help either. Tannis had already moved back and was leaning against the wall, an expression of anticipation on her face.

Alex tugged on Skylar's arm. "Stop him, Skylar."

"Who? Rico or the werewolf? They look pretty well matched to me. Besides, I don't think either of them is willing to listen to reason right now." She breathed in. "Can't you smell the testosterone in here?"

They were all crazy.

Jon took a step closer. His eyes were changing, glowing amber. Feral.

The adrenaline coursed through Jon's veins.

After Al had left, he'd gotten bored of waiting in his cabin and finally ventured out in search of food. Also, he wanted to know how soon he could get off this stinking ship.

But once out of the cabin he had to admit he was impressed with the vessel. She was a Mark 3 Cruiser but obviously extensively customized. The black and silver decor gleamed. The air was fresh—no stinting with the recycling, but beneath the freshness he caught the scent of death. As he'd followed his nose deeper into the ship, the stench grew stronger. Finally he'd arrived at the bridge, and even though he'd guessed what he would find, shock had held him immobile.

Vampire.

It had been decades since he'd even heard mention of them. He'd believed, and hoped, that they'd all died out.

Maybe this was what he needed to clear the last lingering effects of the cryo. What would be ideal is if he could shift and go for a long hard run, but that was hardly going to happen. So a fight would be the next best thing.

And if the vampire killed him, his problems would be over. He wasn't afraid to die. On the other hand, he'd fought vamps before and survived; no doubt, he could do it again. They were almost impossible to kill, especially without the proper weapons, but you could hurt them, make them bleed. Vampires and werewolves were natural enemies—both predators and both territorial—they didn't like sharing their prey. And vampires had a taste for were blood.

His fists clenched at his side. No way was this bloodsucking monster feeding on him. It occurred to him fleetingly that if he seriously damaged the vampire, his welcome on the ship was probably over and he'd be out the airlock without a spacesuit.

His attention had been on the vampire, but for the first time he took in the other occupants of the room.

The "boy" Al was no threat. Now he knew she was a girl, she appeared different—quite striking with her red hair; pale, creamy skin; and huge gray eyes. Not that he was interested. Her gaze caught his, and she glanced away quickly. He moved on to the two women. They were armed with laser pistols, and both looked more than ready to use them, their hands resting lightly on the grips.

One, with her eerie violet eyes, was obviously Collective. His "sister" he presumed. Was no one on this ship who they said they were? He'd have to remember to thank her later, and then find out why the fuck she had lied and busted him out of prison. Not that he wasn't grateful. Anything was better than the Meridian mines and a slow, painful death from radiation poisoning, which was where most prisoners ended up.

The other woman was a GM. The effects of genetic

engineering clear in her sinuous body and cold yellow eyes. He idly wondered if she had a forked tongue.

He turned back to the vampire who appeared relaxed, his lean body loose, but Jon sensed the coiled tension and the eagerness in the gleaming dark eyes. The guy was big, but not as big as Jon, and the bloodsucker was unarmed. Well, except for the fangs. A vamp had bitten Jon once, and he wasn't about to let it happen again. Not that he could be turned—werewolves were immune to that particular side effect—but it had hurt like hell.

His mood lightened. Yeah, this was definitely what he needed. How long was it since he'd been in an honest-to-goodness fight? Killing was his profession, but his business these days always seemed to be from a distance, and it always left a nasty taste in his mouth. Killing the vamp would feel good—real good.

He rolled his shoulders, easing the tension in his muscles, and heard the shirt rip down the back.

The vamp's eyes narrowed. "That's my shirt," he growled.

"Yeah, I thought it must belong to someone puny." He rolled his shoulders again and the material tore a little more. Grinning, he stripped off the rent fabric and tossed it at the vamp. "Have it back. It doesn't fit anyway."

"Nice. Very nice." Jon heard the muttered words of one of the women in the background but took no notice. The vamp didn't try and catch it, and the cloth fell to the floor between them.

He saw the moment when the vamp's muscles tightened and readied himself. Jon's vision narrowed, the rest of the room fading to nothing, his concentration fixed on his opponent.

It still came as a shock when the vamp made his move, and Jon barely had a second to brace himself before the impact. Lightning fast, he slammed into Jon hard, pushing him back step by step, until his shoulders pressed against the smooth curve of the wall.

He took a deep breath and lashed out with his foot, swiping the vamp's legs from under him. His grip slipped, then tightened again, dragging Jon down as he fell.

Jon landed on the bottom, his cheek pressed against the cool metal of the floor. He rolled instantly so he was on his back, just as the vampire reared up over him. Jon clenched his fist and punched him in the jaw. The blow hardly seemed to register, but it nearly broke Jon's hand.

"Can't do better than that?"

Jon gritted his teeth. Grabbing onto the other man's shoulders, he smashed his forehead into the vamp's nose.

Jesus. The guy was like granite. But he heard the crunch of bone and the sharp acrid scent of blood filled the air.

"Fuck, that hurt." The vamp shook his head and blood sprayed across the room.

"Don't look so pretty now, do you?" Jon mocked.

The vamp's eyes narrowed as he licked a drop of blood from his lower lip. Then he raised his fist and punched Jon in the mouth. *Fuck*. A warm trickle oozed down Jon's chin, and he resisted the urge to wipe it away. Instead, he bunched his knees to his chest between them and thrust out, hurling the vamp across the room so he crashed into a chair. Somebody swore loudly, but Jon ignored everything else. He rolled to his feet, charged, and slammed his head into the vamp's belly, and they crashed to the floor again. He was vaguely aware of booted feet scrambling out of the way.

They were rolling, each trying to get a grip. Pretty evenly matched in strength, each tried to get in the punch that would make a difference.

Twisting, Jon freed himself and scrambled to his feet. His eyes stung with sweat, and he blinked. Blood smeared his chest from his cut lip, but the vamp looked no better. His nose was clearly broken.

For a moment, their gazes locked. As Jon watched, the vamp slowly raised his hand to his face and licked the blood from his knuckles. Jon's blood.

Ugh!

The vamp's eyes glowed crimson now. The tension in the room ratcheted.

"Rico!"

Someone spoke urgently behind him, but Rico seemed not to hear. He stalked toward Jon, his lips curled back revealing razor-sharp fangs.

A flash of primordial fear rolled over him, but he held his ground. Shifting wasn't an option in such a confined space, and besides, there was nowhere for his wolf to run. Instead, he concentrated on his right arm, heard the bones crack and the claws pop from his skin until it was covered in thick dark brown fur and ended in vicious claws. He flexed his fingers and smiled.

"Come on. Let's party."

They circled each other with focus. This time, Jon made the first move, diving for Rico and hurtling them both to the floor. They slid along the smooth surface and crashed up against the wall, the vamp on top of him, so close his cool breath skated across Jon's skin. His nostrils filled with the scent of death. He used his free hand to grip the vamp's throat, holding him off while he raised his clawed right hand and tried to get an angle so he could rip into the jugular.

The fangs were only inches from Jon's vein as the vamp pressed forward with inhuman strength. Jon's arm trembled under the strain of holding him back.

A laser pistol flashed behind them. Rico's grip loosened, and he rolled away. The reek of singed flesh filled the air.

Jon lay on his back, staring at the pattern on the black

and silver ceiling. After a few seconds, he pushed himself to his feet ready to resume the fight.

Rico lay on the floor with the Collective woman standing over him, her laser pistol drawn.

"Ow. That hurt," he said, rubbing his backside.

"It was supposed to," she snapped. "I did try and ask nicely."

"I never heard."

"No, you were having too much fun with your new friend over there."

"You know, I'm sure I remember you promising to love me forever. Not more than four hours ago."

"Actually, I said I'd think about it. And don't be such a baby—it wasn't even on full."

"It still hurt."

She grinned. "Don't worry. I'll kiss it better for you later."

"Too right you will."

The vamp stretched out his hand. "Help me up."

The woman reached down and slipped her hand into his. A moment later, she was dragged down onto the floor next to him. Jon watched through narrowed eyes as the vampire kissed her. For a moment, she appeared to relax against him, then she pushed away and scrambled to her feet.

The vamp followed her up and cast a sideways glance at Jon, but the animosity and tension had vanished from his features. He limped across the floor and picked up the torn shirt. He made to wipe his face but changed his mind and ripped it in half, tossed one half to Jon, who reached out and caught it instinctively.

The snake lady strolled over. "So can I take it vampires and werewolves don't like each other very much?"

"I like them well enough for lunch." Rico licked his lips. "Actually, they make good pets as well. We used to keep them back on Earth. Put a collar round their necks. Leash them. You could even train them to do simple things if you were patient enough."

Someone sniggered.

Jon growled, and the Collective woman swung around and raised her pistol so it pointed at his heart.

"I've got a pretty good idea Rico here will survive a laser blast. You"—she waved the gun in Jon's direction—"I don't know. But I'm willing to take the risk."

"Yeah, you can kill him with that," Rico said. "But make it a direct hit otherwise they tend to get snarky."

"Thanks," she muttered.

Jon stepped closer. "Point a gun at me, lady, and you'd better be ready to use it."

"Oh, I'm ready."

"She is," Rico added. "She shot me, and she loves me. Who knows what she'll do to you—probably disintegrate you. That's one tough woman." He grinned with pride.

Jon raised his right hand, still clawed, some inner destructive urge driving him on. Some need to see how far she would go. Her finger tightened on the trigger.

And something slammed into the ship.

CHAPTER THREE

The whole ship lurched sideways, hurling Alex out of her chair.

El Cazador screamed under the strain, and the lights flashed and went out. They spun out of control, and Alex was tossed onto the floor like a doll. Someone landed on top of her, and the air whooshed from her lungs. She gripped on to whoever it was as the ship rolled, and this time she fell, presumably hitting the ceiling only to be flung to the floor again as *El Cazador* righted herself.

"Shit." The word sounded close. Alex thought it was Jon, but in the darkness, she couldn't be sure.

She lay still, waiting for the next hit. It never came. After a minute, the lights flickered back on. Except for people littering the floor, the bridge appeared in good shape.

Searching around, she found Jon a few feet to her left. He was sitting up, rubbing his head. Her gaze clung to him for a moment, taking in the naked chest, then down the length of his arm. The claw was gone—his hand had returned to normal.

For one horrible moment earlier, she'd been sure Rico was going to kill him. Or Jon was going to kill Rico. Either outcome wouldn't have been good. She'd actually jumped to her feet, unsure what she could do, but ready to launch herself between them. They'd probably have torn her to pieces . . . She needed a gun.

Luckily, Skylar had decided it was time to intervene, and she *did* have a weapon. Alex had slunk back down into her seat.

Now Tannis stood up, brushed herself off, and scowled. "That was no freaking warning shot."

Alex brightened a little at the words. Her immediate thought had been that the Church had come back for her. But as the captain said—that was no warning shot. Whoever had hit them had meant business. Maybe it was nothing to do with her.

Rico picked himself up off the floor. "If that's the goddamn Church again, this time I'm blowing them out of the sky."

He flung himself down in the pilot's seat, smashed his fist on the console in front of him, and the monitor flickered into life. A huge star cruiser filled the screen.

"That's no Church vessel."

Alex scrambled to her feet and brushed herself off. She was bruised but nothing worse. She edged around Skylar and peered over Rico's shoulder at the ship on the monitor. It was huge; she'd never seen anything like it.

"No, it's not," Skylar said. "That's a Collective Star Cruiser, and I'm betting it's chock-full of Corps."

"How sweet," Tannis muttered. "Your friends came to say hello."

Rico frowned. "That shot sounded more like good-bye to me."

"They must want him bad," Skylar said, nodding at Jon.

"Yeah, he's a real popular guy," Rico replied. "How the hell did they find us so fast?"

"Maybe he's bugged," Skylar said.

"Jesus. Why the hell didn't we think of that?" Tannis leaned across and pressed the comm link. "Janey, you okay? Well, get down here and bring a scanner with you." She turned back to Rico. "What's the damage?"

"She's holding for the moment, but another hit like that, and we'll have problems."

"Well, let's see if we can persuade them not to. Skylar, can you talk to them?" Tannis asked.

Skylar nodded and closed her eyes, her face clearing of expression. A minute later, she blinked. "They're not interested in talking."

"That's not good news," Tannis muttered.

"Well, the next bit's even better. They've given me five minutes to get off the ship, then they plan on blowing you into little pieces."

"Will they go ahead even if you stay on board?" Tannis asked.

"Oh, yeah. They made that very clear. But they did promise to resurrect me."

"They can do that?"

"As long as there's DNA left."

"Maybe you'd better go," Rico said quietly.

Alex's eyes flashed from Rico to Skylar. Would she go?

"No way," Skylar snapped. "So you'd better be thinking of a way to get us out of here. And in the next five minutes."

"How am I supposed to think when you just shot me?"

"So your brain's in your arse now, is it? Figures."

"Ha-ha. What if we hand him over?" Rico asked, nodding to where Jon lounged against the wall, arms folded. Jon had wiped the blood from his face but it was still smeared across his broad chest. Rico's question didn't appear to bother him in the least.

Alex held her breath as she waited for Skylar to answer and only released it when she shook her head.

"No deal. They're not interested. They want you all dead."

"Any clue why?"

"They're not saying. Maybe they don't even know. I'm guessing the order is coming from up high. Aiden Ross was a founding member—if not a popular one. It might just be in reparation for Jonny over there killing him."

"But why kill us? We didn't assassinate Ross."

"I said it might be. But I don't think so. My guess is Jonny knows something they don't want out. And they probably suspect he's already told us."

They swung around to stare at the werewolf.

"The name's Jon, not Jonny. And it was a job. I was paid to kill some guy. I know fuck-all else."

Janey appeared in the doorway, with Daisy close behind her. "What's happening?"

"We're being attacked by the Collective and are going to be blown into pieces in five minutes."

"Four now."

"Wow," Janey said. She didn't appear particularly disturbed. Alex had never seen Janey less than totally poised, hair and makeup perfect. Janey had red hair like Alex—but that was their only similarity.

Janey lifted the scanner in her hand and waved it. "What do you want scanned?"

"Him." Tannis pointed at Jon, and Janey turned to stare.

"Double wow," she murmured. Alex watched with narrowed eyes as she sauntered over in her high heels, hips swaying. No one would ever mistake Janey for a boy.

"What am I looking for?" she asked, running the scanner over his bare chest.

"Anything that could be used to track us. And take your time. We have four minutes, after all."

"Three."

Beep. Beep. Beep.

"Got it," Janey said. "Turn around and drop your pants."

He looked at her for a moment. "Just don't ask me to bend over, because I'm not going to do it."

Alex told herself she should look away, but somehow her eyes stayed glued as he undid the button and turned around. He dropped his pants and leaned his arms against the wall in front of him. His skin was smooth and golden, his ass firm above long, muscular legs.

"Nice arse," someone said.

"Nice legs."

"Knife." Janey held out a hand. Crouching down behind him, she ran her slender, scarlet-tipped fingers over his skin. Skylar drew a slim dagger from the weapons belt at her waist and handed it over.

"This might sting a little," Janey murmured.

His muscles tensed visibly, but he didn't say a word as she sliced open the skin of his left buttock and probed. After only a second, the tracker popped out, small, about the size of Alex's little fingertip. Janey picked it up and straightened.

"Get rid of it," Tannis said.

Janey dropped it to the floor and crushed it with her shoe as Jon pulled up his pants and turned around.

"So what's the plan?" Tannis asked Rico. "You do have a plan, don't you?"

"Actually, I do."

"Well, sooner might be better than later. Are you going to share?"

"I saw this maneuver in a movie once. A long time ago."

"A movie?"

"An old Earth thing. Anyway, this was one of my favorites, and I've always wanted to try it. Strap yourselves in, everybody."

Alex hurried to the nearest seat and fastened the safety harness, while everyone else did the same.

"So, the plan?" Tannis asked.

"Wait and see."

"Well, don't make me wait too long."

"I just need to check . . . Okay, hold on tight everyone." He hit the boosters and *El Cazador* shot forward, straight toward the star cruiser, her blasters blazing shots at the giant ship.

"What the fuck?" Tannis yelled.

The speed pushed Alex back into her seat, and she closed her eyes, waiting for the crash. Instead, they slowed dramatically, the ship spun on her tail, and they stopped.

She opened one eye and peered through her lashes. Everyone sat still in their seats as though waiting for something to happen.

"Where are we?" Tannis asked.

"We've landed on the back of the star cruiser," Skylar said, and Alex heard the wonder in her voice.

Rico grinned. "We're out of their visual monitors, and their systems won't pick us up amid their own internal feedback. Or at least that's the theory. It should look like we vanished."

They all sat in silence.

"That's the five minutes up," Tannis murmured. "And we're still here. So what do we do now? They'll pick us up as soon as we make a move."

"Well, in the movie, they waited until the rubbish was released into space and then just floated away."

"What rubbish?" Tannis asked.

"Yeah, well. This movie was made a long time ago, and there was a lot of rubbish back then."

"So we sit here for the rest of our lives." Tannis raised one brow.

"Hey, you're alive, aren't you? Quit moaning. I'll think of something. We need to give them time to run some checks first anyway."

They all fell silent. Tannis paced the bridge. Skylar took the seat next to Rico, who was gazing at the monitor, deep in thought. Alex pulled her feet onto her chair, rested her head on her knees, and watched them all. She'd come to care for them so much over the past three months. Tannis who had taken her in when she was starving, Skylar who had befriended her, and even Janey when Alex managed to get over the massive inferiority complex the other woman induced. The thought of going back to the Church, never seeing them again, made her chest ache. She still had to tell them who she was, and she only hoped they wouldn't hate her for lying to them.

After a few minutes, Tannis paused her pacing, and her glance darted between Jon and Rico. "So, while we're waiting, tell us, where do werewolves come from? For that matter, where do vampires come from?"

Rico grinned. "Straight from Hell, darling."

"Really?"

"No, not really. I'm not even sure Hell exists. The truth is no one really knows where we come from, or at least no one I know of, and if they ever did, the information was probably lost when the Earth died."

Tannis frowned. "That's another thing. How did you get out here? How did you escape the Earth? I read that there wasn't room on the ships for everyone and most people were left behind to die. So how did you lot"—she waved a hand to encompass Rico and Jon—"manage to get a place?"

Alex knew Rico was old. Skylar had told her he'd lived over fifteen hundred years—she couldn't imagine being around that long. He'd actually lived on Earth; he must have been there when the Chosen Ones made their exodus nearly a thousand years ago.

Rico settled back in his chair. "Do you know how the planets in the Trakis system got their names?"

"Weren't they called after the spaceships that took the people from Earth?" Janey offered.

"That's right. Twenty-four ships, each carrying ten thousand humans—the Chosen Ones. They were picked by lottery, though the whole thing was pretty much rigged. Anyway, me and a few acquaintances decided we weren't willing to rely on a one in fifty thousand chance, besides which, I think they forgot to enter us in the lottery. So we took things into our own hands."

"Acquaintances?" Skylar asked. "You mean more vampires?"

"Some, but other things as well—you might say we came together for a common cause. Vampires"—he nodded at Jon—"werewolves, and a few others you probably wouldn't want to meet on a dark night."

"So what did you do?"

"Most of the people were to be kept in cryo, except for a small crew to run the ship. So we made one of the captains an offer he didn't want to refuse."

"What? What could you offer someone when the world was about to end?"

"We offered him life. In exchange for dumping half his load of 'Chosen Ones' and replacing them with our people, I gave him immortality."

Tannis frowned as she thought about it, then her expression cleared. "Shit—you turned the guy into a vampire—wow."

"I did, and here we are."

"Yeah, but for how much longer?" she asked, waving a hand at the monitor. "You got any idea how to get us out of this yet?"

"Actually, *I* might have," Skylar said and switched on the monitor so it filled with the huge silver hull of the star cruiser. She clicked between views, studying the layout.

"There." She pointed at the screen. "Can you shift us so we're up against that blaster shield?"

"Sure," Rico replied.

El Cazador inched forward until the screen showed them snug up against a huge projection.

"Hey, clever. You're going to create some rubbish. Why didn't I think of that?"

Skylar slanted him a quick grin. "Just be ready to go."

She fiddled with the console settings, then punched on the blasters. This close they couldn't miss, striking where the hull joined the shield. Alex tightened her fingers on the seat as a shudder ran through the ship.

"Hopefully, they'll think it's damage from the earlier shooting. One more should do it." Skylar hit the guns a second time, and the great sheet of metal broke free.

"Go!" she shouted to Rico.

He punched the controls, and *El Cazador* peeled away. They drifted slowly, keeping pace with the debris. Alex clenched her teeth, waiting for some reaction to the blast, for the space cruiser to come after them, but gradually it grew smaller and smaller in the monitors.

When the vessel was no more than a speck on the screen, Skylar moved to stand behind Rico. "Are they following?"

"No, I think we're clear." He gripped her around the waist and pulled her onto his lap. "You're a genius."

"So are you."

"Jesus, this is gross." Jon's disgusted tones sounded from nearby, and she turned toward him. He was staring at Skylar and the vampire, his lip curled in an expression of revulsion.

"Too freaking right it's gross," Tannis snapped. "Skip it, you two. We have work to do." Tannis ran her gaze over Jon. "And can someone find him some clothes that fit—he's a little distracting like that."

Alex leaped up. The thought of Jon distracting Tannis made her feel distinctly edgy. "I'll go."

"No. You stay," Skylar said. She scrambled to her feet and brushed herself off. "You've got something to tell everyone, remember? Janey can go."

Alex scowled. "I was going to come back."

"Yes, but when? Just get it over with, kid."

"I'm not a kid."

"No? Then act like a grown-up."

Alex squeezed her lips together, bit back a surly response, and then forced herself to relax. Skylar was right, she was acting like a child—the problem was she'd spent too much time immersed in Al's character—it had become second nature. She drew herself up to her inconsiderable height. She could do this.

"So what is it?" Tannis asked.

Alex shuffled from foot to foot. Why was this so hard? Maybe because she admired Tannis so much. Tannis had taken her in when she was alone and hungry, and on the verge of running back to the Church. Except, at the time, she hadn't known which way to run. In the three weeks she'd been alone, it had rapidly dawned on her how ignorant she was of the world. Always before, everything had been done for her, and left on her own she'd had no clue how to look after herself.

Would Tannis be angry she'd lied? Even though she hadn't done it deliberately. Alex hadn't even realized Tannis thought her a boy until they'd boarded *El Cazador,* and she had introduced Al to the rest of the crew.

After taking a deep gulp of air, she looked up, straight into Tannis's eyes. "I'm not a boy."

Tannis frowned. "You're not?" Her gaze ran over Alex, took in the baggy pants and shirt hanging off her skinny frame. "Are you sure?"

Rico lounged in his chair, an amused expression on his

lean, handsome features. "I believe you, but I've got to say"—his gaze roamed her slim figure, lingering on the flatness of her chest—"you sure look like a boy. How about you show us some evidence?"

Alex ignored him and glanced across to where Jon still sat in his seat, his legs stretched in front of him, his expression bored.

Skylar leaned across and switched on the main monitor so a floor-to-ceiling screen lit up in front of her. She tapped a few keys and sat back as an instantly recognizable image appeared. Recognizable to Alex at least, but a quick glance around the room revealed no noticeable reactions.

The image showed a woman in full-length black robes, her hair covered by a dark veil, a serene, otherworldly expression on her small, pointed face. A wave of suffocation washed over Alex as she remembered the weight of those robes—how much she hated black.

Rico was the first to catch on. "No fucking way." He turned to stare at Alex, then back at the screen. "That's you?"

She nodded.

"The Lady Alexia, High Priestess of the Church of Everlasting Life? You're kidding us, right?"

Alex ground her teeth but said nothing.

"There's a reward," Tannis said.

Alex peered closer and read the screen. There was indeed a reward, and it was a huge sum of money. Way more than she would have ever thought they would offer. It didn't make sense. And Alex didn't like the speculative look in the captain's eyes. Tannis was a good person, but if anything could sway her, it was money, and this was a *lot* of credits.

"The Virgin Bride of the Everlasting God," Tannis read out loud, and Alex cringed. "Virgin?"

Somebody sniggered, and two masculine gazes swiveled in her direction.

"A virgin, huh?" Rico murmured, his voice tinged with amusement and a measure of curiosity.

Skylar slammed him in the gut with her elbow. "Get that look off your face."

"What look?" He grinned and shrugged one shoulder. "Virgins? Highly overrated I've always thought. Give me an experienced older woman any day."

"It's only a title, isn't it?" Janey asked. "I mean, it doesn't actually mean she's a real honest-to-god virgin." She shifted her gaze from the screen to Alex. "Does it?"

Alex's toes curled within her boots. For a minute, she studied the floor. When she looked back up, everyone was staring at her. Even Jon's bored expression was replaced with avid curiosity. He caught her gaze and raised an eyebrow. Alex scowled. What was the big deal?

"Hey, give her a break," Skylar said, but Alex could hear the laughter in her voice. "She was married to God. It's not Al's fault he didn't demand his conjugal rights."

"Ha-ha," she muttered.

Janey gave her a sympathetic smile. "Hey, she's only a kid—leave her alone."

"I am not a kid."

"You're not?"

"She's twenty-four," Skylar said.

"No freaking way." Tannis stared at her.

Alex drew herself up as tall as she could, which still left her the shortest person in the room by a good six inches. What was the point? She slouched again, stuck her hands in her pockets, and thrust out her lower lip. And waited for them to get over it.

And for someone to jump to a few conclusions.

No one had yet made the connection between her and the attack earlier. They would eventually, but right now, they were too entertained by the whole virgin thing.

"So what happened?" Tannis asked. "Why aren't you back there doing whatever priestesses do? What do priestesses do?"

Alex shrugged.

"Anyway, I would have thought it was a cushy number."

"She got to wear that great outfit." Janey giggled and waved a hand at the screen where Alex's robe-clad figure still showed. "That would have been enough to make me do a runner."

"Well, she's hardly a fashion statement now. So why did you run?"

"I was bored. It was an impulse thing, but then I got stranded . . ."

"On Trakis Twelve?

She nodded.

"That was three months ago, and it looks like they've been searching for you ever since."

"And now they've found her." Everyone swung around to look at Rico. "That's right, isn't it? They've caught up with you. That's why you're coming clean now."

Alex would have liked to deny it, but he was spot on. It took Tannis a moment to process the information and her expression cleared.

"Shit. You're what that High Priest guy was on about. You're the thing that belongs to them."

Alex nodded again.

"You're the reason the Church came after us." Tannis sighed loudly. "So what do we do now?"

Skylar shrugged. "We keep out of their way."

"Why not hand her over?" Jon spoke for the first time. He sounded genuinely interested. "You get rid of the problem and pick up the reward."

Tannis pursed her lips, her yellow eyes cold as she

considered the question, and Alex peered around at the people in the room as fear gripped her insides. Janey and Daisy both wore identical expressions of sympathy, Rico still appeared amused, and Skylar's face was blank. The captain's expression was hard to read, and Alex waited for her to answer.

"Because he's, or should I say, *she's* crew, and we don't give up our crew. Not to anyone. Not unless they want to be given up." She turned to Alex. "Do you want to go back?"

The walls seemed to close in around her as she thought of the years ahead. The stultifying boredom that would slowly choke the life from her until even the will to live would abandon her. No, she didn't want to go back. At some point, she knew she'd have to, just not right now.

She shook her head. "Not yet."

"Well, you'd better stay then," Tannis said.

At her words, a warm wave of relief washed through Alex.

"Though I suppose we'd better think of something else to call you," Tannis continued. "Cabin boy doesn't seem appropriate anymore."

Alex had a few ideas. Now that the need to keep a low profile was gone, she wanted to learn everything. How to fly. How to fight. Maybe Janey would teach her how to hack into systems. Then when she went back, she'd be able to find out what everybody was up to—at least that might keep the boredom at bay. The ship's mechanic the Trog was already teaching her how the engines worked—there had never been any need to keep a low profile with the Trog— even if he had guessed what she was, he wouldn't have told. The Trog didn't talk much. He basically hid under his scruffy hair and skulked around the engine room on the lower deck. Alex often wondered what he was hiding from.

"Okay," Tannis said. "So now we know why the Church

is after us. Let's just keep out of their way. Hopefully they'll give up—how important can one priestess be, right?"

The question didn't seem to need an answer. Happiness bubbled up inside Alex until she had to fight to keep the grin from her face.

"And at least we know the Church doesn't want you dead, so they're not likely to blow us out of the sky without any warning. Unlike our other friends."

Tannis turned to Skylar. "Any thoughts on why the Collective is so keen to see him dead?" She waved at Jon and frowned. "Why is he still half naked? Janey—go get him those clothes."

Jon admired the sway of Janey's hips as she left the room, then cast a surreptitious glance at Al, only to find her watching him out of those huge gray eyes. Hungry eyes. Heat curled in his belly, but he dismissed it—it had been a long time, that was all.

At twenty-four, she was no child, but he still wasn't interested. If he had to have a woman, he'd choose the other redhead—she'd know what she was getting into. Or the green one. He'd never seen anyone quite that green before—she would have a certain novelty value.

But his eyes were drawn back to Al, and then to the screen where the image of the High Priestess still stared down at them. He was finding it hard to believe they were the same person. Her fear had been obvious as she'd waited for the snake lady to make a decision. She'd been in no way sure whether they wouldn't hand her over, and her relief when she'd learned they would let her stay had been palpable. The decision confused him; he didn't know what to make of these people.

The immediate animosity with the vampire, he had understood, and the fight had been good—had cleared away the lingering effects of the cryo. But now it seemed forgotten. Rico was murmuring to the Collective woman, but his body language was relaxed. As though he sensed Jon watching him, he glanced up, but Jon ignored the implied question in the vampire's eyes.

His butt hurt where the redhead had sliced him open to get at the tracking device, and he stood up, ran his hands through his hair. The fact he was alive, and for the moment at least free, was beginning to sink in.

The snake lady was pacing the floor, presumably waiting for an answer as to why the Collective wanted them dead. He was curious as well. He had a few ideas, but he'd wait and see how this developed before he decided whether to share them or not. She came to a halt in front of him, a scowl on her face. She wasn't beautiful, but she was definitely intriguing. If he looked closely, her skin glowed with a pearly iridescence. Her tongue wasn't forked, which was a pity. He liked the unusual.

"I'm Tannis, captain of *El Cazador*. Rico is owner and pilot. Skylar's in charge of security. Janey, who just went to fetch you a much-needed shirt, keeps the systems going. Daisy"—she waved in the direction of the green girl—"is copilot and Al, or *Lady Alexia,* you've already met."

"Al's fine," the girl muttered.

Tannis raised an eyebrow. "Well?"

"Well, what?" Jon replied.

"Are you going to introduce yourself?"

"No."

"Charming, isn't he?" Rico murmured. "You'd think he didn't like us. How's that for gratitude when we went to all that trouble to get him out of prison?"

"If I'm not a prisoner, I'd appreciate if you would drop me off at the first habitable planet. I have things to do."

"Well, there's a problem with that," Tannis said. "Since

we freed your ungrateful ass, we seem to have become a little unpopular in certain quarters. Very powerful quarters. And we need to know why."

He shrugged. "Lady, you're mistaking me for someone who gives a fuck."

She stepped up close and poked him in the chest with one finger. "Well, give a fuck about this, dog-boy—you're not leaving this ship until we find a way out of this pile of crap. And I'll shove you back into cryo if I have to."

"You could try."

"Yeah, and I'd succeed. Because you know what—I've got one of these." She drew the laser pistol from her belt and shoved it in his belly. "And you don't."

For a moment, Jon considered taking the pistol from her. He was sure he could do it, but he wasn't positive he could take the rest of them. So he kept quiet and waited for her to finish. His time would come.

"If I thought for one moment getting rid of you would get the Collective off our backs, I probably wouldn't even wait for the nearest landfall. You'd be out the airlock. But Skylar doesn't seem to think that would do any good— which means we need to understand why they want you dead. So shall we try again?"

The redhead Janey came back at that moment and tossed him a black, sleeveless T-shirt. He took a moment to pull it on to give himself time to think. It was a tight fit, stretched across his chest, but at least this one wouldn't rip down the back if he took a deep breath.

Jon considered his next move. He might have to work with these people for a while. At least until he could get away. And there was always the chance they might have information that would help him.

"So why did you get me out of prison? Tell me what happened."

Tannis nodded as if recognizing his acceptance of the

situation. "Ten days ago, Skylar approached us with a job. She told us she was part of the Rebel Coalition who are hell-bent on destroying the Church and the Collective and wanted to employ us to rescue her 'little' brother, Jonny, from the high-security prison on Trakis One."

Jon swung around to face the blonde and studied her. She had short, military-cut hair, high cheekbones, and a wide mouth. Dressed in a black jumpsuit, boots, and a laser pistol once again holstered at her waist, she was beautiful in a tough sort of way, but those eyes sent a shiver of unease rippling through him. They glowed violet, almost inhuman. She must have worn contacts or they would have pegged her as Collective in a flash.

"I take it you don't have anything to do with the Rebel Coalition?" he said. The Rebel Coalition was number three on his hate list after the Church and the Collective. They were a load of amateur assholes who gave professionals like him a bad name.

"No." Her gaze wandered down over him in much the same way his had her. She was making a point. "Do you?"

He shook his head. "So why did you break me out?"

"I was under orders."

"Whose orders?"

"My colonel's. I'm an officer in the intelligence unit of the Corps."

Shock hit him in the gut. The Corps were the Collective's elite private army, and nobody wanted to take on the Corps. Not even him. But this didn't make sense. "Why the hell did the Corps want me out of prison?"

"I don't think they did. They told me it was a training exercise—to test the security at the prison. But we were met by an assassination squad—I think they wanted you dead but also wanted it to appear as though you had been killed trying to break out."

"Why?"

"I have no clue. But I'm guessing you know something—or they think you do—that they'd rather didn't get out. Any idea what that could be?"

Jon shook his head.

Tannis sighed and flung herself into an empty chair. "Let's start from the beginning. Who employed you to kill Aiden Ross? Oh, by the way, did I forget to mention Skylar's full name? Lieutenant Skylar Ross."

Jon's gaze flew to Skylar. "You're related to Aiden Ross?"

"Sort of. I was descended from his brother. But don't worry, we weren't particularly close, and I'm not making this personal—yet. So who paid you to kill him?"

"I don't know." She cast him a look of disbelief, and he continued. "That's not how I work. The information comes through anonymous channels, as does the payment. I never contact the customer directly. We need to look at this from the other side. Who would want him dead? You must have some ideas."

"I don't. Though he was never very popular—he was a pompous ass—he also had close dealings with the Church, which may have made people a little edgy." She turned and grinned at Al. "No disrespect, kid, but the Church are a load of assholes."

Al grinned back. The expression lightened her face. "I know."

"Forget about why he was killed for a moment," Rico said. "Could it just be that you succeeded in killing him at all? That's no easy thing, and it's the first time anyone's managed to take out a member of the Collective permanently. How did you know how to ensure they couldn't bring him back?"

"The information was delivered after I'd accepted the job. I was instructed very specifically on how it should be done."

"Well, it worked," Tannis said. "They're supposed to be indestructible, or that's what they've led everyone to believe. So how *did* you assassinate one of the 'impossible to kill' Collective?"

He opened his mouth to answer, but Skylar shook her head. "Keep that to yourself. If I get questioned, I want to be able to answer that the rest of you don't know. Hell, that I don't know for that matter."

"So what if we threatened to release the information?" Rico said. "Or if we just go ahead and release it anyway. Once it's open knowledge there would be no point in coming after us."

"Great idea," Skylar snapped. "How to make friends and influence people. I can guarantee—you put that information out on the open airwaves and they will hunt you down and kill you all, just out of revenge."

"So what about the threat?"

"I'd really rather not go about threatening anybody at this point," Tannis said. "My chance of getting the Meridian treatment will be zero if we piss them off now."

Jon rubbed at the cut on his backside absently while he tried to figure it out. "Anyway, somebody else already has the information. Whoever employed me."

"There is that," Skylar said. "Besides, I can't help thinking there's something else."

Tannis ran a hand through her hair. "I agree. I think there has to be more to it. And it likely has to do with why Aiden Ross was assassinated. If we can find out who ordered the assassination and why, it might give us some leverage. There has to be a way to track down who paid you for the job. You must know who contacted you initially."

Jon thought for a minute. The only way he survived in his profession was by maintaining anonymity and by keeping his contacts a closely guarded secret. But he'd had it with the assassination business. He'd already decided killing

Aidan Ross was his last job, and he'd been paid enough that he could afford to retire, so really he no longer needed his contacts. And one of them had betrayed him. Set him up.

"There is someone we can start with. The initial contact came through him."

"Where can we find him?"

"Last time I heard, he was running a bar on Trakis Two."

"Great," Tannis muttered. "Trakis Two—isn't that right next door to Trakis Five, where those guys who want to kill us come from?"

Jon shrugged. "Well, they won't be expecting us there, will they?"

"Do you really trust him?" Skylar asked Tannis.

"Hell no—of course I don't trust him. But unless you can come up with a better idea, I don't see what choice we have." She pointed a finger at Jon. "But you double-cross us, and I'll deliver you to the Meridian mines myself."

Jon ignored the threat.

"Hmm." Rico switched on the console in front of him and concentrated for a moment. "Trakis Two would work. We need to head somewhere we can do some repairs. Apparently, the main thruster is damaged beyond anything the Trog can fix, and I know somewhere we can hole up on Trakis Two while we fix her up. That's if he's still there."

"A friend of yours?" Tannis asked.

Rico sighed. "Sort of."

"Sort of?" Skylar frowned. "Why does that make me worry?"

"Because you know me so well?" Rico grinned. "Let's just say there's a slight possibility he'll want us dead more than the Collective."

"Just great," Tannis drawled.

Rico flipped a switch on the console, the remaining thrusters fired, and *El Cazador* took off for Trakis Two— the planet that never sleeps.

CHAPTER FOUR

Christ, he was hungry.

Jon was heading back to his cabin, but he really needed to eat. He raised his head, sniffed, and caught the faint trace of food in the air.

The smell led him to the galley at the center of the ship. It took him a moment to figure out how to work the food dispenser, but he eventually managed to get himself a serving of something that resembled stew and tasted almost like real meat. After wolfing down the first bowl, he got another, and sat at the table to eat it more slowly.

Things weren't going too badly. They could be much worse. But even so, his nerves twitched. He didn't work well with people. It was a long time since he'd even tried.

After his pack had been killed, he'd spent the following years tracing the people responsible and making sure they paid. Afterward, he'd lost his urge for killing, but he'd continued anyway because he was good at it and he'd found there were plenty of people around who would pay him— and extraordinarily well—to use his talents. But he always worked alone.

Long ago, he'd taken a vow never to change anyone—he

didn't want any other wolves relying on him, looking to him to save their miserable lives. He'd proven how crappy he was at the whole protection thing. And he'd never come across another werewolf either. The occasional rumor came his way, but if it sounded like his kind, he'd turned around and gone in the opposite direction as fast as he could.

He was better off alone. He liked it that way. Women he took when the need got too strong, but always women who knew the score, who wouldn't ask for more than he was willing to give, which wasn't very much. Women who could look after themselves. Women who were definitely not virgins.

The Virgin Bride of the Everlasting God.

Who would have guessed it—a High Priestess? He waited for the rush of hatred to overcome him. After all, she was Church, and he ought to hate her as he hated the rest of her kind. But she obviously wasn't too keen on them herself or she wouldn't have run away.

His lips curved at the memory of her discomfort. The sensation was strange. He didn't smile a lot. A red flush had swept over her creamy skin as they'd teased her. Whether it had been from temper or embarrassment, he didn't know. Probably both.

He had a flashback to the feel of her lying beneath him, and heat coiled in the pit of his stomach. She'd felt feminine but delicate, small-boned and fragile. The sort of woman who needed protecting. Not his sort of woman. And no breasts. He liked breasts. If he needed sex, then the other redhead would be a much more sensible option. And she'd had breasts. But although he tried to picture her, he couldn't really remember what she looked like.

The cryo was obviously still messing with his head. He needed to forget about women and concentrate on what to do next. Not that he had many choices.

Maybe he could try and get rid of the crew, but he

couldn't manage a ship the size of *El Cazador* alone. Or he could make a break for it. Take one of the shuttles perhaps. But why bother? Trakis Two was his only option, his only lead, so why not go there aboard *El Cazador*? He chewed a mouthful of stew thoughtfully. At least the food was good. For now, this was probably his best bet for getting around. He'd regain his strength. Treat it like a holiday.

And once he'd seen his contact, he could decide what his next move should be. It would be easy to ditch them on Trakis Two. Especially if he acted like he was cooperating now and they lowered their guard.

Unfortunately, cooperation had never been a strong point of his, and he was a crap actor. Maybe he could get the women on his side at least. Maybe he *shouldn't* limit himself to the redhead. From the way the women on this ship were acting around him—freaking out over a damn shirt, he reckoned he could have them all. Well, except Al; he really wasn't going to allow himself to go there. From now on, she could keep out of his way.

Getting to his feet, he stretched. He had a plan. If he could ignore the fact his butt hurt like hell, he might even feel optimistic.

When he reached his quarters, the door to his cabin was open, and he could see Al, down on her hands and knees. So much for keeping out of his way.

"What the fuck are you doing here?"

She jumped, scrambled to her feet, and stood chewing on her lower lip. "I was cleaning . . ." She trailed off and gestured to the mess on the floor where the food had spilled earlier. " And there are more clothes." She pointed at a pile on the bed. "They should keep you going until we reach Trakis Two."

He strolled across the room, picked up a white shirt, and held it to his nose. "Did you pinch them from the vampire?"

"No—they're from the Trog—he's the engineer but he doesn't come out much, so he won't even notice." A smile flashed across her face. "Rico only wears black—I think he likes to match the ship."

"I'll bet."

"I'll just finish . . ."

Crouching down again, she picked up the cloth she'd been using and bundled it into a bag. Her gaze kept flicking up to him as she worked. Her eyes were really quite amazing, the irises almost silver rimmed with black, and very expressive. How had she managed to hide what she was for so long? She must be one hell of a good actress. Shit, she might even be acting now—with those shy, little "I might be a virgin, but I'm willing to change that" glances she kept sending his way. He shoved his hands in his pockets and shifted uncomfortably. These pants were definitely too tight.

Al straightened, wiping her hands up and down her thighs, and he bit back a groan. She still wore a baggy shirt, but the material was thin, almost transparent. Through it, he could clearly make out the outline of a pair of surprisingly full breasts. Where the hell had they come from?

As he stared, unable to look away, she thrust back her shoulders so her dark nipples pushed against the fabric, sending a jolt of heat to his groin. It had been way too long.

He forced his gaze upward and caught a small, catlike smirk of satisfaction on her face. The expression was blanked out as soon as she saw him watching, and a wave of anger rolled through him. The little priestess thought she could manipulate him. She needed to learn she couldn't. Nobody could.

But he hoped she'd learn fast and get the fuck out of here, before his dick exploded out of his too-tight pants.

She was still fussing about the cabin, and he growled low in his throat.

He'd noticed her breasts. Alex was sure of it.

It was such a relief to get rid of the bindings that had been part of her disguise, she hadn't considered this added advantage.

Tannis had given her some breathing space, but that was all it was. Her time was running out. If Hezrai found her once, he would find her again. The Church was powerful, and she didn't want anyone to get in trouble because of her. Next time, she would hand herself over.

But there was so much she wanted to experience first. She had a lengthy to-do list she'd been adding to since she came on board. And today she'd added one more thing.

She gave Jon a small sidelong glance. His hands were in his pockets, and he was lounging against the wall. He should have appeared relaxed; instead, he radiated barely leashed tension.

"Is there anything else I can do?" she asked, her tongue darting out to moisten her lips.

His eyes narrowed. "You can get the hell out of here, little girl."

"I'm not a little girl—I'm twenty-four." Why did she have a feeling she was going to have to repeat those words many times before they would make any impact?

"Yeah, and I'm one hundred and ninety-two."

"Really?"

"Yeah, really. Look, I know what you think you want. But you're wrong."

"What do I want?" Her voice sounded breathless to her own ears.

"You want to get rid of that virginity you find so embarrassing." He shook his head, pushed himself away from the wall, and strode toward her. Up close, he was huge, towering over her, and she had to force herself to stand her ground. This was no time to turn yellow.

He halted a foot away and stared down at her through half-closed eyes.

"You really want it? You want me to fuck you, *little girl*?"

No, actually, she wanted him to make sweet, dreamy love to her, but she had an idea he might laugh if she mentioned that, so she'd take the other if it was all that was on offer. Something tightened low down in her belly at his words and heat washed through her. She didn't think she could get any sound out of her suddenly dry mouth, so she nodded.

His eyes widened as though he hadn't expected that answer. "Jesus, I don't believe this. Are you always so reckless?"

She opened her mouth to argue that she wasn't reckless—this was a well-thought-out plan—but he continued before she got the chance.

"Why me?" he asked, running a hand through his hair. He didn't seem to need an answer, so she kept quiet. "Hell, I bet you can't even say the word, never mind do it."

Alex ground her teeth. "I can."

Jon folded his arms across his chest, a smug, superior expression on his face. "Go on then."

She swallowed. There was nothing hard about this. It wasn't even blaspheming, which she'd probably find impossible. Just because she had never said the word in her life, didn't mean she couldn't. Her mouth opened, but nothing came out, and she closed it again. She hated being a priestess—she was so repressed.

He laughed, but the sound held no amusement, and her fury rose.

"So I can't say it? What's the big deal here? It's not as

though I want to marry you or anything. As it happens, I'm already married."

"Yeah, I remember—to God, right? And he's obviously not giving you any."

"I don't even like you," she continued, deciding to ignore his comment. "But I don't happen to have a lot of options here."

He regarded her, his head cocked to one side. "Doesn't it bother you that I'm a werewolf?"

She smiled sweetly. "No, I always wanted a pet dog."

An expression of outrage flashed across his features, and she had to bite back her grin. "Besides," she added hurriedly, "as I said—I don't have a lot of choices."

"And you're desperate, right?"

She thought about the question for a second then nodded. It was sad but true, and she wasn't going to get what she wanted by lying about it. "Yeah, I'm desperate."

"Jesus," he muttered again. "Let me give you a word of advice. Real men like to do the chasing."

"Real men?"

"Look, you're obviously a good girl. Why don't you go back to where you belong? Back to the Church, like a good little virgin priestess."

The last words were sneered and twenty-four years of pretending rose up inside her. "I am *not* a good girl. For one thing, I'm not a girl—I'm a woman. For another, I am not good. I've never been good. I've just pretended, and I'm sick of it." Alex took a step toward him, and he backed up. She prodded him in the chest—it reminded her of solid rock. "Do you know what it was like?"

He shook his head, a slightly panicked look on his face.

"Every single day. For twenty-four years. I pretended to be good. And every single day I thought of new bad things I wanted to do. I wanted to do them so much that sometimes I would scream inside. And soon, I'll go back, and I'll pretend to be good again—"

"Why?" he interrupted. "Why go back?"

She thought of all the people who had given up their lives for her, of Sister Martha who had basically raised her. Alex was the center of their universe—their reason for being. They believed in her—that she was God's chosen emissary. Even if she didn't believe it herself, could she abandon them?

But there was more to it than that. This time away had made her see things clearly for the first time. One of the reasons she'd hated her life so much was because she'd felt like some sort of drone-droid, unable to take control or change anything. And there were so many things within the Church that needed changing. As High Priestess, she could become a force for good, make things better. But she wasn't telling him that.

"Just because," she mumbled. "The point is, I *will* go back. I'll do my duty, and I'll make believe I'm good. But before I do, I'm going to do a few of those bad things. All I'm asking for is a little cooperation."

He was silent as he studied her. Alex held her breath.

Finally, he shrugged. "Much as I appreciate the honor, I don't do innocents. And I especially don't do needy innocents."

Her fists clenched at her side. "I am *not* needy."

"You're about as needy as they come, darling. Now I'm tired. I'm going to lie down—perhaps you could close the door on your way out."

Jon strolled over, settled on the bed, and closed his eyes as if to shut her out. His muscular body stretched out, his hands clasped behind his head, showing the dark tufts of hair in the hollows of his armpits. There was so much of him.

"Quit staring," he murmured.

Alex sighed. She wanted to argue the needy thing some more, but what was the point? She picked up her bag of cleaning things and trudged to the entrance.

"Hey, Al."

She paused, turned back to face him, a little flame of hope igniting in her chest. "What?"

"Maybe I am feeling a little horny after all. You think you could get me a date with that other redhead?"

It took her a moment to realize he meant Janey. Hurling the bag at his head, she spun around and stalked from the room.

His chuckle followed her as she stomped down the corridor.

"Fucking bastard," she muttered under her breath.

Swearing, she decided, was easy. All you needed was the right incentive.

CHAPTER FIVE

Alex spent the next two days helping the Trog in the engine rooms. She liked the Trog and found his company restful. There had never been any need to pretend with him. Even when she'd been in disguise, she'd known he wouldn't give her away.

Maybe because he was such an enigma himself.

Occasionally, she caught flashes of sadness on his face, but some inner instinct told her that whatever was in his past, he wasn't yet ready to talk about it. She reckoned that was why he spent so much time alone; he had secrets he didn't want to give away either.

They hadn't seen any sign of either the Church or the Collective since their escape. Maybe they'd outrun them. Or their pursuers had lost interest.

El Cazador was managing to limp along, but only the Trog's constant nursing kept her from giving up completely. Even the captain hadn't insisted on him joining them for meals as she usually did. And Alex had used the excuse that she was helping him to stay out of the way.

She didn't want to know if Jon had gotten his date with Janey. But she didn't think so. Occasionally, Janey or Daisy would pop into the engine rooms to fill her in on the gossip. Apparently, Jon was flirting indiscriminately with every woman on board. Well, every woman except her.

Because she was "needy."

Bastard.

At least the whole swearing thing was getting easier. She'd been doing a lot of practicing.

Alex could tell both of them were flattered by his attentions, but she didn't think either had actually done anything about it yet or they'd be boasting. And she presumed Tannis wouldn't be taken in—she had far too much sense. It was obvious Jon was only trying to gain influence—well, or get laid. Even so, the thought of him with Tannis sent an odd little jolt to her belly.

This morning, Rico had called them all together for a meeting, and everyone else was already there when she'd sidled into the central conference room.

Rico sat at the front, long, booted legs stretched out in front of him. "Well, if it isn't our little priestess."

She stopped moving and scowled. "Don't call me that."

"What should we call you? What did they call you back at the . . . ?" He shrugged. "Hey, where did you live?"

"At the Abbey on Trakis Four."

"So what did they call you back at the Abbey?"

Alex caught Jon's gaze, and he raised an eyebrow. She took her hands from her pockets, and gave her best high priestess glare. "They called me Lady Alexia or your Ladyship. Either will do."

Rico grinned. "Yeah, like that's going to happen, *your Ladyship.* I reckon you'd better stay Al."

"No, she's Alex—she has to have a girl's name, now," Janey said as Alex sank down into the chair beside her.

"Why? She doesn't look like a girl."

Janey patted her leg. "Soon she will. But none of our

clothes fit her—they're all too big, so we'll have to get new stuff. We're going shopping on Trakis Two."

Rico shook his head. "Al's not going shopping anywhere and certainly not on Trakis Two. She stays on the ship."

"Why?"

"Because there are wanted posters everywhere—with her picture on them."

"Yeah, but the picture looks nothing like her. No one will recognize her."

"I recognized her," Skylar said. "And if I did, someone else might."

"And Trakis Two is always crawling with church people desperate to get laid," Rico added. "We'll probably bump straight into that High Priest . . . what was his name?"

"Hezrai Fischer," Alex said and couldn't prevent a grin at the thought of Hezrai trawling for pleasure providers on Trakis Two. The expression disappeared fast. She'd been looking forward to going shopping, seeing the sites.

The sun never rose on the dark side of Trakis Two, but still the place was supposed to be hot. Very hot. The permanent darkness attracted the lowlifes from around the universe—anything was acceptable on Trakis Two, and visiting was on her to-do list. Now she'd have to stay on the ship? No way.

But if life had taught her one thing, it was if you planned to do something you weren't supposed to, keep quiet about it. Placing her hands on her lap, she kept her eyes downcast. "I don't mind. I'll stay on the ship."

"Obedient, isn't she?" Jon said, but his tone was skeptical.

She peeked up and caught his gaze. Why did she get the impression he saw right through her? And what did it matter? Ignoring his obvious sarcasm, she smiled serenely—she was good at that—and Jon shook his head and looked away.

"Right," Rico said, "when we get to Trakis Two, we're going to be staying with a *friend* of mine, and I use that term in the loosest sense. So I wanted to give you a word of warning. Well, a few words actually."

"And they would be?" Tannis said.

"Don't trust him. Don't go near him. Don't be alone with him." He stared into space for a moment. "In fact, it might be best if you all stay on the ship while we're there."

Janey muttered under her breath.

"No way," Daisy said. "I've never been to Trakis Two."

Rico must have realized he faced a mutiny. "Well, if you do have to go off the ship, at least stay in pairs."

Tannis frowned. "How friendly are you with this 'friend' of yours?"

"Not very."

"Great."

"But he'll do what he's told."

"And why would he do that?"

"Because he has no choice. Take my word on this one."

"Hmm," Tannis said.

"He's another vamp, isn't he?" Everyone turned to look at Jon as he spoke quietly. "That's right, isn't it?" He stood up and stepped toward Rico. The tension in the room ratcheted several notches. Alex held her breath. "You're taking us to stay with another bloodsucker, aren't you?"

Rico rose to his feet in one fluid move, his eyes narrowed. "So? What's it to you, dog-breath?"

"Well, my guess is—from the warnings—that this one isn't quite as good at playing civilized as you are. For whatever reasons, you've fooled these people into thinking you're some sort of nice guy."

Alex could have jumped in at that point and said that he hadn't fooled her. Instead, she watched as the two faced off.

"But you're not a nice guy, are you, Rico?" Jon taunted.

The silence stretched out between them.

"I think he's nice," Skylar said. "Well, he's nice to me anyway—he gave me a ring." She waved her hand with the huge purple stone and the tension snapped.

Rico grinned. "Thanks, sweetheart. But he's right—not about me—I am a nice guy." He smiled with a flash of fang that totally belied his words. "But Bastion *is* a vampire, and he's not so—"

"Nice?" Tannis finished for him. "Great, just great."

"Hey, it's no big deal. As I said—he'll do what he's told."

"Now why would he do that?" Jon drawled. He studied Rico for a moment. "He's one of yours, isn't he?"

"One of his what?" Tannis asked.

"One of his offspring. You turned this guy."

Rico shrugged. "Yeah, so what? Why the fuck does that matter? What matters is he has a place on Trakis Two, and we need somewhere to hide out while we do repairs. And we don't have a lot of choices here. The *Cazador* isn't going to make it much farther without some serious work. Isn't that right, Trog?"

Everyone turned to face the Trog, who sat at the back of the room. He lifted his shaggy blond head, nodded once, and returned to contemplating the floor.

"So that's agreed? Just be careful and don't let him get you alone." Rico grinned at Jon. "And you'd better be particularly careful, dog-boy."

"Why's that, leech?"

"Bastion's not as fastidious about his food as I am."

Janey nudged Alex in the side and leaned in closer to whisper in her ear. "Do you think this Bastion will be anything like Rico?"

Alex shuddered. "I hope not."

"Rico is dreamy."

Alex rolled her eyes. But her gaze was drawn to where Jon still stood facing the vampire. Now *he* was dreamy.

And she was one sad woman.

Jon had made his thoughts perfectly clear regarding what he thought about her. He was a dead end, so why couldn't she stop staring and move on? Maybe she'd meet someone on Trakis Two. All those men looking to get laid. Still her gaze was drawn back to the werewolf.

"Are we finished?" Jon asked.

"Yeah, we're finished, dog-breath. We should hit landfall in an hour."

"Then I'm out of here." Jon pivoted and stalked from the room.

Alex's eyes followed him—the view was great from the back as well. He moved with the leashed power of some big predatory animal. She sighed, and Janey let out a soft laugh beside her. "What?" Alex asked.

"Well, you're being a little obvious."

"I am?"

Janey smiled. "A little."

"Yeah, I know. And 'real men' like to do the chasing. I know *that* as well."

"Not all of them. But some. You've got to learn to play hard to get."

"I'll try." Another sigh escaped her throat. "But I don't want to play so hard I never get got."

"Don't worry. You'll get got. Just do what I say—I know all about getting a man to chase you."

Alex had no doubt Janey had had hoards of men chasing her; she was the most beautiful woman Alex had ever met, and the cleverest. She'd always wondered what had brought Janey to *El Cazador*. While Alex loved the ship and the crew, it was hardly a glamorous lifestyle. "How did you end up here?" she asked. "You could do anything."

"What's wrong with here?" For the first time since Alex had met her, Janey sounded faintly hostile.

"I didn't mean anything except you're so"—she searched for the right word—"perfect."

"I'm far from perfect. And where should I be? Living in a big house on Trakis Five? Married to some rich guy? Believe me, I've been there, done that, and I don't ever plan on repeating the experience."

"Oh."

Janey's expression was rueful. "Sorry, I didn't mean to snap. It's just a sore point. I married a bastard because I thought he could give me everything I wanted, but it turned out what I wanted wasn't worth the price. And I had no one to blame but myself. But at least he taught me how to make the best of my looks, and that's come in useful."

"You left him?"

The corners of Janey's lips curved up in a small smile. "You could say that. Anyway, I've always been good with computers, so I set up on my own doing freelance jobs, mostly illegal. One day I did some work for Tannis, she offered me a place, and here I am."

"I'm glad."

"So am I. Come on, let's go make a start—your hair could definitely do with a cut—we'll make you so gorgeous, your werewolf won't be able to resist you . . ."

Jon had a bad feeling about this.

He didn't take too much notice as he frequently had bad feelings. More often than not, they came to nothing, and he'd come to the conclusion it was just his miserable nature.

Still, there was something about the view below that wasn't at all comforting. He knew Trakis Two well—he'd done a lot of business here. It was a great place for people who wanted to stay under the radar, but he'd always stuck to the city before. Everyone stuck to the city on Trakis Two. There were reputed to be things out in the surrounding darkness you didn't want to come across. And he had a feeling they were about to knock on the door to the lair of one of those things and ask if they could come inside.

Maybe he should get out now.

Glancing around, he found Skylar watching him, her hand resting on the laser pistol at her waist. They were giving him the appearance of freedom, but he had a feeling if he tried to test it, they'd zone in on him pretty fast. He turned back to the viewer.

Off in the far distance, he could make out the multicolored lights of Pleasure City glowing like a false promise of dawn. But beneath them, a hulking great piece of darkness rose up from the planet's surface. Man-made of dull black rock, it appeared hewn out of the night itself. Here and there across the exterior, a sullen orange light glowed from cavities in the walls.

The skin of his neck prickled. He was being watched and he knew only one person who had this effect. He went still then slowly turned his head and searched the room. At first, he couldn't see her; maybe he'd been mistaken. At the thought, he berated himself for even looking. What did he care if her Ladyship was here?

At the meeting earlier, he'd done his best to ignore her. But he'd still been able to scent her like a bloody bitch in heat. Now, his body was wound up tight, and if he didn't get relief soon, he might explode. Janey or Daisy would have happily obliged at any time over the past two days, but though he'd flirted madly, he'd backed off when they'd responded. Janey, because although she'd been happy to flirt back, he sensed the banter was something that came to her automatically, and he couldn't shake the idea that she didn't actually like men all that much. And Daisy was way too bouncy and enthusiastic; she made Jon feel old.

He'd also tried dealing with the problem himself but only gained a momentary release, and then the itch had come back even stronger.

Shit. There she was. Standing by the door, talking with Daisy. Jon did a double take. Somebody had cut her hair. The shaggy mop was gone, and the skinny cabin boy had been banished forever. Now her hair was no more than two inches anywhere, with tendrils curling around her cheeks. As he stared, she ducked her head and ran a self-conscious hand through her hair, so it stuck up in spikes. She looked like a sexy street urchin. An urchin with flawless skin, high cheekbones, and those huge, slanting eyes.

As though she sensed him watching her, she turned wary eyes his way. Then pursing her lips, she lifted her chin and deliberately turned her back on him. He smiled. She'd obviously taken his comment about men liking to do the chasing to heart.

Yeah well, it made no difference. Even if she backed off, he wasn't going anywhere, except maybe in the opposite direction.

He turned back to the monitors. They were directly over the black compound now, and a fissure had formed as though the rooftop split in two. The sides slid back, revealing a landing pad inside the walls.

They hovered for a minute longer before lowering enough to touch down light as stardust.

Rico was a good pilot—even if he was a bloodsucker.

Jon itched with impatience to get things moving. He wanted some action. He wanted to get into the city, chase up his contact, and find out who had betrayed him. Instead, he was waiting for Rico. Apparently, he wanted everyone to meet this new vampire so he could warn him off. Until then, they were supposed to skulk on the ship as if Jon was afraid of some pathetic blood-sucking leech.

"Did you know, there are more pleasure providers on Trakis Two than in the rest of the Trakis system put together?" Daisy was reading tourist information from the screen while they waited for Rico to join them in the docking bay. "And I bet that's just the registered ones." She prodded Alex in the stomach. "You're not paying any attention to this, are you?"

Daisy was dressed in all black, a sort of mini version of Rico, whom she had a whopping crush on. And she'd obviously been on her sun bed as she was even greener than usual, her skin the color of new leaves, her eyes sparkling like emeralds. She was also fizzing with excitement—but then she was off into the city to have some fun as soon as they'd met their host, while Alex was to be left on the ship.

"I am paying attention." Alex was actually only listening with half her concentration, while she surreptitiously watched Jon with the other half. Her back was to him, but she could see him reflected in the polished black metal of the docking bay loading doors.

He was pacing like a caged . . . wolf.

As Rico and the captain appeared, he stopped and swung around. "About bloody time."

Rico ignored the comment and strode past him. His eyes narrowed as he came up level with Alex and took in the new hairstyle.

Alex couldn't believe the difference a haircut made in her appearance. She couldn't wait to get some new clothes, pink ones—shocking pink that clashed with her hair. And orange maybe. Anything but black.

Rico's brows had drawn together in a frown. "*Christos*," he muttered. "Bastion is going to love you. Couldn't you have waited?"

"To do what?"

"The whole"—he waved in the general direction of her hair—"innocent waif look. Well, it's too late now. Just keep out of his way and don't do anything to draw attention to yourself."

He turned to the side and murmured to Tannis who glanced at Alex and nodded.

At that moment, the docking bay doors slid open, revealing a cavernous area beyond. Alex shivered as they stepped off the ramp and onto the black sand floor. The group had formed around her, so she was in the middle, Rico and Tannis at the front leading the way, Daisy and Janey on either side of her, and Skylar and Jon bringing up the rear.

The exposed skin on the back of her neck tingled.

They came to a halt in the center of the room, and Alex tried to keep her eyes from widening. They were in a great hall, but it was more like standing inside some vast echoing cavern with matte black walls, smooth as glass. The roof was closing over their heads, blanking out the last of the stars so the only light came from small sconces cut into the rock walls. A number of dark tunnels led away like great yawning jaws ready to swallow her whole.

The air was still, faintly musty, and the catacomb silent. Someone laid a hand on her shoulder, and she jumped and let out a small squeak.

"Quiet as a grave," Jon murmured in her ear, and she shivered again despite the fingers that burned through the thin material of her shirt. "By the way—I like the new haircut. Pity I don't go for the 'innocent waif' look."

Alex shrugged off his grasp. "Don't worry," she muttered, "you'll be pleased to know, I've deleted you from my to-do list."

"You have a to-do list?"

"Yes, and you're not on it."

"Playing hard to get, now?" His voice was laced with amusement.

She sniffed. "I am hard to get."

"Well, make sure you remember that when we meet the vampire."

She turned slightly so she could see Jon's face.

"Vamps can be tricky," he continued. "The older ones have this whole seduction thing going. Makes it easier to snare their prey."

"I don't think you need to worry. I'm hardly likely to be attracted to a vampire," she snapped.

In front of her, Rico's shoulders stiffened. Jon chuckled. "Quite right. Satan's spawn, the whole lot of them, and you a good little priestess. All the same, watch him and do not make eye contact."

Rico glanced over his shoulder. "I hate to agree—because he's a dog—but it's good advice. Listen to him and stay at the back where you might not be noticed. Right, here they come."

Muffled footsteps sounded on the sandy floor, and Alex peered into one of the dark tunnels. A flickering orange light appeared, waxing brighter, casting shadows against the surrounding walls.

Finally, a small group came into view. One central figure surrounded by four torchbearers.

"Bloody melodramatic," Rico muttered.

"Asshole," Jon added.

"Holy freaking moly." The captain's voice was filled with awe.

The vampire was tall, with a slender body that moved like a dancer's, beneath a fitted black and crimson jumpsuit and long boots. His pale blond hair hung down to his shoulders. He had white skin and dissipated blue eyes that glittered with malice. Alex had seen faces like his depicted on the walls of churches—fallen angels. A shiver ran through her, and she reached up and clutched the cross she wore beneath her shirt.

The vampire had come to a halt in front of Rico, but he must have sensed her movement because he tilted his head to get a look around Rico. His gaze ran over her body and back to her face, and his lips curved into a lazy smile, revealing the tips of his fangs. Alex swallowed, mesmerized, unable to break the link between them.

"Bastion!" Rico spoke sharply, and the spell was broken. The vampire looked away, and Alex breathed again. She shifted backward so she stood beside Jon, with Skylar, Daisy, and Janey in a line in front of her.

Bastion flicked his cold gaze to Rico then lowered his head slightly. "Sire, you honor me with your presence." Even Alex could tell the words were sarcastic.

"Cut the bullshit, Bastion," Rico replied.

He shrugged one elegant shoulder. "I have a welcome gift for you." He gestured behind him and a woman stepped forward. A naked woman . . . naked except for a red ribbon tied around her throat like gift wrapping. Tall and slender with full, perfect breasts. In fact, she was perfect all over from her long blond hair to her scarlet toenails. Halting beside Bastion, she appeared unconcerned that she was naked in front of a room full of strangers. She aimed her attention at Rico, pouting her full red lips and casting him a smoldering stare out of dark blue eyes, then she raised her head as though showing off the smooth line of her throat.

Daisy made a gagging sound, and Janey sniggered.

Skylar reached forward and tapped Rico on the shoulder. "Even look in her direction, and you're dead."

Rico chuckled. "Sweetheart, I'm dead already."

"Well, you'll be even deader."

Rico shrugged. "Thank you, Bastion, but another time perhaps."

"Like never," Skylar muttered.

Bastion's eyes narrowed and his pale gaze shifted from Skylar to Rico, his lips turning down. "You take orders from your *food*?"

There was a wealth of contempt in the word. Skylar

drew her pistol and stepped forward. "Who are you calling food, dead guy?" Her tone was icy. Bastion looked at her, and then at her pistol. He raised one eyebrow but didn't appear particularly concerned. Unlike the guards surrounding him.

Rico sighed, loudly. "Put the gun away, *querida*, he's just trying to wind you up."

Bastion smiled. "You know me so well. But why not take the woman? I thought we might do a little trade. It's easy to find willing food on this planet, but it tends to be a little . . . used."

"And I thought she was a gift."

"Surely you wouldn't miss a little one." His gaze searched their small group, and Alex took a step sideways so she was hidden behind Janey. It bought her up against Jon, but he didn't move away, and she was comforted by his solid strength beside her.

"Not a chance."

Bastion shrugged. "So what do you want? I'm presuming it's not merely the pleasure of my company. Though, you used to find my company very pleasurable."

Skylar's eyes widened. "Ugh! Rico, you better tell me right now you and dead guy here didn't . . . you know."

"No, we didn't." Rico sounded offended. "We played cards and things. Man stuff. And that was a long time ago."

"And in a faraway place," Bastion finished. "So what is it you *do* want?"

Rico waved at *El Cazador* behind them. "My ship's in need of some repairs. I need somewhere to hole up while we do them. And maybe some information on what's going on in the city."

"I'd stay away from the city if I were you."

"Why's that?"

"There's a bounty out for your ship and crew."

"A bounty? Who from?" Skylar asked.

"Two bounties actually. It appears you're very popular."

"Just get to the point," Skylar snapped.

Bastion shrugged. "Both the Collective and the Church have a price on your heads. The Church wants you found, but the Collective are quite happy to have you dead." He waved a languid hand toward Skylar. "Though perhaps you've sorted your differences with the Collective."

"Shit," Tannis muttered. "That was too freaking fast. They must have the comms out on every planet in the system by now if it's reached here."

"We knew it was likely," Rico said.

"I thought we'd have more time."

"Well, we'll just have to get in and out fast."

Tannis folded her arms and tapped her booted foot. "So why are we standing around like it's some sort of tea party? Let's get moving."

"Aye, aye, captain." He turned back to Bastion, who was watching the interaction, a smile of disdain curling his narrow lips.

"These are my people." Rico waved to encompass the crew. "Keep off them. Don't touch them, don't drink from them, and don't even look at them."

"Really?" Bastion's gaze swept over them, pausing at Jon, and his nostrils flared as he breathed in deeply. His eyes widened slightly.

"You've brought a pet? How nice."

A low growl trickled from Jon's throat, and a smirk flashed across Bastion's face. His gaze shifted to Alex, and he examined her as though she were something interesting or . . . tasty.

"So are we good?" Rico asked.

"Of course. *Su casa es mi casa,*" he murmured. "Now, I must be off. This meeting has made me . . . peckish." He looked again at Alex as he spoke, and a knot tightened in her belly, her breasts ached, her nipples hardening. She tried to turn away, but she was drowning in his blue eyes . . . swaying toward him. A hand clamped down on her shoulder and yanked her back, and she shook her head, trying to clear the haze.

"Get a grip," Jon barked, and the spell was broken.

She brushed his hand away. "I'm fine."

Bastion nodded once then swung around and disappeared the way he had come, his guards following. Alex watched him, her whole body trembling.

"*I'm hardly likely to be attracted to a vampire*," Jon mimicked her earlier words.

Her gaze flashed to his face. For a moment, he appeared furious, but he quickly regained control and the expression was wiped clean.

"Get lost," she said.

He breathed in. "You wanted that bastard. I can smell it on you."

She really hoped that was an exaggeration. Glancing around she realized everybody was staring at her, and she ground her teeth. "Shut up." Shoving her hands in her pockets, she turned her back on him only to come face to face with Tannis and Rico.

"Will he be okay?" Tannis asked, nodding in the direction Bastion had disappeared. "He won't give us up for the bounty?"

Rico shrugged. "I don't think so. To be honest—I don't trust him. But he hates the authorities, so he's unlikely to give us up to either the Church or the Collective. And he won't board *El Cazador*. That's my territory, and there are some lines he won't cross."

"Which lines will he cross? What about the crew?" Tannis asked.

"That's more problematic. The thing is, Bastion just doesn't see people as important. He sees you as . . ."

"Food?" Jon provided.

Rico grinned. "Exactly the word I was searching for. Bastion won't understand why I'd give a shit if he fucks Al's brains out, drains her dry, and then dumps her corpse with the rest of the leftovers."

He held her gaze while he spoke and a shudder ran through her. She knew he was trying to frighten her. And he was succeeding. Her fingers toyed with the cross at her throat. Maybe she should ask if it would help. But she couldn't make herself, in case he made her throw it away—vampires hated crosses, didn't they? Despite her doubts, her cross had been a big comfort over the last few months. Especially when Rico was around.

"So what's the deal with Al? Why's he so interested?" Tannis asked.

"Bastion likes . . . innocence."

They turned to stare at her now, and she fought to keep from squirming. Typical. This whole innocent thing was driving her nuts. It was hardly her fault. She caught Jon's amused stare and glared.

"Hey, don't blame me," he said.

The problem was she did blame him. It was *all* his fault. She whirled around and stalked up the ramp into the relative safety of *El Cazador*, leaving the faint murmur of everyone planning their trip into the city in her wake.

CHAPTER SIX

They took one of Bastion's speeders into Pleasure City, dropped Tannis and Skylar off on the outskirts to visit the shipyards and find the spare parts they needed to repair *El Cazador*, before taking Janey and Daisy to the shopping district to stock up on supplies.

Jon sat beside Rico as they continued into the heart of the city, the speeder gradually slowing to a crawl as the traffic grew heavier. After five minutes of sitting in the tail fumes of an ancient speeder-cab, Rico swerved into a parking space.

"Come on, we'll make better time on foot."

Jon climbed out and was instantly assaulted by the incessant clamor. Noise crashed into him from every side, the raucous cries of street vendors, the roar of speeders, the low throb of music spilling out from the clubs and bars lining the street. Even the air crowded in on him, thick with the stench of fumes and too many people, liberally mixed with a nauseating fusion of every type of food available to man.

Psychedelic lights flashed, making his head spin.

"Don't you love this place?" Rico said. "It's so alive."

"No." Jon hated the place. He'd spent a considerable amount of time doing business here, and each time he visited, he hated it a little more. A sudden longing for the forests and mountains of his home planet washed over him—the clean air, the silence of the nights. He hadn't been back since his pack was slaughtered, and he rarely allowed himself to think of the place.

He closed his eyes and pinched the bridge of his nose, trying to ease the pressure in his head. When he opened them, he found Rico watching him.

"Let's get this over with," Jon said.

"One thing first," Rico replied. He reached back into the speeder and handed a weapons belt to Jon. "You might need it. I don't want to have to protect you if things go bad."

Jon took the belt, strapped it on, and felt instantly better with his hand resting on the pistol. Pleasure City was not a place to be unarmed.

"Just don't shoot me with it," Rico said. "It won't kill me, but it will piss me off. Now where are we headed?"

Jon had commed a few people, so he had a good idea where to find his contact. As long as no one had warned the traitor. Deke was a slimy bastard and liable to slither away if he caught wind someone was asking about him. "A bar called The Longest Night."

"I know it. Let's get this done and get back to the ship."

The sidewalks were thick with people, but the mass parted as he and Rico approached, giving them plenty of space. Jon glanced sideways at the vampire. It wasn't obvious what he was, but it was obvious he was dangerous. A dark aura hung about him—he radiated a barely restrained power.

"Look at that." Rico pointed up at the wall.

A flashing sign filled the whole of one side of a three-story building. It took Jon a second to realize he was staring at a huge image of Al in her priestess persona.

"They really do want her back," Rico murmured. "Who would have thought it?"

"Maybe you should send her back. She would be safer."

Rico shrugged, and they walked on. "I'm not in the business of making people safe. If Al wants to be safe, she knows what to do."

Jon's life would be easier if she went back to the Church. For some reason, Al clouded his thinking. And right now, a vague worry niggled at his mind. They all thought Al was quiet and obedient. That she'd do as she was told and stay on the ship. But Jon knew the obedience thing was an act, like the cabin boy disguise. And she was a good actor. Except when her eyes gave her away. He'd seen her reckless streak, and he didn't think she had the common sense to stay out of the vampire's way. Maybe she even believed Bastion was the answer to losing that virginity she seemed to find so onerous. But surely even she wouldn't be that stupid. Would she?

This was exactly the reason he hadn't wanted anything to do with her. He didn't want to worry about anyone but himself. He wasn't any good at looking after other people. They tended to die on his watch, and he wasn't going to let that happen again.

"You want me to wait?"

He realized he'd come to a standstill in the middle of the busy street. Rico was watching him, one eyebrow raised.

"What?"

Rico nodded to a window where a pleasure provider sat, showing off her wares. Jon hadn't even noticed the woman.

"You seem pretty tense. Perhaps you could do with a little relaxation."

Jon had nothing against them. They provided a service— one he had used often in the past. But he looked at the woman and felt nothing. No stab of desire. It would be easier if he did.

"Fuck off."

He strode off and heard Rico's low laughter behind him. "Fucking vampire," he muttered under his breath. Just because he was getting it regular . . .

"So what planet do you come from?" Rico asked.

"Why the hell do you care?"

Rico shrugged. "Just trying to make conversation."

"Well, don't bother."

They walked in silence. This time it was Rico who stopped. "This one I insist on," he said.

They'd come to a halt outside a clothing shop. Jon peered down at himself. He never really thought much about what he wore unless he was cold.

"You look like a complete dork," Rico pointed out. "It's not good for my image to be seen with you."

Twenty minutes later, they stepped outside. Jon dressed in dark pants and a shirt, adding a black trench coat that covered his weapons. He'd also ordered a whole load of stuff to be sent to the ship.

"Now can we get on with what we came here to do?"

The Longest Night bar stood on the corner of two of the seediest streets. Inside the lights and the music were low, and the place was almost empty. It was a relief to be away from the crowds and noise.

Rico surveyed the bar. "I miss alcohol," he murmured.

"Alcohol?"

"An old Earth drink—banned in the twenty-first century."

As they approached the bar, the bartender looked up. Small and pretty, her glance darted between the two of them as though she couldn't decide which one of them was the safer to speak to. Finally, her gaze settled somewhere between them.

"What can I get you?"

"I want to see Deke," Jon answered.

Her gaze shot to his face, but her shocked expression was quickly blanked out.

"No one here by that name." She flashed him a patently false smile.

Jon leaned across the bar and allowed a low growl to escape his throat. She stepped back as far as she could, which wasn't very far.

"Just comm him and tell him Jon is here and wants to talk."

As she looked from him to Rico, her eyes widened. Jon glanced sideways and saw the vampire was smiling, one sharp white fang in view.

The hand she lifted shook visibly as she pointed at a black doorway across the bar.

"Thank you," Rico said. "And I'll have one of those." He reached out a hand, and she jumped. But he only picked up one of the pinkies—the popular recreational drugs most bars offered—from the bar and popped it into his mouth. "Want one?" he asked Jon.

Jon shuddered as they turned to head to the back of the bar. "No—those things will kill you."

Rico grinned. "I doubt it. Come on. So who is this guy we're seeing. How does he fit in?"

"Deke's a facilitator. People go to him when they want something done and he acts as a sort of middleman. He set up the Ross job."

"Is he likely to know who employed you?"

"Maybe. Though he might need a little persuasion to part with the information. His reputation relies on him keeping his mouth closed."

"Well, we'll have to open it for him." Rico rubbed his hands together with obvious excitement, and Jon's own pulse picked up, all his senses heightening in anticipation of the action to come.

The door was solid metal. Jon studied it, considered

blasting his way through, but as he pulled out his pistol, the two sides slid open to reveal a brightly lit office. Jon stepped inside with Rico beside him.

A huge desk dominated the room, dwarfing the man sitting on the other side. Jon did a quick check of the rest of the room. It was empty, but at that moment, four men pushed in behind them and arranged themselves around the room. They were heavily armed, and Jon had no doubt they were bodyguards. But odds of two to one seemed fair to him—no way would Deke join in if this degenerated into a fight. He doubted Deke had ever gotten his hands dirty or bruised in his life.

The man rose to his feet behind the large desk. He wasn't much taller than Al, with a slender frame, dark hair in a ponytail, and a sly expression.

Jon nodded. "Deke."

"Jon. What a lovely surprise." The tone was so insincere it set Jon's teeth on edge.

His own smile was equally insincere. "It's a pleasure to be here."

"Actually, I'd heard you were heading for the Meridian mines. Not that it isn't great to see you." He waved a hand at Rico. "Are you going to introduce your friend?"

"He's not my friend, and no, I'm not going to introduce him."

Deke had the good sense not to push. "So what are you doing here? You looking for work?"

"No. I'm looking for information."

"Jon, please." Deke sounded pained. "You're a friend, but you know that's not the way it works."

Jon stifled his urge to slam his fist into the slimy bastard's nose. He was sure he would get a chance later. "I know, unfortunately my new acquaintance here"—he nodded in Rico's direction—"isn't so understanding."

Deke cast Rico a quick glance and shrugged. "I'd get

no work if I went around giving out confidential information about my clients."

"You'll get no work if you're dead either," Rico growled and took a pace toward the desk. Resting his hands palms down on the metal, he leaned in close and his lips curled to reveal his fangs.

Deke took a rapid step back.

The scrape of laser pistols being drawn from their holsters filled the room. Jon didn't turn around, and he didn't go for his own weapon. It would be hard for the guards to shoot without risking hitting their boss.

Deke must have come to the same conclusion because he waved a hand at the guards and the tension in the room lessened slightly, though they didn't reholster their weapons. Jon ignored them.

Rico straightened and stood back slightly, arms folded across his chest. He was good at this—knew when to push and when to back down. It occurred to Jon the vampire might be useful to have around. If it wasn't for the fact that Jon always worked alone. And the fact that he hated vampires.

Deke lowered himself into his seat. "I suppose I might be able to find out something for you. You know what? Why don't you go see the sights, get laid, and come back in a couple of hours. I'm sure I'll have what you need then."

And Jon was equally sure Deke would be so far gone from here they would never find him again.

"Sorry, Deke, but Rico here"—he gestured to the vampire—"has taken a vow of chastity. We wouldn't want to put him in temptation's way, now would we? So why don't you tell us what you do know right now, and we'll be on our way."

Deke pursed his lips and nodded once. "What do you want to know?"

The ease of his capitulation confirmed Jon's suspicions

that all he was likely to hear from Deke was a load of crap. Still he'd keep up the act for now—he was interested in just how gullible Deke believed him to be. "The last job I did. The one that ended up with me on my way to the Meridian mines. I want to know who set it up."

"I don't—"

Rico stepped forward again and alarm flared in Deke's eyes.

"Call him off," Deke said. "I was going to say I don't have a name, but I do know who was behind it."

Jon bit back his impatience. "So could you tell us? Preferably sometime this year."

Deke licked his lips. "It was the Rebel Coalition. I recognized the man who met with me."

Jon frowned. Not that he didn't believe the Coalition would have wanted Ross dead.

The Rebel Coalition had grown up in the aftermath of the Church's Purge, which had seen millions of GMs slaughtered. Most of the rebels were GMs themselves and had lost friends and family, and they now dedicated themselves to destroying the Church of Everlasting Life and its followers.

They had no argument with the Collective, but Aiden Ross had been a staunch advocate of the Church, and a supporter of some of its more radical activities. By eliminating him, the rebels would discourage any future collaboration.

Jon had done a lot of background research into Aiden Ross after he had taken on the job. He liked to know as much as possible about the people he was paid to kill. It helped in setting up the job and usually made him feel a whole lot better as he'd never yet researched a target without coming to the conclusion that the world would be a better place with that particular person dead.

No, it wasn't that he doubted the Coalition would have

set up the job. Jon just couldn't see a reason why they would have betrayed him afterward, and why there weren't comms flooding the waves taking credit for Ross's death. But there was nothing. And how would anyone in the Coalition have known how to kill a member of the Collective? Even Skylar claimed she didn't know.

All of which meant Deke was lying his weasely head off.

Deke was supposed to be the middleman who stood between Jon and his clients. If Deke had done his job, no one should have known Jon's identity. But they had known. The only way they could have caught him after he'd done the job was if they'd been following him. And the only way they could have known to do that was if Deke had told them.

Jon considered his options. Maybe they could take the guards, and part of him wanted to try. But the rest of him knew there was a good chance that Deke would get hit in the cross fire, and he needed Deke alive. He forced his muscles to relax and curved his lips into the semblance of a smile. "Thanks, Deke. That wasn't so hard, was it?"

Deke's eyes remained wary as though he didn't quite believe Jon was accepting his story, which wasn't surprising. Jon had hardly come across as a half-wit in their past negotiations. But when Jon remained smiling, Deke relaxed.

"Just don't tell anyone where the information came from or my reputation will be worth shit."

"Would I do that to an old friend?" Jon murmured. He turned to Rico. "Come on, we have what we need. Let's get out of here and after those rebel bastards."

Rico's eyes narrowed, and he glanced from Jon to Deke as though he suspected something. Then he shrugged. "Okay."

Jon led the way out of the office, through the bar, and

into the cacophony of the street. He winced as the noise assaulted his eardrums. They stood for a moment surveying the scene as the river of people divided around them.

"A vow of chastity?" Rico shuddered. "Well, that was easy."

"Too easy, and a load of bollocks."

"So why did we leave?" Rico asked.

"I didn't want Deke getting hit if the lasers started going off. So we need to draw the guards away, then get Deke alone."

"You think they'll come after us?"

"I know they will. Deke wouldn't risk a fight in his office where there's a chance he might actually get hurt, but he's a greedy bastard—he'll want that reward. So yeah, they'll come after us."

Jon searched the streets around him. They were on the main thoroughfare of the city. The road was wide, but every few hundred feet a narrower road would break off. These were well lit with gaudy signs advertising all manner of pleasures. He passed another flashing picture of Al and scowled. They were everywhere.

"Come on." The sooner they got this over with the sooner they'd get back. And Jon would feel happier with Rico keeping an eye on that piece of shit, Bastion.

He led Rico down one of the side streets, then into a narrower alley until finally they left the bright lights behind.

"Are you planning to tell me why we're here? Wherever here is," Rico said.

"Because I want to give the guys following us a chance to catch us."

"I didn't think you'd noticed them."

"I hadn't. But I know Deke."

This particular alley was a dead end, with tall buildings surrounding them and muting the sounds of the city. Jon turned and faced the rectangle of light at the entrance.

"Can we get this over with fast?" Rico said. "This place stinks."

He was right. The stench was rank—as though something, maybe lots of things, had crawled into the alley to die. "As fast as I can."

As he watched, figures detached themselves from the shadows. He counted six, and he glanced at Rico. In the dim light, the vampire's dark eyes gleamed with anticipation.

"You want to run for it?" Jon challenged.

CHAPTER SEVEN

Rico cast him a look of pure amazement. "For fuck's sake—there's only six of them."

Inside, Jon could feel the buildup of his own anticipation—his nerves strung like a taut wire, and he forced himself to concentrate. "We need to take one of them alive."

"I'll try and remember that."

The men came at them like an arrow. A stocky, bald one in the center, clearly leading, halted three feet from where Jon stood. He recognized the man as one of Deke's guards.

"Deke would prefer you alive. So why don't you come along without a fight, and no one will get hurt?"

"Is he for real?" Rico asked. "How about, we stay, we fight, and all of you get hurt bad?" The vampire grinned as he dragged the sword from the scabbard at his back. The blade glinted silver in the subdued light.

The men inched closer and drew their laser pistols, so Jon thought it was time to draw his own. The grip felt good in his hand. He flipped the switch from stun to kill and stepped away from the sheltering wall. Without conscious thought, he found himself side to side with Rico.

He studied the henchmen carefully, recognized the moment of resolve in the leader's eyes, saw his finger tighten on the trigger, and was ready when the first blast came at him.

He blocked the shot with one from his own laser. Then they were coming at him from all sides.

One ventured too close to Rico's blade, and his head rolled to the stinking alley floor. Jon took the leader out with a shot to the chest and then, for endless minutes, chaos surrounded them.

It took him a while to realize the only laser still shooting was his own.

His breathing was heavy, but more from the adrenaline running through his system than from the exertion. He shoved the laser pistol back into its holster and looked around.

Five bodies were scattered around the floor of the alley. Rico was still dealing with the sixth, and Jon turned away from the sight of the vampire feeding. The sweet stench of blood hung heavy in the air, overriding that dead-thing smell. Jon wasn't sure it was an improvement. The scent of death woke hungers he kept locked deep inside, calling to his wolf who growled and paced the confines of its prison.

Unlike younger wolves, Jon had full control of his beast, could decide when and even if he changed. Lately, he'd kept his wolf caged—he demanded too much loss of control, and without a pack to back him up it was rarely safe. Certainly not in the middle of a crowded city.

Now he shuddered with the need to give in. He took a slow, deep breath, trying to calm himself, but the scent of blood filled his head, assaulting the precarious hold he had on his control. How long was it since he had run and hunted and feasted on warm flesh?

For the second time that night, a vision of his homeland flashed across his mind, and a longing to run free under the yellow moon rose up inside him. He pushed the image away. That was another life.

Squeezing his hands into fists, he forced his gaze back to the vampire. He'd finished drinking, but the body still hung limp in his arms. Rico raised his head. His face was stained red, his eyes glowing crimson, and behind them, a darkness lurked. No sign of humanity remained.

An urge to turn and run gripped Jon, but he held his ground and ignored the primeval fear churning in his gut. "We were supposed to take one of them alive." He kept his tone casual.

Rico blinked once then seemed to come back to himself. His lips curved in a savage grin. "I forgot." His grip loosened, and the body slumped to the floor.

Jon shrugged, feeling the tension drain from his limbs. He rolled his shoulders. His body felt good for the first time since he'd woken from the cryo; the anger purged from his system.

And it didn't really matter that the henchmen were all dead. It had been a long shot that these men had any information of value. They were low-level soldiers simply doing as they were ordered. People in that line of business should be prepared to die.

Jon was.

Now they could go back to Deke and have a nice heart-to-heart without his bodyguards getting in the way, persuade him it was in his best interests to tell them everything he knew. That's if he did know anything. There was always the chance that he didn't know who had set up the assassination.

Still, he had to have some information. Credits had changed hands. Where money moved there was always a trail. They just had to follow it.

Rico crossed the alley and leaned down over one of the bodies. His sword made a curious sucking sound as he pulled it from the man's chest. The silver blade was stained dark with blood, and Rico wiped it clean on the dead man's shirt before sliding it back into the sheath at his back. He bent down and picked up his laser pistol, holstered that, and turned to Jon. "What now?"

"Now we pay another visit to Deke. And this time we don't play nice."

"Good. I didn't like the slick bastard."

Jon flexed his fingers. It looked like he was going to get that chance to break Deke's nose after all. He liked the idea.

When they entered The Longest Night for the second time that evening, the bartender glanced up, alarm flaring in her eyes. As she lifted her wrist to speak into the comm unit, Jon held her gaze and shook his head.

She lowered her arm and watched as they stalked across the bar. This time, Jon didn't wait for the door to open. Instead, he drew his laser pistol, blasted a hole in the metal, and kicked in what remained.

Deke was already on his feet when Jon stepped into the room. He stared from Jon's extended weapon to the ruin of his door then to Rico.

"Hey, you're back."

"We're back. Why didn't you tell your men to kill us?" Jon asked. "It would have been the sensible thing to do."

Deke's gaze darted to the monitor on his desk, and Jon edged around so he could see the screen while keeping Deke covered. He read the first few words. "You might want to look at this," he said to Rico.

"What is it?" Rico came around the desk and sank into Deke's huge leather chair. Leaning forward, he read the screen. "It's the wanted notice from the Collective." He scanned it quickly. "You're top of the list, but they actually want us all. It goes on to say that if they get us all together, then dead is good enough. If they don't get all of us, they'd prefer us alive—much better price than dead." He frowned. "I presume so they can use us as bait."

Jon stared at Deke, who was rubbing his hands down the side of his pants. "You'd have handed us over?"

"Of course not." Deke sounded calm enough, but beads of sweat broke out on his forehead. "Actually, I sent my men after you because I remembered a name."

"All six men? To tell us a name? This is a name from the Rebel Coalition?"

Deke nodded eagerly.

Suddenly, Jon had had enough. He wanted away from here, from the stench of greed and corruption. And lies.

He reached across the desk and grabbed Deke by the throat. Concentrating on his other hand, he felt the claws break free from his human skin. He raised the hand, now covered in dark brown fur, to Deke's throat and rested one razor-sharp claw against his skin where he could see the pulse hammering below the surface. The scent of fear drifted in the air.

"Who really set up the Aiden Ross job?" Jon asked.

"The Rebel—"

As he started the lie, Jon pressed down with the claw, piercing the skin so blood welled from the wound. Deke struggled, but Jon held him easily as he scraped down along the line of the vein. The blood ran freely now, and Deke whimpered low in his throat.

"I reckon you've got a couple of minutes before you bleed out. So I suggest you talk fast."

"I don't—"

Jon squeezed, choking off the lies he didn't want to hear. "I don't care what you don't know. Show me what you do.

Who made the payments? Where are the original contact comms?"

Deke nodded frantically, and Jon loosened his grip and shoved him toward the console. He tapped in a few words, and information flashed on the screen.

"There, that's all I know. I swear."

Jon turned to Rico, who still sat in Deke's chair. "What do you think?"

Rico studied the readings for a moment and nodded. He entered a code into the console. "I'm transferring this through to the ship. We'll get Janey working on it. She's the best there is—she'll trace it to its source."

"Good."

Deke slumped against the desk, his head hanging low. One hand clamped over the wound but blood still dripped, pooling on the polished metal.

Deke had set him up.

He glanced at the vampire and nodded to Deke. "You want him?"

Rico shook his head. "Shit no—I'm full."

Deke's eyes wide with fear. "Jon—"

Jon flexed his claws and moved quickly, ripping out Deke's throat. Deke collapsed over the desk, and Jon shifted his hand back, wiping it clean against Deke's shirt.

"Messy," Rico murmured.

"But effective. Let's get out of here."

They'd all gone and left her. Except for the Trog, and as usual he was down in the engine rooms. Alex had no desire to join him. She wanted to be out in the city, seeing the sights. Instead, she moped around the ship, with Mogg dogging her heels. Normally, the cat was confined to Alex's cabin, so he was relishing his unexpected freedom.

Alex let him explore but followed closely and eventually found herself down in the docking bay. The exit was closed, but as she stood watching Mogg chase imaginary rodents, the green light flashed, and it slid open. Trog must be checking the systems.

Alex peered out into the dark cavern beyond. Her feet itched with the need to explore, but Rico's warnings rang in her mind. An image of the vampire, Bastion, as he had looked at her last night, flashed in her mind. So hungry. She told herself not to be stupid. To stay put.

But as she turned away, Mogg spotted something interesting on the other side of the opening and headed for freedom.

"Mogg," she called.

He ignored her and scampered toward the open doorway. Through it, Alex could see the cavernous chamber, almost completely dark now.

"Mogg, come back!"

But Mogg was determined to make his escape, and he was out before she could catch up. Alex hesitated, her eyes adjusting to the dim light as she scanned for Mogg.

The red light on the exit was flashing, indicating it was about to close just as she caught a brief flash of movement. She took a deep breath and ran outside onto the soft black sand. As she stood peering into the gloom, the doors slid shut behind her with an eerie finality.

This place gave her the shivers; she swallowed the lump in her throat and wrapped her arms around herself trying to keep out the chill. Rico had told her not to leave the ship. And really, she hadn't meant to. But would anyone believe her?

She stepped back, reached out, and pressed her palm to the panel. Nothing happened. Leaning in close, she spoke into the comm unit, but the systems must have been knocked out and nothing was responding. She tried the manual switch but the door remained stubbornly closed.

No problem. She'd get Mogg, and they'd sit together until the systems came back online.

Nothing was going to happen.

Peering into the gloom, she searched for the cat, but with his black coat, he blended with the walls and floor. Finally, she caught the flash of his eyes—just as he disappeared down one of the dark tunnels.

"Mogg, no."

Alex stood for a moment, unsure what to do. But the tunnel ran in the opposite direction from the one where Bastion had vanished only hours before, and Mogg was her friend. Had been her only friend when she'd been lost in the wilds of Trakis Twelve. No way could she abandon him now.

She hurried after him, the sand muffling her footsteps. Pausing at the entrance to the tunnel, she couldn't make her feet move forward. A meow echoed from somewhere far ahead, and she took a deep breath and stepped inside.

This place was huge. What were the chances of running into the vampire? Really low, she'd bet. All the same, her hand strayed up and slipped inside her shirt, her fingers clutching the silver cross.

The tunnel meandered for what seemed like miles with Mogg always staying out of reach. Finally, it widened into a large chamber, with a bed at one end. The light was brighter in here, a central lamp casting shadows around the room. Her gaze locked onto the bed where a woman lay on the white sheets. Her head hung over the edge so her fall of blond hair spilled onto the stone floor. A crimson ribbon lay curled beside her. She was perfect—apart from a red wound at her throat. It was the woman Bastion had offered to Rico. And she was dead.

Alex swallowed and tried to control the shiver of fear that rippled across her skin. She needed to get out of there.

"Are you looking for me?"

At the softly spoken question, she whirled around. Bastion emerged from the shadows at the edge of the room, his blond hair glowing pale against the dark walls.

Alex froze in place, her muscles locked solid.

The deep blue of his eyes threatened to mesmerize her, and she shook her head, trying to clear the haze from her mind. She took a slow step back, and a smile played across his face.

"Don't run away. I won't hurt you . . . much."

Fumbling, her fingers refused to obey her, but finally she managed to pull the cross from beneath her shirt.

His eyes narrowed slightly, but there was no other reaction. No running away . . . and her last hope fled. She was going to die here. Before she had even lived. Briefly, the idea of praying crossed her mind, but she dismissed it. Why would God answer her now when he'd been silent her entire life?

Bastion's eyes trapped hers once more. "Take it off."

Her mind screamed in denial even while her hands lifted the chain over her head. She wanted to clench it tight, but her fingers opened, and the cross fell to the floor. Bastion laughed softly as he stepped closer, and Alex shuffled back until she came up against the cold stone of the wall.

His hand gripped her shoulder and pulled her upright, so for a moment she hung from his fist. One finger glided over her cheek, and needles of ice prickled her skin.

The finger trailed over her throat, lingering on the pulse point before moving lower to hook into the neck of her shirt then rip the fabric to her waist.

She bit back the small scream, determined not to beg. Besides, she knew instinctively it would do no good. All she could hope was the pain wouldn't be too bad and she could go with some dignity.

"Pretty," he murmured. His hand cupped her breast, where no man had ever touched her before. She didn't want to respond, but jolts of sensation raced down to her belly and settled between her legs. Her nipple hardened under his touch, then he pinched it between his finger and thumb and pain shot through her.

He lowered his head and kissed her there. She looked down at the blond head against her breast and wanted to cry. Bastion scraped a fang down over the creamy flesh and a trail of blood welled up. He lapped at it with his tongue, and his eyes changed from blue to crimson.

She struggled, and he laughed again.

"Go ahead," he murmured. "I don't like them too docile."

Subduing her with ease, he spun her around, and slammed her face-first into the stone wall, pressing his icy cold body against her back.

He leaned in close and kissed the back of her neck. "Please me," he murmured against her ear, "and I may keep you alive for a while. Would you like to live?"

Not at any price, she realized. Besides, she didn't know how to please him. She didn't know how to please anyone.

He positioned her as though she was a rag doll, tugging her head to the side with a hand in her hair. His other hand reached around to squeeze her breast, slick now with blood—the fingers digging in cruelly so she couldn't prevent the scream from rising up in her throat.

His cool breath whispered against her throat, and she tried to distance herself, to pretend this was happening to someone else.

She screamed again as his fangs pierced her skin, but more from shock; there was no pain, just a rhythmic tugging that pulled at places deep inside her.

"Oh God. Oh God." As she closed her eyes tight, a vision of Jon filled her mind. She latched onto the thought, tried to pretend it was Jon; he was kissing her neck, not draining her lifeblood.

But Jon's touch would be hot, not bitterly cold.

She didn't want to die. Too late, she realized she *would* do anything for the chance to live. Now it was just a matter of how much she would have to endure before death finally took her.

CHAPTER EIGHT

Rico and Skylar had vanished as soon as they got back to the ship. They'd been all over each other in the speeder. No prizes for guessing what they'd be up to right at this moment.

Jon didn't blame them. There was a close link between sex and violence; a good fight always made him horny as hell. Not that there was a lot he could do about it right now, so instead he was unloading the supplies from the speeder, trying to keep his mind off the subject of sex. He didn't trust himself to behave in a rational manner, so the best thing he could do was keep busy.

"I can't find Al."

Janey stood in the open doorway, chewing on her lower lip, her normal composure was gone, and fear flared inside him.

"What do you mean?"

"She's not on the ship. We've checked everywhere."

His fists clenched at his sides. He'd known she wouldn't do as she was told. What had she said—she wanted some excitement before going back? But even she wouldn't have gone looking for excitement with a murderous vampire.

Would she? "Jesus," he muttered, staring around the enormous area, as if he could will her to appear.

A hiss behind him made him turn. A small black cat stood a foot away, back arched. It hissed at him again. Cats never liked him.

Janey frowned. "It's Al's cat." She crouched down. "Here, Mogg."

The cat slanted him a green-eyed glare then tiptoed toward her. Janey picked him up and stroked his head. "He must have gotten out, and Al followed him."

Jon had a bad feeling about this, but he forced his fear down. He needed to stay focused. Maybe it wasn't too late.

"Go find Rico," he said to Janey. "Tell him Al's missing."

"She'll be all right, won't she? We shouldn't have left her."

"Just go," he growled.

When she'd disappeared inside the ship, still clutching the cat, Jon turned and studied the cavern. Breathing in deeply, he caught a faint lingering scent of Al. He followed it, moving methodically around the room, until he came to a tunnel where her scent hung in the air mixed with the musky stench of vampire.

"Fucking stupid little bitch," he snarled.

His fear and fury rose in equal proportions as he took off, racing down the dark tunnel. Would he be in time? He'd seen the way the vampire had eyed Al earlier. But maybe he wouldn't drain her. Not all vamps killed their victims. Then he remembered Rico's warning and knew Bastion would kill her. Hopefully, not straightaway.

Why couldn't she have left the cat?

"Goddamn fucking imbecile."

Her scent was stronger now, tinged with the faint odor of fresh blood. Jon considered shifting, but he didn't know what he would find. Then a scream echoed down the tunnel, and he broke into a dead run.

Finally, he turned a last corner and spotted them. He took in the scene immediately. Al appeared tiny clutched against the vampire. She was pressed faceup against the wall. Her head was back, her eyes closed as the vampire fed, but Jon couldn't tell if she was conscious. At least she was still alive. Vamps didn't drink from the dead.

One pale hand gripped her hair, and Jon lost his tenuous hold on his control.

Roaring with rage, he dived across the room, his hands shifting into claws as he flew through the air. The vampire didn't have time to turn. Jon's claws dug into his shoulders, and he dragged him away from Al and hurled him across the room.

Al crumpled to the floor, and Jon cast her a quick glance. Her shirt was torn open to the waist, baring the vulnerable curve of her breasts and white-hot fury scorched through his veins. But at least he could see the shallow rise and fall of her chest as she breathed. She was alive. He turned around just as Bastion launched himself across the room and slammed into Jon hard. Jon held his ground, his fury giving him strength.

His claws raked down over the vampire's chest, sinking into the flesh while he brought his knee up into his groin. Bastion groaned and doubled over. Jon kicked him hard in the face, reveling in the crunch of bone.

The vampire fell back and Jon made to follow, but Al moaned, and he turned instinctively toward her. When he looked back, Bastion was vanishing down a tunnel opposite. Christ, he was fast.

He stared longingly after him but shook his head and went to Al, crouching down beside her. Her eyes were open now but blank and unseeing. Jon gave her a quick examination; blood pulsed from the wound at her neck and one full breast had bite marks vivid against her pale skin. He swore softly.

A sound behind him made him whirl around. Rico appeared from the tunnel. Part of Jon wanted to stay close to Al, but the rest of him was consumed with the need to kill the bastard who had done this to her. He quickly tugged Al's shirt together and stood up. "Look after her," he said and headed off after the vampire.

Bastion was about to die.

Alex's whole body ached. She rolled onto her side, wrapped her arms around her middle, and tried to work out what had happened.

She was still alive. That was about all she knew.

Jon had been there. Had he saved her? As she blinked open her eyes, a pair of tall black boots appeared in her line of vision. Rico stood staring down at her, his face expressionless.

When he saw she was awake, he crouched down. Alex flinched as he reached out to touch her but didn't have the energy to do anything more. He placed a finger under her chin and turned her head so he could examine the wound on her neck.

It was still bleeding. She could feel the slow trickle of blood down her throat.

Rico picked her up and straightened so he held her against his chest. Alex struggled. Logically, she didn't think he meant her any harm, but the reaction was instinctive. His grip tightened as his head lowered toward her, and she fought then, desperate to free herself of his hold.

"Hold still," Rico snapped. "This will stop the bleeding."

She forced herself to remain still, while every cell screamed to fight him. His tongue stroked over the wounds, and the sharp sting subsided. When he raised his head, his dark eyes were tinged with crimson, and she couldn't prevent the whimper that escaped her throat.

"Don't look at me like that," he growled. "I'm not going

to finish the job. Though that's what you deserve. Come on. Let's get back to the ship."

"Is she okay?" Tannis asked as she emerged from the tunnel, breathing hard.

"She'll be fine. Though she doesn't deserve to be. Fucking imbecile."

Alex closed her eyes as he carried her along the dimly lit tunnels, only opening them when they were safely back aboard the ship. He lowered her down onto a chair. Some of her strength had returned, and she clutched the arms and sat up straight.

They were in the conference room. Rico and Tannis were watching her. She didn't know what either of them were thinking. Janey and Daisy were both staring at her wide-eyed. Alex peered down. Her white shirt was stained crimson and ripped open to the waist. She pulled the tattered edges around herself. Bruises were already forming like bracelets around her wrists where Bastion had held her, and she knew there would be others all over her body. She'd have been dead if Jon hadn't come after her.

Panic flared inside her. Where was he?

"Jon?" she asked.

"He's gone after Bastion," Rico said.

Tannis frowned. "Shouldn't you go after them?"

"I doubt he'll find him in these tunnels. The place is a maze, and Bastion knows them too well."

Alex shivered, her teeth chattering together as though she'd never be warm again.

"Come here," Rico said.

She looked up at the sharply spoken words and shook her head. No way—she didn't want to go anywhere near him. But his gaze caught hers, much as Bastion's had, and when he spoke again, she had no choice but to obey.

She stumbled to her feet and tried to stop her shuffling steps, but her body refused to obey her mind. She came to a halt in front of him, holding the tatters of her shirt around her.

"Which part of 'stay on the ship' did you *not* understand?" Rico's tone was gentle, but she could sense the fury beneath his words.

"I didn't mean to leave. I followed the cat."

Rico's eyes widened. "You followed the *cat*? What fucking cat?"

"Oh, God. Mogg. I forgot about Mogg. He's still out there."

"No, he's not," Janey said hurriedly. "He came back—I put him in your cabin."

She sagged with relief.

"First dogs. Now cats. Bloody ship's turning into a zoo." Rico pulled something out of his pocket. "Did you really think this would protect you?"

The cross dangled from his fingers. He must have picked it up from the floor where she'd dropped it. Holding her gaze, he clenched it in his fist. His skin hissed at the contact, the reek of scorched flesh assaulted her nostrils, and nausea roiled in her belly. He opened his hand and flung the cross against the wall. His palm was a mass of burned, smoldering flesh, but as she watched, the damage healed leaving only the faint but perfect brand of a cross.

"I bet you've been wearing that thing all this time— thinking it would protect you against me. Well, know this—the Church can't protect you. Nothing can."

Alex's breasts hurt, her nipple throbbed, the wound at her neck ached, and she was filled with an overwhelming urge to sob uncontrollably. She bit her lip. She wouldn't give him the satisfaction.

Besides, she deserved his fury. If she'd died, it would have been her own stupid fault. And if Jon was harmed going after Bastion she would never, ever forgive herself.

"Leave her alone, Rico," Tannis snapped.

"Why the hell should I? Stupid little cow—"

"Just shut up."

Tannis shoved Rico out of the way and wrapped her arms around Alex. For a moment, she stiffened then relaxed. It occurred to her that in her whole life, she couldn't remember anyone ever hugging her. The thought broke down the last of her defenses, and she was crying, great heaving sobs that racked her whole body.

Another first—she never cried.

She was sure that Tannis wasn't big on hugging either—the embrace felt awkward as Tannis patted her on the shoulder, but that made it all the sweeter.

Rico swore. "Oh for God's sake—stop her crying."

Tannis ignored him, but a moment later she went still. Alex raised her head. Jon stood in the open doorway, a wary expression on his features.

"Did you get him?" Tannis asked, dropping her arms from Alex and stepping back.

"No. He vanished. The place is like a maze." He studied the two of them, his gaze flashing between Rico and Alex, lingering on her face. She knew she must look a sight, and she ducked her head.

"What's the matter? She's all right, isn't she?"

"Rico made her cry," Tannis answered.

"Hey, that's right—make like it's all my fault."

Tannis shrugged. "You're only so pissed off because you're blaming yourself for bringing us here. You knew what he was like. I thought he had to obey you?"

"Tricky bastard must have been feeding day and night to overcome his sire's compulsion." Rico sighed, running a hand through his hair. "It was unexpected. Anyway, she would have been fine if she'd stayed on the ship. Like she was told. It wasn't as though I didn't warn her. She's like the rest of this fucking crew, incapable of taking fucking orders. What happens next time? Maybe she gets us all killed. She's like a fucking kid who hasn't a clue about real life."

Tannis rolled her eyes. "Get a grip."

Alex wiped her sleeve across her face. No more tears, but she couldn't prevent one last sniff. Rico swore again then pulled a silver flask from his pocket and took a long swallow before holding it out to Alex.

"Drink it," he said. "It will make you feel better."

Tannis raised an eyebrow but didn't say anything as Alex took the flask and lifted it to her nose, breathing in the potent fumes. She put it to her lips and took a big gulp. The liquid stung where she'd bitten through her lip and burned like fire down her throat, warming the coldness in her belly. She took another swallow and held out the flask to Rico.

He shook his head. "Keep it. But drink some water as well—you need to replace the fluids."

"Thank you," she said.

"Yeah, right, I'm a bloody doctor now as well." He turned and stalked toward the door.

"Where are you going?" Tannis asked.

"I'm going to stake me a vampire."

"Do you need any help?"

"And share the fun? Hell, no."

CHAPTER NINE

Alex stood in the shower, letting the hot water wash away the blood and scent of fear. She was feeling stronger with every passing minute—and more stupid.

Rico was right.

She was too naive to live.

But he was wrong about one thing. She wasn't a child. She didn't think she had ever been, and maybe that was the problem. She'd been cosseted, cared for, never exposed to the realities of life, but she had also never been allowed a childhood filled with mistakes.

Never experimented, tried things—discovered for herself what was safe and what wasn't. One thing she had learned at an early age was obedience. Every waking moment someone had told her what to do and how to do it.

That was the real reason she had left the ship today. Oh, Mogg had given her the excuse, but she'd wanted to break the rules.

From as long as she could remember she'd been told she was important—this great priestess whom everybody worshipped. When she'd run away, it had been a total revelation. One that had nearly killed her. No one had worshipped her. No one had cared whether she lived or died. Until Tannis had found her and given her a home. And she'd repaid that kindness by jeopardizing everyone.

Two fang marks marred the smoothness of her breast, vivid against the white skin. At least Rico hadn't tried to lick *them*. Hadn't even seen them, she hoped. Her skin was darkening as bruises formed. A handprint on her other breast, each finger clearly marked where he'd dug into her flesh. She touched her fingers to the wounds on her neck. It had always been a complete mystery to her why women let Rico bite them. But the actual bite hadn't really hurt at the time. Not much anyway, and she realized that what she'd hated the most wasn't the pain, but the feeling of powerlessness. That Bastion had had the strength to do whatever he liked with her, and she could do nothing to stop him.

After drying herself, she pulled on some clean clothes, curled up on the bed with Mogg held tight against her stomach, and closed her eyes.

They'd come to save her. Jon and Tannis. Even Rico. At the thought, her eyes pricked again, but she blinked away the tears. That was the last time she cried.

From now on, she wouldn't give anyone a reason to call her stupid.

Rico's silver flask stood on the table by her bed, and she picked it up, took another swallow, and leaned back as the warmth spread through her system.

She sipped until the flask was empty, lay down, and shut her eyes. The room swam behind her closed lids.

And then she was dreaming about Jon. He was rescuing her again. It was a good dream. In this one, it was Jon who picked her up, held her cradled against his chest. Jon who kissed and licked her throat, his tongue warm and wet, until the pain went away.

She woke abruptly and jumped, then forced herself to relax. It was only Daisy and Janey.

"How are you feeling?" Daisy asked.

Alex pulled herself up and took a quick inventory. Bits of her still ached, and there were one or two sharp twinges, but otherwise, she felt fine. "I'm okay."

"Good, because we're here to take you shopping," Janey said.

"We checked with Tannis," Daisy added. "She says it's okay."

"What about the wanted posters?"

Janey held up something that bore a strong resemblance to a dead animal. "Skylar donated this. And she's coming with us to keep guard. You'll be safe."

Alex recognized it now. Not a dead animal, but Skylar's long blond wig. She took it from Janey's outstretched hand and plonked it on her head. "What do you think?"

"It's good." A small frown played across Janey's face. "Are you okay though? Are you up to this? If we're going, we have to go now. The Trog reckons he'll be finished in a couple of hours, and Tannis wants to get away from here. But if you just want to sleep, we'll understand."

Alex thought about it for a second, nodded, and adjusted her wig. "There's time enough to sleep when you're dead."

Or stuck back at the Abbey.

The image of her tear-drenched face was lodged firmly in his mind. Jon hated women who cried.

He should have left her to the vampire. It wasn't his business, and she meant nothing to him. But he hadn't thought. Just gone running straight in there like some fucking goddamn hero.

And what now?

Like the stupid dick he was, he'd gone and asked Tannis how she was. The snake woman had looked at him as if he was mad and then informed him that Al had gone shopping.

Shopping.

She'd just had a near-death experience with a crazed vampire, and she'd gone *shopping*?

Tannis had told him to keep an eye out for them and comm her as soon as they returned. Apparently, the ship was fixed and ready to go. All they needed was the crew.

Rico had gotten back half an hour ago, his expression blank.

"Is he dead?" Jon had asked when Rico made to walk past him without a word.

Rico had nodded curtly, and disappointment stabbed Jon in the gut. He couldn't believe how much he had wanted to do the deed himself. But he reckoned it was Rico's right as Bastion's sire. If it had been one of his wolves, he would have wanted to do the job himself. Rico and Bastion obviously had history, and he guessed this had been a long time coming.

He had a thought. "What was the name of the ship you left Earth on?"

Rico looked at him with resignation. "The Trakis Two."

"And I'm guessing Bastion was the captain you changed?"

"Yeah, and the biggest bloody mistake I ever made. Not that we had much choice."

"What happened?"

"He kept eating the Chosen Ones. He'd wake them up from cryo and drain them dry."

"And you objected to that?"

"Hell, yeah—there was no need. I put up with him for a hundred years, then I'd had enough. I stuffed him in cryo—he's never forgiven me. Anyway, it's over now." He looked around. "Is Skylar on board?"

"No. They've gone shopping."

"*Shopping*?" Rico sounded suitably incredulous. "Who's gone shopping?"

"All of them. Well, except the captain."

"Al?"

Jon nodded, and Rico stalked off muttering about women under his breath.

Jon was sitting on the ramp still waiting when the speeder pulled up and spilled out its cargo of women. To his annoyance, he immediately searched for Al. And found her.

Last time he'd seen her, she'd been red-eyed and blood-stained. Bruised and battered. And he wasn't sure this was an improvement. Al was gone forever.

Her hair was slicked back. Someone had covered the bruises on her cheeks and chin, though her lower lip was still puffed and swollen. But her clothes were the biggest difference. She'd replaced the baggy shirt and pants with a pink jumpsuit, skintight, molded to her high, full breasts—breasts he'd seen naked only hours before—and her slender thighs. The pants tucked into boots that had four-inch heels and came up to her knees.

She appeared animated, chatting to Janey as they unloaded bags from the speeder, but the smile slid from her face as she caught sight of him watching her.

"Pink?" he said.

"Hot pink."

He turned away and headed inside the ship, not understanding the anger that pricked at him. Tannis met him in the open doorway. "Get on board. We're out of here."

"What's going on?" Jon asked.

"I guess someone knows we're here. There are about a hundred Collective ships orbiting right above us. We're leaving. Now. And Rico wants everyone on the bridge."

Jon followed, feeling the rumble beneath his feet as the engines fired. Rico was already seated in the pilot's seat when Jon arrived. He took a chair across from the vamp and strapped himself in. He'd seen enough of Rico's flying to know a safety harness was a good move. The notion stopped him. Since when had he cared anything for his own safety?

He'd never gone hunting for death, but neither had he avoided it. Now he realized—he didn't want to die.

Which was a real goddamn pity, because right now, he could see no way they were going to get out of this alive. The monitor showed a mass of small cruisers milling in the space above Bastion's stronghold. At least a hundred, maybe more. Rico might be the best pilot in the universe, but there was no way *El Cazador* could break through that lot.

He wondered who had contacted the Collective and given them away. It could have been Deke or Bastion. It was good to have friends.

It didn't seem right that he'd saved Alex, only to have her die like this. Maybe if they told the Collective that she was some important priestess, they would let her go. But if they were willing to kill Skylar, one of their own—even if there was a good chance they could regenerate her—then they were unlikely to save Alex, who was nothing to them.

Jon almost wished he'd given in. Made love to her. It seemed sad that she should die without experiencing anything of life.

The rest of the crew came in and took their seats. There was a sense of controlled urgency, but no one was panicking overtly. They must know they were about to be space dust. He sensed the moment Alex sat down across from him, but he purposefully didn't look her way.

Rico swiveled his chair to face them. "Good of you to join us," he said to the room in general. "All the shopping done?"

Skylar grinned. "Yes, boss."

He looked straight at Alex. "Bastion's dead."

Her eyes widened, and then she nodded. "Thank you."

"My pleasure." He turned back but carried on speaking. "I wanted you all in here because it's come to my notice recently that you're all crap at taking orders. So I want you where I can see you. And if I tell you to do something—do it."

"In your dreams," Tannis said. "You know, we're never going to get through that lot."

"We're not going to go through them. We're going to go around them, and hopefully they won't even notice. Skylar, can you contact someone up there and tell them we're coming out. We want to give ourselves up."

She frowned. "I told you. They don't want us to give ourselves up. They want to kill us. We go out there, and we're dead."

"What did I say about taking orders? Does 'just do it' sound familiar?" He sighed. "I want them to think we're going out there, but we're not actually going out there. I'm not a total moron."

Jon didn't see what choice they had. That many ships, with that much firepower, it didn't really matter where they attacked them, in space or on the ground. They were as good as dead.

"But you've got a plan, right?" Skylar asked.

"Have faith," Rico murmured. "I'm too young to die."

"Why the hell not?" She closed her eyes. A minute later, she blinked and nodded. "They're expecting us."

"Good." Rico pressed the comm unit on his wrist. "You ready, Trog?" He listened to the reply. "Let's do this."

A second later, the lights went out, plunging the bridge into near darkness, the only illumination from the monitor, which still showed the massed ships. Covered by the darkness, Jon gave in to the urge and turned his head so he could see Alex. Her eyes gleamed in the dim light, but she didn't appear scared.

Through the viewing window at the front of the bridge,

he could see the cavern, or rather the Stygian darkness where he knew the cavern should be. Then a faint light filtered down from above. The roof was opening, only a narrow slit at first, barely revealing the star-strewn sky, but the gap widened with each second.

The ship was moving, but not upward. Instead, they were crawling along the cavern floor. Up ahead was the opening to one of the many tunnels, this one far wider than most. They were heading straight for it, hovering no more than a dozen feet from the ground.

"Shit," he muttered. The crazy bastard couldn't really mean to go down there. Could he? There was no way they would fit.

"Okay, breathe in, everybody."

Jon clenched the arms of his seat, waiting for the screech of metal on rock, his eyes glued to the vampire's back. Rico's shoulders were tense but somehow, he managed to keep the ship in the center of the tunnel. Once inside, the ship's external lights came on, and Jon watched without breathing as they wound and twisted for miles.

Finally up ahead, the tunnel came to an abrupt end. He waited for the ship to slow. Nothing happened. They weren't going fast, but all the same, if they hit even at this speed, they would disintegrate.

"Shit, Rico," Tannis muttered. "Shoot it out."

"Can't. They'll see the explosion."

"They'll also see the explosion if you crash straight into a solid metal door and blow us up."

"Actually, I'm hoping it works on proximity sensors. Otherwise we're fucked." He nodded to Alex. "Hey, maybe you could try a prayer right about now. We could do with a little divine intervention."

Alex put her hands together. Jon realized she was actually going to pray. Did she really believe there was a God out there? And if there was, did she think He'd be listening and would give a toss whether they lived or died?

"Dear God," Alex murmured. "Please open the doors. Rico says he's sorry for all the bad things he's done, and he promises to be better in the future."

Shock flared inside him at her words. They were about to die, and she was joking.

Rico laughed. "Thanks, sweetheart, but I think that might have done the trick. God loves us after all."

Jon forced his gaze from Alex back to the viewer. A thin crack appeared in the doors, and then they slid back.

Seconds later and they were out into the open sky. Jon waited from them to speed up to make a run for it. Instead, Rico kept the speed slow and hugged the contours of the land. He was a brilliant pilot, sticking so close to the ground that they wouldn't show up as a separate entity. Still, Jon found his heart beating fast as he waited for them to be spotted, waited for the horde to swoop down and annihilate them.

The monitor was back on the cruisers above them. They still hovered above Bastion's place, but at any moment, they would realize the *Cazador* was gone. Time crawled by as they inched over the barren landscape.

Sweat beaded on his forehead, and he wiped it with the back of his hand. He was actually afraid. Jon almost didn't recognize the emotion. He hadn't been afraid of anything in a long time.

How can you fear when you have nothing to lose?

His mind refused to process the implications of that. Nothing had changed. There was still nothing to lose, and he planned for it to stay that way.

The tension in the room slowly rose as each second stretched taut. Finally, Tannis snapped.

"Shit, Rico, that has to be far enough. Get us the hell out of here."

"Getting to you?" He grinned. "Okay. We should be far enough not to be picked up. Hold on, children."

The engines roared, and they headed out into space at full speed.

"Looks like we're in the clear," Janey said a minute later, and Jon released the breath he'd been holding for what seemed like hours.

Next to him, Alex was grinning like an idiot. Didn't she have the sense to know they'd nearly died?

He unstrapped the harness and stood up. Everyone's eyes locked on him as he stalked across the floor, but he kept his lips clamped together. If he opened his mouth now, he was sure something stupid would come out.

In the privacy of his cabin, he shrugged out of his coat and tossed it on the bed. His skin was clammy and cold at the same time. He'd been certain they were going to die back there, and they hadn't. Why wasn't he feeling euphoric?

He didn't know what he felt, but he was sure fucking *joy* didn't describe it.

Edgy. Scared. Stupid. The list was endless, and none of it was good.

Pressing his fingers into his eyeballs, he tried to reduce the pressure. Behind closed lids, he saw pink, hot pink, and he ground his teeth together to banish the image.

He had to get out of there. He functioned better alone. If he could get away from these people, he'd be fine.

They weren't going to kill him, at least he didn't think so. If they ever managed to get the Collective off their backs, he was sure he'd be free to go. So all he had to do was track down who'd set him up, find a way to get out from under this bounty—keep to himself, not get involved—and afterward, he could go back to his life.

The thought filled him with no pleasure. That part of his life was over. It was time to move on. Which didn't mean he had to throw all sense aside. Money was no problem; he had accounts all over the universe. Killing people was a lucrative profession, and he'd been good at what he did. The future was limitless; he could do anything he chose.

But he'd do it alone.

He threw himself down on the bed and stared at the ceiling. Closing his eyes, he tried to sleep. No way. The notion came to him that he was waiting for something, and he was unsurprised when the buzzer sounded.

Rolling to his feet, he smashed his hand down on the panel without checking the viewer. He knew who was out there—he'd been expecting her. No doubt come to parade herself in front of him and expect him to be all turned on by her tight little body in those tight little clothes.

"What the hell do you want?"

Even in the four-inch heels, she only came up to his chin, and he had to look down to sneer at her. Straight into her cleavage. He tried to remember her breasts last time he'd seen them, bloody and marked by the vampire, but he couldn't summon the image to his mind.

The fastener of her top was lowered so the creamy mounds almost overflowed the hot pink jumpsuit. Jon forced his gaze upward. Her eyes were downcast, almost demure. Another act. She tilted her head to look up at him. For the first time, she was wearing makeup, her eyes ringed with smudged black, making them appear even bigger. Like great limpid pools of neediness.

She licked her lips. "Can I come in?"

"No."

"Please. I just want to say thank you for saving my life."

"Then say it and go."

Alex blinked up at him, her eyes glistening with unshed tears, and a wave of horror threatened to roll over him and suck him under. He wanted to yell—don't do this. Instead, he gave in to the inevitable, stepped back, and gestured for her to enter the room. Leaving the door open, he turned back to face her, folding his arms across his chest, doing his best to look formidable.

She stood, nibbling on her lip as if unsure what to say now that she'd wheedled her way in. Finally, she took a deep breath. "I know you think I'm a kid. But I'm not—I'm a woman. You'd know that if you took a moment to look."

He didn't want to look. Or maybe he wanted to look too damn much. This was exactly why he should have nothing to do with her; she clouded his mind. Confused issues that were normally crystal clear.

Her hand went to the clasp at the front of her jumpsuit, fiddling with it, and his gaze followed the movement. The fit was so tight, he could see her nipples clearly defined under the material.

Heat pooled in his groin, and his balls ached viciously. He had an almost overwhelming urge to toss her skinny ass on the bed and lose himself in her. Except her ass wasn't skinny. It was surprisingly full. Like her breasts.

She wouldn't know what had hit her.

And that was the problem.

The little fool had no clue what she was asking for.

Maybe she'd tempted Bastion the same way. And the poor sap had died because of it. He almost wanted to kick himself for that betraying thought.

Slowly, she lowered the fastener farther, until he could make out the shadowy curves of her breasts.

His dick was already rock-hard. Luckily, she wasn't looking in that direction.

As she stepped closer, her scent teased his nostrils. She smelt like warm woman.

"I was so frightened," she murmured. "I thought I was dead. I was sure I was dead. And he was hurting me." A shiver ran through her small frame, and she gazed at him with those limpid eyes. "And then I thought we were going to die back there, and all I'd ever know about sex was pain. I just want to forget." The fastener was lowered another inch. "I know you like to do the chasing. But one kiss? Is that so much to ask? To help me forget. Then I'll go, I promise."

She was manipulating him, but he could do absolutely nothing about it, and when she licked her lips again, he groaned.

"You are the dumbest woman in the universe," he muttered before giving in to the unavoidable. Her mouth was soft. He had every intention of keeping his own lips closed, but her small tongue pried them open, thrusting into his mouth so he tasted her sweetness.

His cock twitched, and he shuddered with the effort of keeping his arms by his sides. She was rubbing up against him now like a bitch in heat.

The cradle of her pelvis rocked against his shaft, and he groaned into her mouth. She went still before drawing back to peer down the length of his body, and his cock twitched again. When she peeked back up at his face, her eyes were wide, and for a moment, something flashed in her expression. Then she lowered her lashes so he couldn't see what she was thinking.

But she was as turned on as he was, the hard points of her nipples pressing against the soft material.

Jon couldn't help himself. Sliding his hand inside the open top, he cupped her breast, rubbing his palm over the beaded nipple, squeezing gently. She winced, and he went still then dropped his hand and stepped back.

She moved in close again. "Please," she whispered.

He parted the material and stared down at her. Dark bruises marred the perfection of one full breast. The other sported a double fang mark where the blood-sucking bastard had bitten her.

"It doesn't matter," she said.

"The hell it doesn't matter. It's all that matters. You're a kid in need of protection. And I'm not in the business of protecting anybody."

"Too late. You already saved my life."

"Then I'm not in the business of protecting you again. Go find someone else."

"You won't need to. I've learned my lesson."

"Darling, people like you never learn."

"People like me?"

"Reckless people."

She frowned. "I'm not reckless. I'll have you know I'm the most unreckless person ever."

"Yeah, right. That's why you came begging me to fuck you, hours after we'd met. And that's why you went running into a vampire's lair. And no doubt, why you stowed away on that ship in the first place. It's only a matter of time before you do something else stupid, and as Rico said, next time maybe you'll get us all killed."

Hurt flashed across her face, but he ignored it. Time she learned the realities of life. He reached out and pulled the jumpsuit closed, right up to her neck.

"Now you've said your thank you. Get out."

She opened her mouth. Then snapped it closed again, whirled around, and left the room.

Jon took a deep breath and slammed his hand on the panel to shut the door. His body ached. He couldn't remember ever feeling like this. Needing some sort of relief, he shoved his hand down his pants, wrapped his fist around his erection, and closed his eyes.

An image of Alex played across his mind, on her knees in front of him, her soft pink mouth wrapped around his engorged cock. He'd bet she'd never done that before either. No doubt, he'd have to tell her how he liked it, but she'd be a fast learner. He could almost feel her small fingers stroking his balls, while her tongue . . .

"Oh, hell."

A minute later he came.

Alex got halfway down the corridor and stopped. Instinct told her she'd nearly had him; he'd been so close to losing control.

She had a brief twinge of guilt over the tears. Especially when she had sworn she wasn't going to cry again. Maybe she would burn in hell. But Janey had suggested crying if all else failed. She'd said most men went to pieces if a woman cried, and that had certainly been true of Rico earlier. He'd been shocked.

Shocked was better than no reaction at all.

Her lips still tingled, and she touched them with her finger then pressed her hand against her breast.

His mouth had been hot and hard, the taste of him unforgettable. But there was also a gentleness in the way he touched her that was at such odds with his words and size. He'd said he wasn't in the business of protecting anyone, but he had rushed in and rescued her. And kissed her.

Her first kiss.

Beneath her palm, her heart gave a little jump and unease shifted inside her. This thing with Jon was supposed to be simple fun—it was never meant to touch her heart.

CHAPTER TEN

"So what sort of fighting do you want to learn?" Skylar asked.

Since their escape two days ago, they'd headed out into deep space, the idea being to keep a low profile while Janey worked on the information they'd gotten from Jon's contact. She was searching for anything that would give them some idea of why the Collective wanted Jon—and the rest of the crew—dead so badly.

Everyone was on edge, waiting for something to happen, and Skylar had jumped at the chance to teach Alex some fighting moves. She'd led her down to the docking bay, where there was more room, and spread some mats on the floor.

Alex frowned at the question. "What sort of fighting is there?"

"Well, to my mind, there are only two kinds. The kind you start, and the kind you try and finish. That's offensive and defensive."

"Defensive, I suppose."

"You don't sound too sure?"

Alex thought about it. Mainly, she wanted to know how

to defend herself. She never wanted to feel as helpless as she had with Bastion again. Even if she couldn't win against someone so much stronger, she'd still rather go down fighting. On the other hand, she had to admit that there were a few people she wouldn't mind starting a fight with. Hezrai for one.

Skylar grinned. "Okay, we'll do both. But you've got to realize that you're at a serious disadvantage in any hand-to-hand."

"I am?"

"Yeah. You can build up your strength, but you'll never be a match for most guys. Probably your best bet is to play on that. Try to look weak. Lull them into a false sense of security."

Alex sighed. "Only trouble is the sense of security would hardly be false."

"Don't worry. You just have to learn to use your strengths and play down your weaknesses."

"I have strengths?"

"Course you do. I'm betting you're fast, and you're bright. We can work with those. Okay, so the first thing you have to learn is that physical combat should only be entered into as a last resort. A professional soldier—somebody who does this stuff for a living—will almost always back down from a fight he isn't absolutely compelled to take part in."

"He will? I can't imagine Rico running from a fight."

"I did say professionals. Rico's not a professional—he's a . . ."

She seemed at a loss for words.

Blood-sucking maniacal monster?

The words hovered on Alex's tongue, but she bit them back.

Skylar shrugged. "There's also a danger that you might learn to enjoy it. The adrenaline rush can be like nothing else—it's addictive. Which is fine if you're a six-foot-four vampire with big teeth. Or a six-foot-four werewolf with big teeth. Not so good if you're a . . ." She trailed off a second time.

"A five-foot-one woman with small teeth?" Alex supplied for her.

"Yeah. So your first tactic is avoid situations which might lead to violence."

"You mean stay on the ship when there's a scary, bad vampire outside."

"Exactly. If you can't help but put yourself in harm's way, the next best option is—run. As fast as you can. But if you absolutely have to fight, try and get it over with fast. Take the initiative, and once you've committed, don't hesitate."

Alex nodded.

"Right, I want you to come at me. Pretend I'm about to do something you don't like, and you have to stop me."

Alex had no clue, but she gritted her teeth and hurled herself at Skylar. A moment later, she was flat on her back on the mat. She wasn't even sure what had happened— Skylar had moved so fast—but she suspected she'd swiped her feet out from under her.

Staring up at the black and silver ceiling, she wondered whether she should stay down here.

A hand appeared by her nose, she clasped it, and Skylar pulled her to her feet.

"Don't take it too bad," Skylar said. "I've been fighting since I joined the Corps over a hundred years ago. Come on—try again. This time you know what to expect."

Thirty minutes later, Alex was a sweaty, heaving mass of aches. She hadn't landed a single blow on Skylar though the last two times she had managed to stay on her feet for at least thirty seconds—a huge improvement. She pulled the clingy material of the jumpsuit away from her breasts and fanned her hot face, then got ready to try again. Despite the pain, she was actually enjoying herself.

A sound from the open doorway behind her made her turn, breaking her concentration, and Skylar swiped her legs from under her, dropping her on her ass for about the twentieth time. Rico chuckled, and she ground her teeth.

"Hey, that's not fair," she muttered. "I wasn't ready."

"Life isn't fair, and you've got to learn to be ready whatever happens. Use every advantage to take the other person down, and don't let yourself be distracted," Skylar said. "Keep your focus on your opponent."

Alex dragged herself to her feet and rubbed her sore backside as Rico sauntered over and flung himself into a chair close by.

"Hey, Al's got breasts."

She went still and looked across to where he lounged, arms clasped behind his head, an amused expression on his face. "Who would have guessed it?"

Skylar turned around to stare at him through narrowed eyes. "It's Alex not Al. And you'd better stop staring at her breasts, or you'll get another laser shot across the butt."

"I wasn't admiring them or anything—I was just surprised. Though now that you come to mention it . . ."

Skylar made to draw her laser pistol, and he raised his hands in mock defense.

Alex had been terrified of him when she first came on board. She still was, but not nearly so much. He had changed since Skylar joined them. Before that, he'd been a dark and mysterious figure who'd kept to himself and refused anything to do with the crew, well, except for the captain.

Obviously, all he'd needed was the love of a good woman. Perhaps that's all Jon needed as well. Trouble was, she wasn't sure she was good. Besides, she wasn't looking for love. All she wanted was a new experience before she went back to real life. Love didn't come into it. How could it when she didn't even believe in love? She shoved aside the memory of the queer little twist of her heart when he'd kissed her. Or to be more honest—when she had kissed him.

"You know," Skylar said, "I can teach you some basic moves, to use as surprise tactics, but you really need something more." She studied Alex, hands on her hips. "Hmm, I'm thinking serious firepower. And a blade, maybe two."

"Why do I find that seriously scary and an enormous turn-on at the same time?" Rico drawled.

"Because you're a pervert?" Skylar suggested.

"Oh yeah."

Alex personally liked the sound of serious firepower, and she followed Skylar across the room to the weapons cabinet tucked in the corner. Together they studied the contents.

"Here," Skylar said and handed her a weapons belt with a laser pistol.

"Are you sure that's wise?" Rico asked from behind them.

"Of course it is." Skylar watched as Alex wrapped it around her waist. "Just remember, never aim at someone you're not willing to shoot."

Alex liked the feel of the gun at her waist. She rested her hand on the grip and practiced a quick draw.

"What's going on?"

Jon stood in the open doorway, and the muscles clenched low in her belly. He'd showered and his hair was wet and slicked back from his face. He wore black leather pants and a white shirt, the sleeves rolled up over his dark forearms, a laser pistol strapped to his waist. Alex swallowed.

"Skylar's teaching *Alex* to fight," Rico replied.

"Is that wise?"

"Exactly my question."

"Wow," Skylar said. "Great minds think alike."

"She any good?" Jon asked, coming into the room.

To Alex's amazement, Rico didn't immediately jump in and say she was crap. Instead, he shrugged. "Well, she's fast."

"Useful for running away."

Alex's hand tightened on the laser pistol. But she remembered Skylar's words, and she didn't think she was quite ready to shoot Jon yet, though she was getting close. Instead, she shoved the pistol back in its holster and wiped some of the sweat from her forehead.

At least he seemed to have stopped flirting with the others, or he didn't do it when she was around. Which was just as well, as she reckoned that would be legitimate cause for a laser blast.

He was watching her now, a disdainful expression on his face. "She'll never be a fighter. She doesn't have the instinct."

Rico grinned. "Oh, I don't know, looking at her expression right now I think the instinct's there."

Jon stepped farther into the room and shrugged. "The only way to fight is to presume you win or you die."

"Not everyone would agree with you."

"Yeah, they're the sort who do the dying."

"And what sort are you?" Skylar asked.

"What do you think?"

Skylar nodded toward the mats. "You want to have a go?"

He grinned. "Why not?"

Skylar led the way, and the two stood facing each other. Skylar was at least six inches shorter than Jon and half the width, but she faced him with an easy confidence that stirred a flicker of jealousy in Alex.

Rico patted the seat next to him. "So how are you feeling?"

Alex glanced at him warily, but sat down on the edge of the seat. "Why?"

"I just wondered. Some people react strangely to a vampire's bite. They get cravings."

"Cravings?" Then she realized what he meant and a shudder of disgust ran through her. "Ugh!"

He gave a short bark of laughter. "Well, that puts me in my place."

There was actually something Alex had wanted to ask since the attack—now was as good a time as any. "That thing you and Bastion did . . ."

"Thing?"

"Where you made me do what you said." She nibbled her lower lip. "How far does it go? Can you make me do *anything*?"

"You want me to test it?"

"No!"

He grinned. "Don't worry—it only works for simple physical acts. If too much thinking is involved, the brain takes over and breaks the compulsion. That make you feel better?"

It did—the idea that Rico could make her do anything just by telling her had played on her mind. She nodded and turned away to watch Skylar and Jon. They were circling each other now. "She won't hurt him, will she?"

Rico grinned. "You don't have much faith in your boyfriend."

"Jon's not my boyfriend."

"But you'd like him to be." Her gaze flew to his face, and he raised an eyebrow. "You're not exactly subtle."

"I don't have time to be subtle," she muttered.

"Forget the wolf. When this is over, we'll get some downtime. Visit one of the bigger planets. You can find a nice boy."

Was he being deliberately obtuse? "What are you, a matchmaking service? Besides, I don't want a nice boy."

"No, that's obvious. But let me tell you a bit about wolves, especially lone wolves."

Alex was torn between wanting to watch Skylar and Jon and wanting to listen. Rico wasn't always so talkative, he might never open up again, and she wanted to know. "What's a lone wolf?"

"Well, your normal wolf is a pack animal. The pack gives them structure, a purpose and a place in life, and a strict set of rules to live by. Pack wolves, especially alphas, can be bad news, but at least they're predictable—their one purpose is to protect their pack. But you know the only thing more dangerous than an alpha werewolf protecting his pack?"

Alex was sure he didn't expect an answer, but she shook her head anyway.

"An alpha werewolf without a pack to protect. A lone wolf lives by nobody's rules but his own. Most of them have a death wish."

"Jon doesn't have a death wish."

"No? Going one-on-one with Skylar isn't exactly sensible." He shrugged. "Maybe he doesn't have a death wish, but he doesn't care if he lives or dies. And that makes him dangerous. Also, I'm betting he isn't shifting regularly."

"Shifting? You mean turning into a wolf?"

"Well, I don't expect he can turn into anything else. Back on Earth, they had no choice—they had to shift at the full moon. Out here, the older ones don't need to change, but if they resist, it builds up inside them. My guess is our boy over there"—he nodded to where Skylar and Jon were still circling—"isn't shifting, except for that fancy hand stuff. It's one of the reasons he's so bad-tempered right now. And one day he's going to blow, and you don't want to be around when that happens."

Alex considered mentioning that Jon was hardly a "boy"—he was a hundred and ninety-two. But she supposed to someone of Rico's age, that would seem very young. Besides, something else he'd said interested her.

"One of the reasons?" she asked.

Rico turned to her, his gaze sliding down over her body to linger on her breasts pointedly. She resisted the urge to cross her arms. "My guess is he's hankering after the one thing he's told himself he can't have, and it's making him a little testy."

Alex opened her mouth to ask what he meant, but at that moment, the two fighters stopped circling.

"At last," Rico muttered. "Now watch."

Alex watched, her gaze glued to Jon. He was beautiful to watch, all leashed power.

Skylar made the first move; she whirled and kicked out. Jon evaded her easily. Then they were moving fast, almost a blur of speed. Each too quick to get caught by the other, until Skylar landed a punch on his right shoulder. He appeared to fall back, but as Skylar followed through, he swiped her legs from under her, and she crashed to the floor. She was up in an instant and they were circling again. This time Jon made the first attack, diving for her, the weight of him driving her down to the ground.

"There—that's where size will always win in the end. Sheer brute force," Rico murmured from beside her.

For a moment, it seemed like the fight was over, but Skylar got her knees between them and heaved him off. He landed on his back, and she was on him in a flash, a knife appearing in her hand. She crouched over him. The point pricked his throat so a bead of blood welled up. "Yield?"

Alex cast Rico a quick sideways glance. "Isn't that cheating?"

Rico shrugged. "I think she's probably trying to illustrate a point. There's no such thing as cheating in a real fight. Just winning or losing."

"Well?" Skylar nudged him with the tip of the knife. He winced, then nodded.

"Have I missed the fun?" Janey asked, strolling into the room. As usual, the other woman had the instant effect of making Alex feel small, scruffy, and decidedly unfeminine. She'd had to work hard at the beginning not to hate Janey for that. And she'd succeeded. But since Jon had come on board, she seemed to have regressed.

"Why? Do you want to learn to fight as well?" Rico asked.

"I don't think so." Janey shuddered and smoothed down her black dress then grinned at Alex. "You're learning how to fight? You are keeping busy. She had me teaching her how to hack into systems this morning."

"Very useful talent for a high priestess," Rico murmured.

Alex wasn't going to try and explain the intrigue and political infighting that went on within the closed walls of the Church. When she went back, she would make sure she wasn't at a disadvantage and having access to knowledge would help.

"What's going on?" Skylar asked Janey, as she rose gracefully to her feet. Jon still lay on the floor, but he rolled onto his side and propped his head on one hand to watch them. Alex had expected him to be furious at Skylar for beating him, but he appeared more relaxed than she'd ever seen him, the harsh lines on his face smoothed out, as though the fight had released some of the pent-up tension inside him.

"Tannis sent me to find you. I'm picking up a ship following us," Janey said. "It's right on the outer edge of our scanners at the moment, but whoever it is they're closing in on us fast."

"Collective?"

"I'm pretty sure it's not. The Collective is somewhere behind us. This lot are coming at us from the side."

Skylar sighed. "Okay, let's go see who's after us this time."

Alex trailed behind them to the bridge. She wished she had a more important role on the ship, but what would be the point of pushing for that if she were leaving soon? Still, it irked her when everyone else was doing stuff, and she had nothing to contribute.

"You could always pray."

She jumped at the whispered words and spun around to find Jon standing beside her. Lost in her thoughts, she hadn't even noticed him.

"How did you . . . ?"

"I didn't, but you looked sort of lost and jealous and . . ."

"Useless?" she finished for him.

"Yeah, useless."

"They all know what to do. I wish I had something I could add, but I'd only get in the way."

"Stop feeling sorry for yourself. I'm not doing anything, and it's not bothering me."

"There they are," Janey said.

"That's not Collective," Tannis replied. "That's our other current best friend. High Priest what's-his-face. Only this time he's got company."

"Okay," Jon murmured. "Now, you can feel sorry for yourself."

"Thank you," Alex muttered sourly, then shifted closer until the monitor was visible. She recognized the space cruiser from their previous attack, but not the two ships on either side. They were big and nasty, and a shiver of unease ran through her.

She was still shocked by how much trouble the Church was going to to get her back. It should be making her feel all warm and fuzzy. Instead, anxiety gnawed at her insides as though something wasn't right with the world.

Tannis was pacing the bridge. "They're bigger than us and faster than us. And those new ships don't look like Church."

"No," Rico agreed. "They're mercs." He turned to study Alex. "You sure are popular, honey."

Alex squirmed under his direct stare, but after a moment, he turned back.

"Can we outrun them?" Tannis asked.

"You just said it—they're faster than us."

"Outfight them?"

"Not a chance. There's one thing on our side though—presumably they want their priestess alive, so they won't shoot us down. And out here in open space, it's going to be hard to give them the slip. Besides, if we do manage to evade them—chances are we'll run straight into the Collective."

"Shit," Tannis said. "We'll never be able to get away with them both dogging our every move. This is not earning us any money. We need to get rid of these guys for good." She turned to Alex. "What if you come right out and tell them you don't want to go back? Can't they just get a new priestess?"

Alex shook her head. "No. It's hereditary. The old priestess has to die, and at the exact same moment, a new one is born."

"So what—they go searching for a baby born at the same time. And that's it? If you have the misfortune to be born right then, you're stuck with this priestess shit?"

"Yes," Alex said, trying not to sound morose. "But there's usually something else."

"Like what?"

"Some sort of sign or mark."

"And you have one."

"Yes. I have a birthmark in the shape of a cross. Here." She pointed to her right thigh.

"Can we see it?" Rico asked.

"No, we can't." Tannis ran a hand through her hair. "Next time I see someone starving in the streets—you know what—I'm going to leave them there."

"I'm sorry."

"Don't worry, kid," Tannis said. "It's not all your fault."

Alex winced at the "kid," but decided now was not the time to argue about it. Tannis had turned her attention to Skylar. "And next time someone comes to me with a job that sounds too good to be true, I'm going to turn and run as fast as I can in the opposite direction."

"Unless they offer you a lot of money," Skylar drawled.

Tannis glared for a moment and then grinned. "Yeah, I guess that would do it. So how do we get out of this one?"

"They're on comms now," Janey said. "You want me to ignore them for a minute while you guys come up with a plan?"

Alex wanted to ignore them for a lot longer than a minute. A lifetime would be nice. She gnawed on her lower lip as she waited for Tannis to respond.

"No," she said. "Let's hear what they have to say. At least we'll know what we're up against."

"This is Hezrai Fischer, High Priest—"

"Yeah, we heard that bit the last time," Tannis interrupted. "What do you want?"

"Only what belongs to the Church."

"Did we mention before—we don't have anything that belongs to the goddamn Church?"

"Then let us board and see for ourselves."

"You're not setting one holy foot on my ship."

"You think you can stop us?"

Alex recognized the smug tone of Hezrai's voice. He believed he had already won, and she hoped he was wrong.

A sense of suffocation enveloped her, and she forced herself to breathe deeply. She glanced down at her jumpsuit—this one burnt orange with scarlet piping—and could almost feel those horrendous black robes wrapping themselves around her, burying her alive.

Tannis turned off the comms link. "This guy is starting to seriously piss me off. Any ideas?"

"Well, we have someone who might stop them boarding," Rico said.

Tannis tapped her foot. "And are you going to reveal who that is?"

"We have a representative of the Collective on the ship, flash them a live feed of Skylar if you have to, and tell them if they board us by force, she'll be filing a formal complaint."

"Then what?"

"Tell them we've no argument with the Church, and if we have this thing of theirs, we're willing to negotiate. Set up a rendezvous point."

"And then what?"

"Jesus, I don't know. But this will at least give us a chance to come up with a plan."

Tannis switched the comms back on. "Look, we're not even sure what it is you think we've got. But we're willing to come and discuss it with you."

"Why can't we discuss it right now?"

"Because I don't like you, and I don't want you on my ship. And just so you know, we have a member of the Collective with us, and if you make any attempt to board, she'll be filing an immediate complaint."

Hezrai didn't speak for a minute, though Alex could hear the rasp of his breathing. He was upset. Good.

"So what are you suggesting?" he asked.

"Let's arrange a rendezvous point, and we'll meet you there." Tannis moved across to the captain's console and pressed a few keys. "How about the third moon of Trakis Four. That's neutral ground. And only a few hours away."

"Agreed. But you try and move out of tracking distance and we will attack immediately."

"Yeah, right. I'm *so* scared." Tannis switched off the comm and flung herself into her seat. "You know this guy?" she asked Alex.

She nodded. "All my life."

"You get along?"

"He hates me. Apparently the first time we met, I threw up on him."

Tannis sniggered. "Good for you."

"I was only four weeks old at the time." Alex defended herself. "But things never really improved after that."

"Right, so we have about six hours to think of a way to permanently get this piece of shit off our backs. So get thinking."

Alex waited until everyone was busy and headed for the door, needing time to think.

She didn't go back to her cabin; instead, she headed for the docking bay and slipped inside the shuttle where she was pretty sure she wouldn't be bothered. Both Jon and Skylar had watched her as she left the bridge, but she didn't want to talk to anyone. Jon was unlikely to follow her—why would he? But she had a notion that Skylar would come in search of her. And she didn't think she could cope with anyone trying to persuade her out of what she was about to do.

Or even worse, not trying to persuade her. What if she told Skylar she was going back, and Skylar said, "Good idea, kid?"

She couldn't bear it. This way she could at least tell herself she had been part of something, and that they'd wanted her to be here. Even if she had no choice except to go. The thought had been churning in her mind ever since that kiss with Jon.

Everything had changed with that kiss.

Or rather, not changed but become clearer. It was why she had stayed away from him these past few days. She needed to understand what she was feeling and what the ramifications were.

Maybe she was wrong, and with a little distance she'd realize she wasn't coming to care for him. That she just had a serious case of hero worship, because he was gorgeous and exciting and had saved her life.

Before the kiss, she'd thought she could have a little fun, learn what it felt like to be a real woman. And afterward, she would go back and do the job she was born to do, with a few happy memories to look back on. Eventually, she would forget her time on *El Cazador* and forget Jon.

But she knew it wasn't only hero worship. It wasn't love either—yet. The problem was, she suspected she wasn't the sort of person who could separate sex and love however much she wanted to. Now, if she stayed and if she did somehow manage to persuade Jon to give in and make love with her, she doubted she would ever have the strength to walk away. He would shatter her heart without a thought, and she'd be left broken and useless.

It wasn't as though he would ever allow himself to care for her. While she might persuade him to have sex, for him that was all it would be. Jon was a hard and bitter man. Somewhere in his past, something had broken him. Alex couldn't change that. She wouldn't even know how. Anyway, he'd told her as soon as this was cleared up he was off on his own again. The way he liked it.

Why could she never be the person she wanted to be? Why did everything have to matter so much to her? The recent interaction with Hezrai had crystallized her thoughts, until they were like sharp little daggers stabbing at her tender brain.

Tannis had said they couldn't escape from both, so at least by going back she could do some good.

If she gave herself up to Hezrai now, maybe he would leave her friends alone, and without her dragging them down, they would be able to sort out their issues with the Collective.

So she was doing this to save her friends. Why did she always have to think that the whole world was her responsibility? Maybe that's what happened when you were brought up as a priestess and told you were the divine hand of God.

You can't save the whole world, Alexia.

Sister Martha's words echoed through her mind. The old sister had said them so many times when Alex had been growing up. Whenever she'd wanted to make changes, make things better. When she was younger, she had argued. As she'd grown older, she'd argued less as it seemed more and more futile, and she'd come to believe she couldn't save anything, never mind the whole world.

Now she wasn't so sure.

At least she planned to try.

CHAPTER ELEVEN

Alex disappeared from the bridge soon after the comm ended.

She'd appeared sad and defeated. And who could blame her; if he'd spent most of his life with assholes like Fischer, he'd be suicidal by now. The thought worried him. Jon couldn't even begin to imagine what her life must have been like. She'd said that she intended to go back, but he presumed she hadn't really meant that.

He'd almost decided to follow her when Skylar rose to her feet and headed out. Skylar would be much better for Alex; she'd be able to talk without the other thing clouding the issues.

Alex had been avoiding him the last couple of days. He'd gotten himself all built up to fend off her advances, and he'd hardly seen her. If she was in a room when he entered, she somehow managed to slide out and vanish.

That was a good thing, wasn't it? At last, she'd realized he wasn't some sort of puppy dog she could play with. But he hadn't been happy.

Then today he'd come up with the brilliant notion that

what she was really doing was letting him do the chasing. After all, that's what he'd told her to do.

So he'd gone looking for her today. Not really understanding the impulse but knowing he had to see her. Probably to tell her she was wasting her time, and he wasn't the running sort. In any direction.

He'd seen her with Rico. At first, he hadn't noticed Skylar was present as well. Alex had been all hot and sweaty, and sexy as hell, and he'd been shocked by the fury that had roared through him at the sight. Luckily, no one had noticed him before he'd spotted Skylar and managed to get his rage under control.

In that moment, he had accepted that he was fighting a losing battle.

Why not give her what she wanted?

The truth was they would sort out this thing with the Collective, and he would be on his way eventually. Or they would all die. Either way, having a little fun with Alex wouldn't do any harm whether she decided to go back to the Church or not. He wouldn't be here anyway.

Once he'd accepted the idea, the tight knot of tension had unwound inside him, and he was filled with a lightness he couldn't remember.

He'd welcomed the fight with Skylar to blow off a little steam, but it was a measure of how unsettled he was that she'd beaten him. His mind had been on other things.

Walking behind Alex to the bridge, he hadn't been able to drag his gaze from her tight little ass, knowing it was only a matter of time before it would be his. And he'd been feeling the pressure ever since.

Now, he was lying on his bed, an hour later, his hand down his pants, trying to relieve a little of that pressure when the shrill of the buzzer rang through his head. He knew who it was without looking. She was the only person who ever came to his cabin.

"Shit."

Bad timing. He'd explode if she came near him now.

Jon released his grip on his cock, rolled to his feet, and pulled his shirt down over his pants in an attempt to be a little discreet. He didn't want to scare her off now that he'd decided he didn't want her scared off.

She stood in the doorway, hands in her pockets. Despite the clothing, she reminded him of Al the cabin boy.

"Can I come in?" she asked. "I have a proposition for you."

A proposition? That sounded more like it. Still, he couldn't quite get rid of the idea that something wasn't right with the world in general, and his immediate plans for the future in particular. Stepping aside, he gestured for her to enter.

She gave him a wide berth as she passed, and he frowned again. For once, she'd fastened the jumpsuit right up to her neck; no sign of cleavage on show today. Though it molded to her full breasts, and his cock twitched inside his pants.

He reached out for her, but she stepped back, and he dropped his hand to his side, shaking his head in confusion. Why, when he thought he had a grip on things, did the rules have to change? He took a deep breath. Maybe she needed to talk about it first. Women liked to talk. Didn't they?

"So this proposition . . . ?"

She nibbled on her lower lip. "I want you to take me to the rendezvous point with High Priest Fischer."

For a moment, he didn't think he'd heard right. Maybe because he'd been expecting words more along the lines of: *I want you to take me to bed and fuck my brains out.* Well, maybe not that exact wording, but similar. Now, he had to try and get his head around this. At least his hard-on was subsiding.

Was it some sort of more oblique approach? Maybe he should tell her he'd decided to give her his full coopera-tion. Or perhaps he could show her. He stepped toward her, but once again, she backed away.

"You were right," she said.

"I was?" Well, that had to be a first.

"I have to leave before I get you all killed."

He pressed his fingers to his scalp. "Let me get this straight. You want me to take you and hand you over to the Church."

She nodded.

"Why? What's changed?"

"Nothing really. I told you I was always going to go back."

"So why now?"

"They know where I am. And they obviously won't stop coming after everyone until they have me back. Once I re-turn, they'll leave you alone. You'll be able to concentrate on sorting out the Collective rather than avoiding the Church."

"You can't give yourself up."

Uncertainty flickered in her expression. "Why?"

She no doubt wanted to hear something soft and roman-tic like he couldn't bear to see her go. But that wasn't who he was. Hell, even before his pack had gone he'd never been one to articulate his feelings.

"Because I can't stand the thought of that slimy bastard getting what he wants."

Disappointment flashed in her eyes, but she shrugged. "Anyway, I'm not giving myself up. I'm going home. It's not as though I'm in any danger."

He paced the room for a minute, before turning back to face her. "Why come to me?"

"Because I don't know how to fly the shuttle."

"But why me? Why not one of the others?"

"Because the others might try to talk me out of it. I know you won't. You told me to go back, after all."

"I didn't mean it."

"Yes you did. And you were right." A frown formed between her brows. "What's the problem? You'll even get a reward for handing me over. It's a win-win situation for you."

Jon rubbed his chin. In a way, she was right. She would be safe if she went back to the Church, unlike the rest of them who were not likely to survive much longer with the Collective after them. As long as the Collective never found out her involvement, and they were unlikely to make a connection between The High Priestess of the Church of Everlasting Life and a motley crew of space pirates. No, she'd definitely be safer, so why was he searching his brain for reasons why she shouldn't go back?

Why wasn't he elated? Instead he felt as though he was about to lose something. Something he'd never actually had.

He forced himself to think through it logically.

The truth was, he didn't want her to go.

But if she stayed here, she would die with the rest of them. He'd be unable to protect her, just like he'd been unable to protect his pack.

"I'll take you," he said.

He'd hand her over to the Church, he'd pick up the reward money, and he'd keep right on going, head off on his own. That was how it should be.

She nodded. "I'll meet you in the docking bay in half an hour."

Alex had to get out of there. If she'd stayed any longer, she might have broken down and decided she should stay after all. She'd thought he would leap at the chance to get rid of her. But he hadn't. In fact, he'd been downright reluctant, and she'd sensed her resolve weakening. She'd wanted to wrap her arms around him, bury her head against his chest, and let him tell her that everything was going to work out.

Of course, she hadn't. Because he couldn't tell her that.

Back in her cabin, she dragged the bundle out of the small cupboard, while Mogg watched her from the bed. These were her only possessions when she'd come aboard— now she wished she'd tossed them away on Trakis Twelve. She shook out the black robes. The material was the finest available. It didn't help—she loathed them.

Glancing down at her lovely orange jumpsuit, a wave of loss washed over her so strong she staggered under the weight of it. She knew she was doing the right thing, but this way she wouldn't even get to say good-bye to her friends. And they were friends, probably the first true friends she had had in her entire life. Maybe she'd send Skylar a comm, to apologize, once she was safely back in the Abbey.

Everyone was still on the bridge discussing how to evade the Church. Soon they wouldn't need to. She hoped they'd be grateful and not angry with her.

As she stripped off the jumpsuit and boots, she cast a quick look down her body. All she wore was a pair of scarlet panties. She'd keep those on. No one would know what was beneath her robes. Except her.

She pulled the black dress over her head and tugged her boots back on. The robes were old-fashioned in design and buttoned up the back. At the Abbey, she'd always had people to help her dress. Here, she'd have to ask Jon. She crumpled up the headdress, shoved it in her pocket, and she was ready to go.

Mogg rubbed up against her legs as though he could sense something amiss. She had to leave him behind, and she couldn't bear it, even though she knew Daisy would take care of him. She sank onto the bed, pulled him onto her lap, and stroked his silky fur.

Then she gave him one last hug, put him down on the floor, and ran from the room before she could change her mind.

Jon was waiting for her, dressed in his black coat and leaning against the side of the shuttle. When he caught sight of her, his eyes widened. He stood up straight, staring at her outfit in disbelief.

"Jesus Christ," he muttered.

She ignored the comment, slammed her hand into the door panel, and heaved a sigh of relief when it slid open. The Trog had assured her he'd adjusted the systems, but she hadn't been sure he'd really understood what she needed. Standing to the side, she gestured for Jon to enter, then followed him inside.

"You do know they'll notice as soon as the outer doors open?" Jon said. "They'll very likely stop us. If they threaten to shoot, I'm turning straight back."

"No, they won't. The Trog's shut down the external monitors."

"Why would he do that?"

"Because I asked him to. But we have to leave now."

The interior of the shuttle was small—about ten feet by ten feet. With two seats facing a bank of consoles. Jon sat down in the pilot's seat, and Alex took the one next to him. It hadn't occurred to her to ask if he could actually fly one of these things, but he appeared quite competent, and soon they were speeding away from *El Cazador*.

Alex still hadn't asked him to fasten the dress. Now she stood up and turned her back to him. "Would you do me up?"

"What?"

"Do up my dress—I can't reach the buttons."

"Do I look like a goddamn lady's maid?"

She peeked over her shoulder to where he slouched in the chair, his expression vaguely hostile.

"Please?"

She turned around again and waited. Finally, she heard him rise to his feet. He stood behind her, not moving, not touching her, but close enough so she could feel the heat from his body on her bare skin.

"Aw fuck. What the hell."

At his words, she made to turn around, but his hands slid down to rest on her hips and hold her in place. She should move away, but she couldn't make her feet take the necessary steps. Holding her breath, she waited to see what he would do.

He reached across and slammed his hand down on the controls. The engines died. The shuttle drifted, and still she waited.

One finger stroked down the length of her spine, sending pleasure shooting along her nerve endings. All the way down, until it delved beneath the edge of her panties to tease the cleft at the top of her buttocks.

A small whimper escaped her mouth, and she bit down on her lower lip.

She couldn't have moved now for anything.

The finger trailed back upward, and both of his hands slid inside the gaping dress. For a second they rested, flat against her rib cage, burning heat searing her flesh. They glided around over her sensitized skin, and he cupped her breasts and squeezed gently. Alex shuddered as exquisite pleasure melted her insides.

Her nipples ached with need, and he rubbed them with his palm so they hardened. He rolled them between his fingers and thumbs, then tugged at the stiff peaks, sending darts of sensation shooting down through her belly to settle between her thighs.

Jon leaned over her, so his hot breath feathered along the back of her neck, and her whole body shivered in response.

"Do you like that?" he murmured against her skin, and he gently pinched her nipple.

"Yes." Her voice sounded breathless to her ears.

He laughed softly and kissed her throat, his mouth open. Her head fell back, and she squirmed against his hands. She'd never imagined a man's hands could feel like this. That his mouth could drive all logical thought from her mind, reducing her to nothing more than a mass of nerve endings, each one craving his touch.

"What are you doing?" She forced the words out.

"Everyone is allowed one good deed in a lifetime of bad ones. This is mine." He licked her throat. "Something to remember in your lonely bed, back at the Abbey."

One hand left her breast and tugged the material of the dress down over her shoulders and arms so it fell to her waist. Now, her breasts were bare, cupped in his big hands, her skin pale against his darkness. Mesmerized, she watched as he played with her, rubbing the pads of his thumbs over the taut peaks, then scraping his nails over them gently.

A pulse throbbed between her legs, and she clenched her thighs together to intensify the feeling. He must have sensed the movement, because his hands went still.

"Do you want me?" he whispered in her ear as one hand skimmed beneath the dress, over the flat plane of her belly. She couldn't answer, the power of speech had deserted her, but she didn't need to. For a second he cupped her in his hand before pushing beneath the panties. His fingers found her and slid between the folds of her sex.

Her knees gave way, and she almost fell, but his arm around her waist held her steady while his clever fingers moved between her thighs.

"Open your legs," he murmured and pushed one leg between hers, widening her stance.

She was frozen in place as one finger pushed up inside her, then withdrew to draw lazy circles around that point that throbbed and pulsed. The sensation was overwhelming, everything was out of control.

"I can't . . ."

She didn't know what she couldn't do, then he found the exact spot, rubbed once, twice, and she exploded.

He held her tight while her body convulsed. Only when the tremors eased did he turn her around in his arms and hold her loosely so she could look up into his face.

A lazy smile played across his lips. "Well, that was easy."

Alex hadn't known it could feel like that. That her body would respond so readily to a man's touch. Not any man's, only this one, she reminded herself.

She wanted to hold him and lie in his arms and never let him go. The thought was like ice water poured over her. She wrenched herself free and stepped back, dragging the dress up over her naked breasts. "I can't do this."

"Yes, you can."

"We have to stop."

"No we don't."

"You don't understand. I've got to go back, and I don't want to, and this makes it harder and"—she paused then said the only thing she could think of that would make him back off—"and I think I might be falling in love with you."

He'd been reaching out to pull her back to him, but at her words, his hands fell to his side, his eyes wary as he studied her.

"Turn around," he said.

"Why?"

"Because I'm going to fasten your dress."

CHAPTER TWELVE

He could still smell her arousal in the air, stirring his blood.

They hadn't spoken since he'd fastened her dress. Now, as the ship settled on the soft sand of the moon's surface, he switched off the engine and glanced sideways to where she sat strapped into the seat beside him. Alex faced straight ahead, a fixed expression on her small face.

She thought she was falling in love with him.

Even if she stayed, he couldn't offer her anything except a very likely death.

Nothing had changed, and everything had changed.

He wanted to be angry. But he also wanted to understand.

"Why?" he asked.

She turned and blinked as if coming out of a trance. "Sorry?"

"You told me you always planned to go back—what I don't understand is, why? Once you got away, why not turn your back on the whole rotten lot of them? Don't tell me you actually believe the crap the Church spouts."

"Most of the crap, and most of the time, no—I don't believe it. But a lot of people do. The Church gives hope to many."

"Yeah, and it kills a whole load more."

"That's my point. I've done a lot of thinking and reading since I've been away, and I've come to realize that the main reason I was so unhappy was because I was a drone. I did what they told me to do, and it all felt so futile. But it doesn't have to be like that."

"You reckon you can change things?"

She nodded, and some of the animation returned to her face. "Generations ago, the High Priestess had more power than the High Priest. Something happened, and she became a mere figurehead. I'm going to change that. I'm going to get the power back and make things better."

"Jesus," he muttered. "I knew you were naive the first moment I saw you. People don't want things better. People want money, power, and immortality."

"Is that what you want?"

The truth was he no longer knew what he wanted. Right from the start, she'd confused him, twisted his thoughts, and made him believe that things could be different. He could be different.

None of that changed the fact that he couldn't protect her from the Collective or the Church hell-bent to have her back under their thumb. An image of his slaughtered pack flashed across his mind. He'd been their alpha—it had been his job to protect them, and they had died. All but him. He couldn't keep her safe. This time, he doubted he could keep himself safe.

The best he could hope to do was go into hiding, but the Collective wielded so much power that eventually he would be found. Unless he kept moving, kept running. What sort of life was that?

She was so young. At least this way she would have a life.

"I just want to be left alone."

Her lips tightened then she visibly relaxed. "Well, that's good because in a few minutes, I'll be leaving you alone for good."

"Off to save mankind." Why couldn't he leave it alone? He was goading her but couldn't seem to stop.

"The ones who want saving—yes."

"And will that be enough?"

"It will have to be." She unfastened the harness and got to her feet, brushing down the ludicrous black gown. He couldn't help but remember what was beneath it—a pair of tiny scarlet panties, and a whole load of bare skin.

"You can still change your mind. I can take you back to *El Cazador.*"

"No, I can't. I can't do that to them. Without me, they might have some chance of keeping ahead of the Collective."

It was on the tip of his tongue to say they could disappear together, take the shuttle and vanish. But he swallowed the words down. It was a stupid thought. He heaved himself up. "Let's do this."

She nodded, pulled a scrap of material out of her pocket, shook it out, and placed it on her head, covering her vibrant red hair. He hadn't thought she could look any worse, but he'd been wrong. God, those clothes were ugly.

"Suits you," he said.

She cast him a look of disbelief, but all she said was, "Thank you."

The moon had an atmosphere ideal for supporting human life, but nothing else—no water, no soil—so it had never been colonized. It was a bare, desolate landscape of ochre rock bathed in perpetual twilight.

The air was cool outside the shuttle. Jon checked the readings to get a fix on the rendezvous point and headed

off. After a few minutes, he realized she had fallen behind, and he slowed his pace to accommodate her.

"Not exactly built for convenience, that outfit—is it?"

She didn't answer, just picked up her heavy skirts and
followed him.

They walked slowly across the soft sand, neither speaking until up ahead he saw the outlines of two ships. He
stopped while he studied them. One was small, obviously a
shuttle from a larger ship, and bore the cross of the Church
on the side. The other was bigger, squat, black, and ugly. An
unmarked Mark One cruiser, capable of deep space travel.

Unease stirred inside him at the sight, but he forced the
feeling down. He was just looking for excuses.

"There they are," he said.

Alex had come to a halt beside him. Her face appeared
serene, but her small hands gripped the black material of
her skirt so hard, her knuckles showed white in the dim
light.

She must have perfected that expression at an early age.
Learned how to hide what she was really feeling.

"Come on," she murmured. "Let's get this over with."

Without waiting for him to answer, she marched off in
the direction of the ships.

For a moment, Alex thought he wasn't going to follow. She
kept moving and finally heard his slow steps behind her.
Keeping her breathing slow, she tried to calm the panic
clawing at her insides, willing her to turn around and run.
Even in the cool air, her skin felt hot and itchy under the
heavy dress and with each step she neared the ships and
the robes grew heavier.

The ships had landed in a large clearing surrounded by
steep rocks. The entrance was through a narrow gap between two of the great stones. As she stepped between

them, a small group of men appeared from behind the larger ship. She hesitated, and Jon stopped slightly behind her and leaned in close.

"Is that the High Priest guy?"

"Yes."

He gave a short, humorless laugh. "The creep looks just as I imagined."

Alex had known Hezrai Fischer her entire life, and she had stopped noticing his appearance as you do with people you see on a day-to-day basis. Now she studied him as though seeing a stranger for the first time.

Hezrai liked to think himself an ascetic. He ate sparingly, took no drugs or stimulants. He was over a hundred, but his body beneath the robes was lean and strong, the body of a much younger man. Yet his face had developed an intemperate cast as though something rotten inside him was trying to escape.

Alex had hated him for as long as she could remember. She'd wanted to like him, but even as a child, she had sensed his dislike of her. More than dislike—he hated her. Technically the High Priestess stood above the High Priest in the hierarchy of the Church and she reckoned that fact had festered in Hezrai's mind. But if she had been a drone, then it was Hezrai at the controls, and if she was going to somehow change her position and actually take back some of the power, then it was Hezrai she would need to wrest it from.

He stood in front of the shuttle. At his back stood three men, and she frowned. She didn't recognize them. The Church had a small army of private soldiers, but she knew most of them. These men she had never seen before, and they didn't wear the uniform of the Church's army. Besides, they looked bad. Maybe Hezrai had had to bring extra people on to search for her. Maybe he did care. There must be some reason he had gone to so much trouble.

So she smiled as she came to a halt in front of him. "Hezrai, how nice to see you."

Something flashed in his eyes, before he blanked the expression and smiled at her—with his lips at least.

She'd thought about what to reveal regarding her little time away and decided her best bet was a mix of the truth laced with a few embellishments. The hardest bit would be convincing him that she'd somehow wandered onto his ship by mistake that day. If she could get him to believe that, the rest was easy.

Afterward, she'd got lost on Trakis Twelve and been picked up by the crew of *El Cazador*. She'd been scared, unsure of what they would do if she revealed who she was, so she'd disguised herself as a cabin boy. And she'd been waiting for a chance to leave the ship and contact the Church when Hezrai had found her.

She wouldn't have believed a word of it, but Hezrai had always liked any evidence that she was stupid, so maybe he wouldn't question her story too closely.

He bowed before her. "Your Ladyship."

Beside her, Jon sniggered. Alex ignored him and bowed regally in return.

"Hezrai, this is Jon . . ." She realized she didn't actually know his second name, and she glanced at him.

"Decker," he provided.

"This is Jon Decker—he offered to bring me to you. In return for the reward, of course."

Hezrai's pale gray eyes flicked to Jon and back to her. "You don't feel you should return our priestess for the glory of God."

"Do I look like a complete idiot?" Jon growled.

A spasm of anger flashed across the priest's face, and his eyes narrowed. "I sense a difference about you. Are you entirely human, Mr. Decker?"

Jon took a step forward so he stood beside her. "Why don't you come a little closer and find out?"

Behind Hezrai, the three men moved as one, their hands shifting to rest on their laser pistols, and the tension rocketed. Alex peeked sideways at Jon, expecting his own hand to be on his gun, but they hung relaxed at his side. A small smile played across his lips as though daring Hezrai to move against him.

Rico had told her Jon had a death wish, but she still didn't believe that was true. Rather, she suspected it was more that he was an arrogant ass.

Hezrai waved the men down. "Not everyone can believe in the Lord," he said. "I will pray for your salvation, Mr. Decker."

"Thanks."

"In the meantime, if you would give me an account number, I will see that the payment is made." He pressed a button on his wristband and a small screen appeared on his right palm. "The number, please."

Jon hesitated and looked at her, as though expecting her to say something, but there was nothing left to say, so she kept her mouth tight shut. After a second, he shrugged and reeled off a list of numbers.

Hezrai turned his palm toward them. Jon glanced at it and nodded.

"Good," Hezrai said. "Then we'll be saying good-bye. I'm sure you have important things to do, and we must get our little priestess back where we can take care of her properly."

Alex ground her teeth together at the syrupy words. She didn't want to be taken care of. Why did no one think she was capable of taking care of herself? But there would be time to exert her new independence once Jon was safely away from here, so she swallowed down the words.

Besides, she was fighting an almost overwhelming urge

to grab hold of his hand and drag him with her far away from here. It was dawning on Alex that this was the last time she would see him, and she hadn't realized it would be so hard. The thought made her chest tighten and her stomach churn. Everything seemed to narrow.

Jon didn't speak although she could feel his eyes on her. Then he moved. Out of the corner of her eye, she saw him turn around and walk away.

Keeping her eyes on the pale sand at her feet, she held herself very still as though if she moved at all she might unravel and never manage to get herself back together. But at the last moment, she had to see him one more time.

She whirled around and ran after him, clumsy in the stupid dress. "Jon!"

He stopped walking. "What?"

"Just this." Her hands grasped his shoulders, she reached up and kissed him on the cheek. "Thank you."

"Don't thank me—I did it for the money."

"I meant for the orgasm, of course."

"Well, if you were really grateful, we could nip behind that rock over there, and you could repay the favor. I'm sure your friend would wait for us."

"I'll pass. Besides, I don't think he likes you. Go," she said. "Be safe."

She turned around and trudged back to where they waited for her. Hezrai was speaking into his comm unit when she got back. This time when he looked at her, he made no attempt to hide the loathing in his eyes, and unease shifted inside her. He'd always at least made some small effort to mask his hatred.

"Stupid fucking little bitch," he snarled and lashed out with his right fist.

The blow caught her by surprise, taking her across the cheekbone. Pain flared, and the force flung her to the ground in a tangle of long skirts.

She pushed herself up on her hands and spat out the sand that had filled her mouth. Fire burned along her cheek, and she stayed where she was for a moment, trying to make sense of what had just happened.

And failed totally. Hezrai had never laid hands on her before. Maybe it was a mistake.

Swallowing, she forced herself up just as a booted foot kicked her hard in the side. She went down again, instinctively curling into a ball to protect herself as he kicked her again, this time in the belly. A sickening pain shot through her, and she bit her lip to keep from screaming.

"Do you know how much trouble you've caused me, bitch?"

She lay, listening to his heavy breathing, and prayed it was over. Then the rush of air before his boot caught her in the ribs. The crack of bone sounded loud in her ears, and for a moment, she blacked out.

Unfortunately, it was only a moment.

When she opened her eyes, his boots were directly ahead of her, and she tensed, waiting for the next kick. When it didn't come, she rolled cautiously onto her hands and knees. The movement sent searing pain shooting through her body. A wave of heat washed over her, followed by chilling cold. Her stomach turned liquid, and she vomited over the polished black boots.

Hezrai swore loudly but stepped back from her.

"Get up."

Unsure if she could, she wrapped one arm around her ribs and used the other to push herself up. She'd managed to get halfway when he grabbed her by the elbow and dragged her the rest of the way before dropping her arm as if he couldn't bear to touch her.

"Why?" she asked.

"You always were a snooping little bitch. Shoving your nose in where it wasn't wanted." He studied her for a moment, eyes narrowed. "Or were you spying on me that day? Did someone put you up to it?" He reached for her, gripped her shoulders, and shook her, so she had to grit her teeth against the pain that shot from her ribs to every nerve in her body. "Tell me."

What was he talking about? "Put me up to what?"

"You eavesdropped on my meeting with—" He glanced behind him at the men who stood watching silently and broke off. Alex followed his gaze and nearly threw up again. They were big men, and their faces held identical expressions—cold and ugly, but eager as they stared back at her. She forced her gaze back to Hezrai and choked out, "I don't know what you're talking about."

"No, maybe you don't. You always were slow. But I can't take the risk."

Unable to help herself, she stared at the point where Jon had disappeared only minutes ago, willing him to return. He must be back at the shuttle by now—he'd probably already forgotten her.

Hezrai brushed his robes and peered down his nose at her. "I'd like to say I'm sorry for what's about to happen, but the truth is—I wish I could stay and watch. Unfortunately, I need to be able to stand before the council and say I don't know how your death happened."

Her mind refused to work fast enough to catch up with what he was saying. She licked her lips. "Death?"

"You ruined everything. It was all arranged." His voice rose with each word he spoke. Then he snapped his mouth closed, and the tension drained from his narrow shoulders. "I was going to live forever." He turned to the men behind him. "I don't care what you do to her, but I want her dead at the end of it. Afterward, send the body to the Church and disappear."

He stalked away, black robes swirling around him. Alex stared after his retreating back, wanting to scream at him not to go. To tell her this was a bad joke, but she knew it would do no good. She had no clue what he was talking about, but that didn't make her situation any less real.

Nobody moved as Hezrai disappeared inside his shuttle, but she could feel their eyes on her, and she shivered, tightening her arms around her middle.

Okay, she was scared. She admitted it. But her mind was sluggish, and she couldn't make sense of what had happened. Refused to consider what was about to happen.

The engines flared, and the shuttle lifted off and still nobody moved. Finally, Alex straightened her shoulders and turned slowly to face the three men. Her breath was coming short and fast, and she slowed it trying to clear her mind.

After one lesson in fighting, she doubted she was in any position to take down three men, each one at least twice her weight and all heavily armed. She would have to talk her way out of this one.

"The Church will pay to get me back unharmed," she said.

"We've already been paid," the tallest one said.

"They'll pay you more."

A cold smile twisted his lips. "That would hardly be honorable, would it?"

"Honorable? You call this honor?"

"In our way—yes. We're paid to do a job, and we do it. It's nothing personal."

"I have friends—they'll come after you."

"Your *friend* just sold you for a whole load of credits. Besides, the priest ordered his shuttle to be destroyed."

Her mind reeled in shock; she wanted to run, scream, somehow warn him, but how could she? Maybe they were lying. "I don't believe you." She didn't want to believe them, but it would be like Hezrai. The double-crossing slimeball.

"They're giving him time to get safely back, then—

bang. So give us what we want. We'll have a bit of fun, and then we'll kill you quick."

They circled her. She stood still, her gaze darting between them. The man who had spoken was obviously the leader. He was the one she had to convince. But staring into his cold, set face, she had a sinking feeling there was no way that was about to happen.

"Look, sweetheart," he said, and she shuddered at the endearment, "you're as good as dead. This is going to happen, so why not make it easy on yourself?"

"Because I don't want to die."

He took a step toward her. Keeping her gaze fixed on him, she backed up, then jumped as hard hands settled on her shoulders. She held herself still, unsure what to do. One thing she did know was there was no way she was giving them what they wanted. They'd have to take it. She tensed herself to fight when off in the distance, she heard the roar of a blaster. Her gaze shot upward as a white light streaked down from somewhere in orbit, followed by an explosion on the surface that sent orange flames shooting into the twilight sky.

The shuttle.

Jon would have been back by now, probably readying for takeoff. Her mind refused to register more than that. Jon couldn't be dead. Not at the hands of someone like Hezrai. Inside her mind screamed in denial. Instinctively, she tried to rip free from the hands that held her as though she could somehow go and save him. Drag him out from the wreckage, touch him one last time.

But the fingers tightened on her shoulders, digging into her flesh, and she fought harder. Pain ripped through her from the cracked ribs, and she had no chance against someone so much stronger. The struggle was futile, and finally she stood still, breathing hard now.

Why hadn't she worn her laser pistol? Because she had

thought she was safe. It had never occurred to her that Hezrai would harm her. She was a fool, and some of her pain and fear was swamped beneath a wave of rage that rose up inside her.

The man in front of her had been watching the explosion. Now he turned back to her, a slight smile curling his thin lips. He stepped closer.

"There, it's just you and us now. I've never had me a priestess before." He reached out, tugged the headdress from her hair, and tossed it to the ground. "Red," he murmured as he caught sight of her hair.

She'd told him the truth—she wanted to live. At least long enough to rip Hezrai into bloody little pieces for what he had done to Jon. But the man standing in front of her wasn't offering her life in exchange for her cooperation, just a quicker death.

Barring divine intervention, she couldn't see any way out of this. And with that realization, some of her panic left her and her brain could function again.

She wouldn't beg. Well, maybe she would, but only to give herself a chance to take at least one of them down with her.

Forcing her grief over Jon to the back of her mind, she stared at the ground until she was sure she had control of her expression. She wiped the anger from her face, allowing fear and pain to fill her eyes as she raised her gaze. "Please, don't hurt me."

His smile broadened. "That's more like it."

Alex examined him—he had a weapons belt at his waist with a laser pistol and a large knife. She needed one of those weapons, preferably the pistol, but she'd take the knife.

He raised his hands to the neck of her dress and yanked, trying to rip it down the front, but the material refused to tear. "What the hell *is* this stuff?" he muttered.

Alex could have told him it was wool from the Abbey's sheep, woven with silk, spun by the Abbey's own silkworms, bred from worms brought from Earth more than a thousand years ago. But she didn't think he'd be interested in the history lesson.

She didn't want to do this, but it was the only way to get them to lower their guard. "The back," she said meekly. "It buttons down the back."

For a moment, suspicion flashed across his features. Maybe she was being too cooperative, but he nodded over her shoulder and the other man released his grip on her arms and stepped away.

Hands slipped inside the neck of her dress and ripped the cloth so the cool air brushed against her bare skin. She hugged the dress to her then unwound her arms from her middle, tugged the sleeves down, and let the bodice fall to her waist, baring her breasts.

A quick peek at the men showed they had moved to the front of her now and were staring at her bare breasts. Her nipples tightened in the chill air, and the leader licked his lips.

Alex hesitated, but in the event that she did get a chance to escape, she'd have a much better chance unhampered by the heavy robes. She pushed the dress down over her hips and stepped out of it to stand before them in her scarlet panties and knee-high boots.

Her hands instinctively wrapped around her waist again, though she could no longer feel the pain from her ribs. Her body had gone numb as though this was happening to someone else, and she could only hope it would stay that way.

They were circling her again like hungry wolves.

"Please, you promised not to hurt me, and I've never done this before."

The leader stopped moving. He nodded to the ground at his feet. "Lie down."

She focused on the pistol at his waist as she lowered herself to the ground. The sand was silky soft at her back. Her breath was uneven, and her panic was rising again. This couldn't happen. Squeezing her eyes shut tight, she saw an image of Jon. Loss and grief threatened to overwhelm her, and she shoved the image aside. The man kicked her legs apart and dropped to his knees between them. Then he was on her. His face pressed against her throat, his erection against her belly. He groped between their bodies to free himself, his hand trembling.

All her life she'd believed that killing was wrong. Now she felt no compunction as she shifted so she could free her hand. She clenched her teeth as she realized there was no way she could reach his laser pistol; besides it was on the side where the other two men stood drooling like hungry animals.

But her hand managed to grasp the hilt of the knife. He was fumbling between her legs now, grunting with excitement. Anger flared; she didn't want him touching her there, where Jon had touched her such a short time ago. She drew the knife and hesitated. She couldn't reach his heart, and if she stabbed him in the side, it was unlikely to do any lasting damage.

In the end, she lifted the knife and gauged him in the side of the neck, twisting the blade as it entered.

He reared back and his hand reached for the knife embedded in his throat. Alex wriggled from under him, scrambled to her feet, and ran.

Something slammed into her lower legs, hurling her to the ground. She rolled over but was shoved back down by a booted foot.

The furious face of the man she had stabbed stared down at her. One hand held a cloth to his neck, and she recognized the black material of her headdress.

"So I take it you don't want it easy after all."

The boot pressed down hard on her cracked ribs, and this time she screamed.

Jon had every intention of flying away and not looking back.

Alex would be okay. She was with her own people and didn't need his protection any more. Which was just as well because he was crap at protecting people.

Jon repeated variations of the same thought over and over in his mind on the way back to the shuttle.

But he wasn't convincing himself.

He'd seen the hatred on the priest's face when he'd first caught sight of Alex. The hatred had bordered on insanity. The man had hidden it quickly enough, but that didn't mean it wasn't still there.

And what was with the mercenaries? The Church had its own army. There was no reason for them to hire mercs.

Unless it was for a job not sanctioned by the Church.

Then again, maybe their own army was spread thin searching for their lost priestess. Maybe they'd had to take on extra people.

He'd actually arrived back at the shuttle when the roar of a ship taking off broke the silence behind him. She was gone, and something inside him screamed in denial.

Then he realized only one ship had left—the priest's. Which meant the Mark One cruiser was still here. The ship belonging to the mercs.

Why?

What reason could there be to hang around?

Plenty of reasons. Maybe the ship had a problem or . . .

He sat down in the pilot's chair, leaned forward to switch on the engine, but stopped.

He'd known that he had to go back and check, even though he was almost sure he would find her gone along with the priest. And that would be that. Still, once outside the shuttle, he found himself running in the direction he had come from. All he could think was he had to save her. Protect her.

A streak of light blazed down from above, and behind him came the boom of an explosion. For a second he hesitated, glancing back to see flames roaring into the sky. The shuttle. Then he was running again.

He was almost there when the shrill scream of agony filled the air. Stripping his clothes as he raced across the sand, he didn't think, didn't consider his actions; he was beyond that. He shifted as he ran, until he had to pause to kick off his boots, shrug out of his pants.

Despite his fear, a wave of euphoria washed through him as his wolf scented freedom. It had been so long. His back arched as the bones snapped and realigned. There was no pain, just a feeling of rightness as finally he stood on all fours, head up, sniffing the cool night air.

His senses sharpened, and his nostrils filled with the scent of blood and fear. Throwing back his head, he howled.

In some part of her mind, Alex was aware she had given up, had accepted the fact of her death. But she would go down fighting.

She managed to get in a well-aimed kick, and he swore, drew back his fist, and punched her on the side of the head. Stars flashed in front of her eyes, and she rolled onto all fours and shook her head. When she looked up, they stood in a circle around her.

They weren't in any hurry. They knew she was beaten. Now they would take their time. Their hands reached for her. She didn't know whose; they had all merged into one attacker. She tried to struggle, but she had no strength left.

Off to the right something howled, the eerie sound bouncing off the rocks surrounding them.

The man holding her went still. He stared off to where the noise had come from, but when nothing further broke the silence, he shook his head and turned back to her.

A faint glimmer of hope had awoken deep inside, but she dismissed it. It was only her imagination that had made the sound remind her of a wolf. There was no life on this planet. No wolves to save her.

Staring over his shoulder, she tried to make her mind go to another place, a far-off place, where she didn't feel the hands that pawed at her breasts and belly.

Something stirred in the space between the rocks at the edge of the clearing, moving too fast for her to make out. Just a huge dark streak that flew through the air toward them; a brief impression of savage amber eyes and a snarling mouth, white teeth before the thing crashed into them. She was wrenched free from the grip as the man who'd held her was borne down to the ground under the weight and sheer speed of the beast.

Warm blood sprayed across her face, blinding her. She wiped her eyes clean with the back of her hand. Her attacker was dead, his throat ripped to a bloody mess.

The beast caught her gaze, and she saw a flash of humanity in the gold-flecked eyes. It leaped away, turning in midair toward where the other two men stood, shock holding them immobile.

One managed to get off a single blast with his laser. The shot went wide, and the animal slammed into him, crashing him to the ground.

Alex crawled toward the dead man and tugged his laser from the holster at his waist. She pushed herself up onto her knees, her fingers fumbling with the controls as she switched the weapon from stun to kill. The third man was trying to get a shot at the beast but the two figures rolling on the floor were inseparable, the clearing filled with snarling and snapping. He'd obviously forgotten Alex even existed. But she wanted him to see who killed him, wanted to look into his eyes as she did it.

"Hey!" she shouted.

He turned toward her. Alex braced herself and squeezed the trigger. The blast hit him square in the chest, and he went down.

She closed her eyes as shock and relief drained the last of her strength. It took her a moment to realize that the clearing had gone quiet. The fight was over, and she forced her lids open.

The men were dead. The wolf stood, legs braced, head cocked to one side, watching her.

He was the most beautiful creature she had ever seen. Dark brown coat streaked with red-gold, deep amber eyes. When she didn't move, he padded toward her. His movements slow and controlled as though he didn't want to scare her away.

Even if she'd wanted to, she had no energy left to run.

A foot away, he stopped and looked at her again as though waiting for her to make a move. When she remained still, he sank down onto his haunches. His muzzle was stained crimson, and he licked it with a long pink tongue, flashing the biggest, whitest teeth she had ever seen. He licked his paw and cleaned his face, his golden eyes never leaving her.

Her mind was slowly starting to work again. To come back from that place of death and accept that she was going to live.

He'd saved her.

Again.

She dropped the pistol, dragged herself the short distance between them, wrapped her arms around his thick neck, and burrowed her nose in his silky fur. He smelled warm and musky, vaguely of Jon, but more of wild animal.

He'd gone still when she hugged him, but as she backed

slightly away he nudged her with his cold nose then licked at her chin with his warm tongue, washing away the blood.

When she was clean, he rose to his feet and stalked a little distance from her. She sat on the sand, knees to her chest, arms wrapped around her, and watched as the beast became a man. The change happened with ease, one form flowing into the other, the fur and claws receding. Only as he straightened to stand upright did she hear the snap as bones realigned themselves.

And Jon stood before her. Legs braced, head thrown back, fists clenched at his side.

Gloriously and totally naked.

Alex didn't look away. If nothing else, the last hour had given her a real insight into her own mortality. She had known she was going to die.

Now she lived, and she was determined to make the most of it.

Maybe she'd never get to do more than look, and if she was honest with herself, she wasn't sure she was up to more than looking anyway. The adrenaline rush was draining away, and every bit of her ached. She was sure her ribs were cracked if not broken—a sharp stab of pain accompanied her every movement.

Still, she could look.

He was broad at the shoulder and narrow at the hips. His chest and shoulders bulged with muscle. More muscle ridged his flat belly. His sex hung heavy between his thighs. As she stared, it twitched and grew, filled with blood, until it stood straight, pale against the hair-roughened skin of his stomach, thick and long.

"Holy Meridian."

He made a noise, a mix of a snort and a laugh, and her gaze shot to his face. He watched her out of half-closed eyes, gold gleaming behind thick lashes, then he stalked toward her.

She wanted to meet him halfway, and she unwound her arms and put her palms flat to the sandy ground. When she tried to push herself up, a small squeak of pain escaped her lips.

He stopped in his tracks then hurried toward her and crouched down. "Are you all right?"

"Well, I'm alive. That's 'all right' enough for me at the moment."

His gaze ran over her, and she fought the urge to cover herself with her hands. Jon appeared unperturbed by his own nakedness, and she wished she could be the same. Maybe it was a werewolf thing. If you had to strip off to change, you probably got used to wandering around without any clothes on. There wasn't a single person in her entire life who had ever seen her naked.

Jon straightened up and held out a hand to her. She slipped her palm in his and allowed him to tug her to her feet, but still couldn't prevent a little moan escaping her lips. He reached out and stroked a finger over her bruised cheek, across her swollen lower lip.

"You saved me," she said.

"Yeah."

"Again."

His gaze roamed around the clearing. "So what happened?"

She shrugged. "I guess Hezrai hated me more than I thought." There had to be more to it than that, but she needed to think things through, try and make sense of what had happened and why. "He told those men they could do what they liked as long as I was dead at the end of it."

"Bastard. Did they rape you?" he asked, his tone harsh.

She shook her head. "No, you stopped them in time."

"Good. So where does it hurt?"

"Here," she said and put a hand on her ribs. "It hurts when I breathe in. I think I have some broken ribs."

His touch was gentle, his fingers stroking over the lines of her bones beneath the skin. "Stay there."

He wandered away, searching the clearing, and came back carrying her black dress. He tore strips of the material from the bottom hem.

"Raise your arms," he ordered.

Alex turned slightly to the side, lifted her arms as high as she could before the pain made her stop and blackness threatened to engulf her. She steadied herself then stood still while he wrapped the strips of material tight around her rib cage. The pain eased immediately, and she took a cautious deep breath.

"Better?"

She nodded and peered down at herself. Scarlet panties, knee-high boots, and a black bandage around her middle. Very nice. Not.

Looking up, she found his gaze on her breasts. Her nipples were already tight in the chilly air, but they stiffened under his hot stare.

"How much better?" he asked.

Her gaze dropped down the length of his body. His erection had subsided while he'd tended her, now it was back. Heat pooled at her core. She swallowed.

"I'd probably be okay if I could lie down for a minute."

At her words, the tight knot of tension inside him unwound. He knew she was giving her consent.

Just as he knew he shouldn't be doing this.

She was hurt, probably traumatized. He should be caring for her, getting her away from here in case that bastard came back.

But he always found his urges harder to control after he'd shifted. Usually his mind controlled his body, but after a shift, those roles were reversed. It had been so long, he'd forgotten what it was like. His body felt stronger, bursting with life force, clamoring for some sort of release.

Back with the pack, there had always been a woman available, an unmated female happy to oblige the pack alpha. Now there was Alex. He studied her. Physically she was nothing like the women he'd gone for in the past. She was small, fine-boned with slim hips and a narrow waist that emphasized the fullness of her breasts. The marks from Bastion's fangs had faded, but new bruises blossomed across her pale skin, and his fury rose again at the thought of others touching what was his.

He'd told her she was weak, but she was strong. She'd been half dead, yet she'd still managed to take one of those men down.

He'd sworn never to have anyone rely on him again, but now Alex was his. The need to take her, mark her rose inside him. He would be quick. And gentle. But he had to have her.

His gaze settled on the horror of a dress. He picked it up, took her hand, and led her out of the clearing. Once away from the carnage and the stench of blood and death, he spread the dress out on the sand.

"You're sure?" he asked.

She nodded, and he picked her up and lowered her gently to the ground, before coming down beside her.

"I'll be gentle. I won't hurt you."

"I know."

Warmth washed through him at her trust. How could she know? After everything she had gone through—the betrayal, the attack—that she would trust anyone amazed him.

Stretched out on his side beside her, he studied her for long minutes, his gaze snagging on the purple mark of the cross that marred the skin of her right thigh. He stroked a finger over the slightly raised skin—such a little thing to have such an impact on her life.

"Kiss me," she whispered.

Careful not to touch her anywhere else, he leaned across and his lips met hers. He nipped her with his teeth, and her lips parted beneath him so he could slide his tongue inside and stroke the velvet softness of her mouth, taste the sweetness of her. Her tongue moved tentatively against his, but he forced himself to keep his movements slow and languid, thrusting gently into her.

His fingers barely touched her skin as he stroked down the line of her throat, over the swell of her breasts. He rubbed his palm over a nipple, then tugged it between his finger and thumb. Leaning over her, he kissed the marks that marred the perfection of her flesh as though he could take away the pain. He licked a slow stroke of his tongue across the tightly swollen bud, loving the sound of her indrawn breath.

Her eyes were closed, her lashes dark shadows on her cheeks, her lips slightly parted, her breath short and ragged.

He took a nipple in his mouth and bit down softly, laved it with his tongue, then suckled her until he could feel the tiny lifts of her hips in time with the movement.

His lips moved lower, over the black bandage that bound her ribs. He kissed the sharp jut of her hip bone, the hollow at the top of her thighs. Burrowing his nose in the silky red curls at the base of her belly, he breathed in the warm scent of her arousal, and his cock jerked in response. He needed her and soon, but first he wanted her hot for him, so hot the horrors of the day would be driven from her mind. He shifted down her body, parted her thighs, and kissed the mound of her sex.

Her whole body arched, and a small squeak left her mouth. "Ow." Her eyes were wide-open now. "Sorry. A twinge. Don't stop. Please don't stop. I never . . ." She trailed off.

He lowered his face to her and pushed between the folds of her sex with the tip of his tongue, the salty sweetness sending another rush of blood to his shaft. Parting her with his fingers, he licked a long, slow stroke from the cleft of her buttocks, stopping short of the small swollen bundle of nerves. He repeated the action until he thought the taste of her would make him burst.

Alex had gone still, but her murmured, almost frantic pleas rang in his ears, and he placed a soft kiss right on the center of her desire. She was so close, and he shifted his hands to clamp her hips so she wouldn't move and hurt herself when she came.

Then he took the tiny bud in his mouth and sucked. She exploded, and he held her tight as she shivered and trembled against him. After bestowing one last kiss, he raised himself on all fours and moved up her body until he crouched over her. Her eyes were glazed with desire, her cheeks flushed.

"Ready?"

She nodded, and her small fingers fluttered along the length of his shaft. His muscles locked solid. He shifted over her, fighting to keep control, as he reached between them, his fingers opening her, readying her for him.

"Jon."

Alex whispered his name, her tone filled with urgency. He opened his mouth to reassure her, and they were bathed in a bright white spotlight from above as the sky filled with the hum of an approaching ship.

For a moment, he didn't move. Maybe it wasn't anything to do with them, and it would disappear if he ignored it. The hum grew to a roar as the shuttle hovered directly overhead.

"Goddamn, fucking crap."

CHAPTER THIRTEEN

Alex's first thought was that Hezrai had come back, they were naked, and the laser pistols were back in the clearing. Her hand tightened on Jon's shoulder, then she forced her fingers to loosen as he pushed himself off and jumped to his feet.

"If that's the priest back, I'll rip the bastard limb from fucking limb," he growled.

Alex squinted up at the sky. She recognized the shuttle instantly, and some of her panic receded. "It's Skylar."

"What?" Jon stared down at her, his dark brows drawing together.

She nodded up at the shuttle hanging in the air above them. "That Skylar's shuttle."

Her panic was replaced by a deep sense of disappointment. Why couldn't they have waited a little while longer? God hated her. That was it. She was being punished.

Her body still thrummed with residual pleasure. She never imagined anything could feel as good as the warm, velvet rasp of his tongue against her flesh. A shiver ran through her at the memory.

Jon had also obviously recognized the ship now, and

some of the tension drained from his figure. The knowledge didn't appear to improve his mood though. "Shit. I feel like ripping *someone* limb from limb."

As the shuttle landed, he paced the area like a caged beast, which she supposed he was in a way. At least she was getting used to him naked. It seemed somehow right. She was also naked, apart from the bandage around her ribs, and she wasn't anywhere near as comfortable with that. She lifted her bottom, pulled the black dress from under her, and clutched it to her front.

The shuttle doors slid open. It wasn't Skylar who stood in the open doorway, but Tannis and Rico.

"Great fucking timing," Jon snarled.

Rico turned to Tannis. "Hey, we came to rescue them, and this is the thanks we get."

"Did we look like we needed rescuing?" Jon moved to stand in front of them, hands on his hips, oblivious to the fact that he was naked.

"Actually, Tannis wasn't sure what was going on. I had to explain." Rico patted her on the shoulder. "Poor thing. It's been so long, and she's forgotten what happens. She thought you were eating Al or something." He cast an amused glance at Alex.

She had an instant image of Jon's mouth between her legs. A wave of heat washed over her, and her fingers tightened on the black cloth.

"Any chance of anyone putting some clothes on around here?" Tannis said, her gaze wandering down over Jon's naked figure. "We don't want Rico getting an inferiority complex."

"Yeah, like that's going to happen." Rico grinned as he looked him over, but at least it took his attention from Alex, and she managed to wriggle into the dress. It was cut short at her knees now, where Jon had torn it for bandages. As she struggled to her feet, Jon hurried over and helped her up.

"Are you all right?" he asked.

The pain in her ribs was back with a vengeance. Her legs shook. Her breasts ached. She nodded.

"I'll go find my clothes. I'll be back in a minute."

Alex watched him walk away. The rear view was as spectacular as the front. She sighed and turned back to the shuttle where Rico and Tannis lounged in the open doorway. Rico was watching her, a lazy smile curling his lips. Tannis was watching Jon disappear, until he vanished behind one of the huge rocks. Finally, she turned her attention to Alex and her lips twitched in amusement as she took in the bedraggled mess before her. Then she frowned.

"So, are you going to tell us what the hell happened? And who blew up my goddamn shuttle? And why you stole my goddamn shuttle in the first place?"

"Mine, actually," Rico murmured.

Tannis scowled but ignored the comment and pointed to the clearing. "And there are three dead guys over there. Who the hell are they? And who killed them?"

Alex didn't answer any of the questions. A wave of exhaustion washed over her, as much emotional as physical. She wanted to be alone, to go over what had happened. Try and work out why Hezrai wanted her dead. There was no way she could return to the Church now. What did that mean for the rest of her life?

And Jon? He'd come back for her. Saved her life a second time. Nearly made love to her. Now, with reality setting in, she wasn't sure how she felt about that. While he might have come back for her, that didn't mean he would stay. Jon hadn't suddenly changed—he was still the same man she'd decided she couldn't risk falling for. The man who would no doubt break her heart. Was it worth the pain?

"Well?" Tannis asked.

"Sorry." Alex shook her head. "I—"

"Leave her alone," Jon said, striding toward them. He

was fully dressed and was strapping a laser pistol around his waist.

Alex smiled at the sight of him. Jon didn't smile back. His features had settled back into their habitually closed, slightly wary expression. But that didn't matter. She could accept that he wasn't a smiley man. It was enough that he was there, rather than dead. And so was she.

They had both come close today. Things could have turned out so differently.

At the thought, dizziness washed over her, the world darkened around the edges, and she swayed, putting her hand out to rest against his warm, hard chest. The steady beat of his heart drummed against her palm.

Jon scooped her up and held her close in his arms. "Go to sleep," he murmured.

He carried her past Rico and Tannis and into the shuttle. Once inside, he didn't put her down, just stood with her wrapped in his arms as they took off and headed back to *El Cazador*. Headed home.

For now, she was safe. She closed her eyes and slept.

When she awoke, she was in the sick bay back on the ship. The hated black dress lay crumpled on the silver floor while she lay on the examination table—naked, except for a light sheet covering her—and Janey was running a scanner over her body.

"Hey, you're awake," she said. "Welcome back."

Alex made to rise, but Janey pressed her down with one fingertip. "Not yet. I'm not finished."

She collapsed back. In truth, she felt as weak as a baby—her body weighted and heavy. Everything ached, with the occasional sharp pain added in. "So how am I?"

"Three broken ribs—they're the worst damage. The rest is just bruising. But there's a lot of it. Bastards."

Yeah—that about described them. "Jon killed them," she said.

"He told us that you killed one of them."

"He did?" She waited for the guilt to strike her, but nothing happened.

"Yes. Good for you."

"So, where is everyone?"

"Having a conference in the meeting room. Or rather waiting for you to join them, and then they'll have a conference in the meeting room. Jon said we had to sort you out first. He was most insistent. You know, he likes you, right?"

"Maybe."

She didn't want to think about it right now, there was too much else to consider. They were waiting for her, and they would want answers. Answers that she didn't have.

"I'm going to give you a shot for the pain. A stimulant to wake you up, and five minutes radiation to sort out the bruises and speed up the healing on those ribs. Okay?"

Alex nodded.

Daisy popped her head in the door when the radiation switched off, saw Alex sitting up on the examination table, and came in. "Clean clothes," she said and tossed a bundle onto the end of the table.

Alex jumped down to the floor with not even a wince of pain. A sense of anticipation bubbled up inside her; she tried to push it down but couldn't quite manage. "You know," she said as she tugged on the pink jumpsuit, "I thought I'd never be back here, I'd never see you all again, and I'd have to wear horrible black, heavy robes for the rest of my life."

She pulled on her boots and ran her fingers through her hair before glancing at the other two. "Do I look okay?"

"You look fine—well, at least you don't look half dead anymore. And you'd better get over there fast. Rico's telling everyone how they arrived to rescue you only to catch you two at it. I'm sure he's only doing it to wind Jon up. But it's working." Daisy grinned. "He's prowling around like a frustrated werewolf."

Actually, when they reached the meeting room, Jon wasn't prowling. He sat in one of the chairs, his booted legs on the table in front of him, hands shoved in his pockets, a scowl on his handsome face. He didn't look up as she entered.

No doubt, he was regretting his actions. But it was too late now.

Alex took a seat across the room, where she could observe him without being too obvious. They were all watching her, and she lifted her chin. There was no reason to hide what she was anymore. No more cowering.

Everyone else sat, apart from Tannis who paced the floor fizzing with nervous energy. She came to a halt in front of Jon and her eyes narrowed. "So what happened to my shuttle?"

"It got blown up." Jon shrugged, appearing almost bored. "You can have the reward I got for Alex. It's enough to replace the shuttle."

Tannis appeared slightly mollified. "Okay." She turned to face Alex. "So, are you going to tell us what happened?"

Alex wanted to say no, but she didn't think that was an option.

"What do you want to know?"

"How about, why didn't you come to us if you decided to go back?" Skylar asked. She was seated on the floor, her back resting against Rico's knees, his hand on her shoulder, and she sounded almost hurt.

"I thought you might try and persuade me not to."

"And would that have been so bad?"

Alex gave a half grin. "Well, in hindsight, no. But I wasn't exactly expecting what happened."

"And what did happen?" Tannis asked.

"He wanted me dead."

"Who wanted you dead?"

"Hezrai. The High Priest."

"The guy who's been following us?"

Alex nodded.

"So why would he want you dead?"

"I don't know. I've been thinking about it ever since, and it doesn't make sense. Oh, I've always known he hates me—"

"Why?"

"I don't think it's entirely because I threw up on him when I was a baby, though I did it again today—it's the effect he has on me." Well, that and being kicked in the belly and threatened with imminent rape and murder. She shuddered at the memory. "I think maybe he just hated sharing the power, however nominal."

"That's hardly reason enough to follow you across the universe and pay a bunch of mercs to murder you."

"He told me I'd eavesdropped on a private meeting. That he couldn't take the risk . . ." She shook her head. "I don't know what he's talking about."

But she'd reached the conclusion that it must have been something to do with the day she'd run away. She frowned as she tried to remember what had happened.

"You've thought of something?" Tannis said.

"Maybe. It must be about the day I left the Abbey. But I can't see why, or what was so important."

"Okay. Take us through it slowly. See if we can spot anything."

Alex rested her head against the back of the seat and forced her mind to go back. "It was the day after the feast of the Everlasting Life. That's our biggest celebration, and it seemed like I'd been praying for an eternity. I needed to get out into the open, or I was going to scream, which wasn't acceptable behavior in a High Priestess. It wasn't easy in the Abbey—I had people with me everywhere I went, but I managed to give them the slip and sneaked out onto the roof where I could see the landing bay." Jon was now sitting up straight in his chair, leaning toward her as he listened, and she spoke directly to him, needing him to understand who she was. "I often went up there to watch the ships come and go. I'd wanted to go into space for as long as I could remember, but I'd rarely left the Abbey since I was brought there as a baby, and then only to the cathedral."

Night had been the best time; she'd liked to sneak out and lie on the tower rooftop, stare at the stars, and imagine what it must be like out there. On a good night, she would maybe catch sight of a ship's lights far off and would try and imagine the places it would travel. But she didn't mention all of that—she had an idea it might come under the heading of "needy."

She looked from Jon to Tannis, who had finally stopped pacing and was perched on the edge of a chair listening. "I didn't intend to go for good or anything. It was an impulse. But there was a ship waiting. The doors were open, and there was no one around. I honestly only meant to have a quick look and get off, but somehow I was still on board when the engines started up. The doors were locked, and I had no choice."

It wasn't entirely the truth. She could have still gotten off at that point or told them that she was there, and they would have taken her back. But she remembered back to the thrill of excitement when the engines had roared into life and the floor beneath her feet had vibrated with power. All mixed with the fear that she'd be found and the adventure would be over before it had begun. So instead, she had hidden in one of the cabins.

"And when we landed, I just meant to have a quick look around—"

Jon snorted and her gaze flew to his face.

"What?" she asked.

"Well, that seems to be a recurring theme in your life—I didn't intend to go for good; I didn't intend to get eaten by the vampire; I just wanted a quick look around . . ."

There wasn't a lot she could say to that, so she shrugged and continued. "I even found some clothes I could change into—my robes were a little conspicuous—and I was going to explore and be back in time for the homeward trip."

Of course, she'd missed the trip home. She still wasn't convinced that it had been an accident. Her feet had carried her farther and farther away from the ship. But she had expected more time.

"When I got back, the ship was gone, and I was stranded."

Tannis frowned. "Well, that doesn't tell us much. Who was on the ship?"

"Hezrai and the crew, that's all."

"Okay, so what happened when you landed?"

"I waited until Hezrai had left the ship and followed him. We were in some sort of compound. It looked deserted—as though no one had lived there for years. There was one other ship, and a man standing in front of it."

"Were there any markings on the ship? A name . . . anything?"

Alex shook her head. "It was plain black and small like Skylar's shuttle."

"Describe the man."

"I only saw him briefly. I got out of there pretty fast. He was tall, maybe as tall as Jon and Rico, but thinner, and he had short blond hair."

"There must be more."

Alex closed her eyes and pictured the scene. "I think he saw me for a second, before I ran. There was some sort of mark on his face"—she touched her finger to her right cheekbone—"maybe a scar like a lightning bolt."

Jon jumped to his feet. "Fuck me. You know who she's describing?

Tannis swung around to stare at him. "No. But I take it you do?"

"Aiden fucking Ross. I know. I studied the bastard."

"Aiden Ross? The Collective founding member you assassinated?"

"Yes."

"He's right," Skylar said.

"He can't be," Alex said. "This man wasn't Collective. His eyes were dark, not violet."

"Yes, well, we know how easy that is to fake," Tannis said and cast a sour glance at Skylar. She crossed the room and switched on the console. A screen flashed up, and a minute later the image of a blond man stared down at them. "Is that him?"

Alex had no doubts. This was the man Hezrai had met on Trakis Twelve. "Yes."

They were all silent for a minute.

Tannis ran a hand through her hair. "So, what would the High Priest of the Church of Everlasting Life and one of the founding members of the Collective have to discuss in secret? Because this *was* a secret meeting. Obviously Ross didn't want to be recognized as Collective and Trakis Twelve is about as out of the way as you can get while still being within easy reach." She turned to Skylar. "Any ideas?"

"Not really—none of this makes sense. Aiden was always the Church's chief advocate within the Collective. It was well known and made him far from popular, but he was always open about it. I can't think of any reason he would need to meet in secret. Did you overhear any of the meeting?" she asked Alex.

"Nothing. I told you, I ran." She shrugged. "I wasn't interested in the meeting—I wanted to see the planet, explore. But Hezrai must have thought I'd heard them talking—he said I'd eavesdropped on a private meeting. He accused me of spying on him and asked me if someone had put me up to it."

"When was this?" Jon asked.

"We picked Alex up a little over three months ago," Tannis replied. "How long were you on Trakis Twelve, Alex?"

"About ten days."

"And I was approached with the contract offer about a month ago. There's a big gap in the timing. Could the two things be related? Could the Church have set up the hit?"

"Or someone inside the Collective who found out Ross was up to no good?" Tannis sounded almost excited about the idea. "I don't know. But there might be something in this that would give us some leverage to get the Collective off our backs for good. Maybe if we can give them whoever killed Ross, they'll be so grateful, they'll be our friends for life. We just need to find out what Aiden Ross was up to."

"Well, Aiden's not talking."

"No," Jon said. "There's only one person still alive who knows what went on at that meeting." He grinned at Alex. "And luckily for me, he's someone I'd really like to meet again."

Alex would never be safe while Hezrai lived. But there was also the other side to think about. While he lived, she had the perfect excuse for never going back to the Church. She could stay on *El Cazador* forever, or at least until someone else came along and killed them. But the thought made her squirm inside. Was she so weak that she couldn't make the decision for herself? Wasn't it time she started making her own choices? She'd never really considered not going back, had never thought of it as a valid option. The Church was her life. But maybe that wasn't the case anymore, and she could have a life elsewhere.

Jon stood in the center of the room. He caught her gaze and raised an eyebrow, and a little fire came to life low in her belly. She did her best to ignore it.

She wasn't foolish enough to think that she could have a life with Jon. Just because he'd kissed her a few times didn't mean he was ready to promise her forever. Besides, her forever and his were drastically different propositions. Did she want to take up with a werewolf? Strangely, she didn't mind the wolf bit; she had found him wild and beautiful. But Jon was already far older than her and could live for a whole lot longer, while she would grow old and die.

She needed to back off, keep her mind clear while she decided what she wanted to do with her life.

But one thing she was clear on—Hezrai needed to die. He was evil. Without him, maybe the Church could grow to be a better place.

Everyone was watching her, as though waiting for her to make a decision. It warmed her, made her feel part of the team. She nodded.

"So it's agreed—we're going after the priest," Rico said. "Good, I never liked the slimy bastard."

Once the decision was made, the meeting appeared to be over and people drifted away. Alex knew she should get up and leave, but instead, she stayed seated as one by one the others left the room, until only she and Jon remained. He stood watching her, hands shoved in his pockets, his face blank, so she had no clue what he was thinking.

Suddenly, she felt shy as she remembered what they'd done together. Her eyes were continually drawn to his mouth, and little shivers of pleasure ran along her nerve endings. She did her best to ignore them as she tried to persuade herself to get up and leave.

"I have something for you," he said, breaking the silence that stretched between them.

"You do?"

He pulled his hand out of his pocket and held up a small disc. "Here."

Alex took it from his outstretched hand, turned it over in her fingers. The disc was plain, unmarked. "What is it?"

"Information. Don't use it unless you have to and don't tell anyone you have it. I just thought, if anything happens to the rest of us—if you're ever left alone and the Church is still after you . . ." He shrugged, looked uncertain. "Anyway, I just wanted to give you this—it might come in handy."

Without waiting for an answer, he strode from the room, leaving Alex staring after him.

CHAPTER FOURTEEN

The cathedral was packed. The air thick with the stench of too many bodies mixed with the heavy, sweet, cloying scent of incense. The light was dim. Outside darkness had fallen, but inside a thousand candles cast their flickering light, adding to the almost unbearable heat.

It was Christmas Eve, according to Alex one of the biggest festivals of the Church's year. When some guy called Jesus was born. Jon didn't give a shit. He just wanted to pick up the priest and get the hell out of there.

On the bench beside him, Rico twitched. The vampire's jaw was set, and his fists clenched at his sides. Despite the place being full to bursting, the people around them had somehow managed to inch away, leaving a good space around them. Even so, he could see Rico was making them nervous.

"What's the problem?" he whispered.

Rico turned to face him, lips curled in a sneer. "Nothing," he snarled. "Why? Do I look like I have a problem?"

"Hell, yeah. We're supposed to be blending with the crowd. You're scaring the shit out of them. Lay off the dead-guy vibes."

Rico flashed a fang and growled low in his throat. For a moment, Jon thought the vampire might attack him right here. Then Rico took a deep breath, and the tension eased from him.

"Sorry." Rico shrugged. "I hate churches. They have a bad effect on me."

"What's up with that?" Jon was curious. Rico usually gave the impression of being laid-back to the extreme. He was anything but laid-back now. Jon hated the Church as well. They had been indirectly responsible for the slaughter of his pack—stirring up the local community into a senseless mob. But he didn't really blame them—he blamed himself.

Rico settled back on the bench and made a visible effort to relax. "I grew up in a time when the Church was very powerful—even more than now—and back then they were assholes." He went silent for a moment. "They murdered my wife, said she was a witch and burned her alive."

"Sorry."

"Don't be. It was a long time ago. And they all died much worse deaths than Maria."

"My wife was killed in the attack that turned me." One more person he'd failed to protect.

"Sorry."

"Don't be. It was a long time ago. And they all died much worse deaths than Sarah."

Rico laughed. The sound held no amusement, but at least the air around him no longer vibrated with tension.

"Anyway," Jon said, "I thought your lot couldn't enter churches. Aren't you allergic to holy ground or something?"

"To some extent. But it's not really the place or the thing—it's the person in control of it, if they believe. My guess is the guy in charge of this show doesn't believe shit."

He raised his hand and held it out. The faint mark of a cross showed on his palm. "That's from Alex's cross."

Jon's gaze flashed to the vampire's face. "When did you get anywhere near Alex's cross?"

Rico grinned. "The day Bastion attacked her. She wasn't wearing it at the time."

"Good. Anyway, Alex doesn't believe in this stuff." He waved at the church around him. "She might have had to pretend, but she knows it's a load of crap."

"Does she? And is it? If that's the case, this should never have happened. As it is, I'm marked for life."

"So vampires can be hurt?"

"Yeah, we can be hurt, and we can be killed if you know how. Why, you still thinking you'd like to have a go?"

Jon opened his mouth to answer but a commotion at the front of the church stalled him.

"Here they come," Rico said.

Up at the front of the church a procession wended its way to the central podium. A tall figure dressed in black robes broke away from the mass and climbed the steps to address the congregation.

Jon clenched his teeth as a rush of hatred hit him headlong and every instinct screamed to take the priest down. But wolves who acted rashly on their instincts didn't live long. A balancing act had to be learned: when to temper the wolf's strengths with man's ability to reason logically. Though logic had never really been a strong suit of his . . .

It had felt so good to shift. He realized he'd missed the sheer exhilaration of his other form. After his pack was killed, he'd turned wolf and stayed in that form until he'd dealt with his grief and guilt. Then he'd shifted back and done what he needed to do to come to terms with what had happened. He'd hunted down those responsible and killed them. But still he'd found no peace. After that, he'd lived among men and avoided changing. And he'd sworn never to have another pack.

"That's him?" Rico asked, dragging Jon from the past.

"Yes."

Rico raised his hand and pointed a finger at the priest. Skylar stood by the door at the back of the church and nodded when she saw the gesture.

"*Christos*, this guy is boring," Rico muttered a few minutes later.

"Imagine growing up having to listen to this shit every day."

Rico grinned. "Yeah, it's a wonder Alex hasn't turned out even weirder than she is. This stuff is enough to drive anyone crazy."

But Alex wasn't crazy; she was strong. Jon still found it hard to believe she'd killed one of those men. When he'd seen her, she'd looked near dead, and the panic he'd felt when he'd thought he was too late had nearly made him lose control.

They'd come to check out it was actually Hezrai Fischer taking the service. Now, Skylar was to contact him, pretend to be a representative of the Collective, lull him into a sense of security while Jon and Rico worked out how to join them—no way would Jon get past security.

But having achieved their objective, there was no reason to stay and listen to this crap. "Let's get out of here. We can wait for Skylar outside." Without waiting for an answer, he got to his feet and headed out, pushing his way past the people in the pew nearest to him. The place was packed. All these people drawn here by the false promise of eternity.

Pathetic.

He breathed in deeply as he came out into the relatively fresh air. The cathedral was at the very center of the planet's main city, at the intersection of the four major walkways where a fog of speeder fumes hung like mist, swirling in the overhead lights.

Across the way, a young woman stood watching him. Small and slender, she wore a bright pink jumpsuit, knee-length boots, and a laser pistol strapped to her waist. Her blond hair hung down her back.

"Shit," he muttered, striding across the busy street. "Which part of 'don't leave the shuttle' did you not understand?"

She flipped the blond hair over her shoulder and smiled. The smile didn't reach her eyes, but still, it was the first smile she'd given him since they'd arrived back on *El Cazador,* and for a moment his anger wavered, then returned even stronger. "This place is crawling with Church people; any one of them could recognize you and blow this whole thing."

"They're hardly going to recognize me like this."

He opened his mouth to order her back as Rico came up beside him.

"Let her stay," Rico murmured

A mutinous expression settled on her face, and she swung around to face Rico. "Let? Who are you to 'let me' do anything?"

Jon waited to hear the answer.

"The owner of the ship you fly on, sweetheart. So get used to doing what you're told or find another berth."

The answer deflated her. "This has more to do with me than any of you."

"Hey, I said stay, didn't I? It's your boyfriend you need to argue with." He turned to Jon. "You know, I think I liked Al better. Al did what he was told, when he was told. Sort this out now. We need to get after Skylar."

"I need to hear what Hezrai has to say," Alex said. "And I can be useful. I know him—I'll be able to tell if he's lying."

What she said made sense. The way he was feeling didn't. Well, that wasn't entirely true. It made a weird sort of sense—at least he understood what he was thinking and why. If he knew Alex was somewhere safe, he could function better. There would be no need to worry about protecting her; he could get on with the job he was here to do.

He could no longer tell himself that he felt nothing. What he needed to decide was whether he had passed the point where he could walk away.

Alex wasn't the sort of woman who would be happy to play it safe. In fact, he was finding it hard to understand how she had lived within the confines of the Church for so long without exploding, but she obviously also had an amazing amount of willpower when she took the time to apply it. Unfortunately, she more often acted first and thought about it afterward.

She'd make a crap werewolf. So it was just as well he'd sworn never to change another person. He wouldn't risk it anyway. Only about half of those attacked survived a werewolf bite. Many died or went insane and had to be destroyed. That's what had happened to Sarah, his wife. The wolves who attacked them hadn't intended her to die, but she had reacted badly, and in the end, they'd had to kill her.

His chest tightened at the memory. He never wanted to feel that overwhelming loss for another woman again.

He couldn't believe he was even thinking about this.

"Come then," he said. "But keep out of the way."

Not waiting for her to answer, he whirled around and stalked off down the street, only stopping when he realized he had no clue where he was going. When he turned back, they were both watching him. Rico appeared amused. Alex had a puzzled frown on her face. Yeah, he wasn't making a lot of sense these days.

"Follow me," she said.

They headed back toward the cathedral. The service was over, and people were spilling out of the open doorway. A waft of hot air buffeted him as they passed. Alex led them straight past the doorway, around the side, and down a narrow alley that ran between the cathedral and the next building. She appeared to know where she was going, which was hardly surprising; Trakis Four was where the main headquarters of the Church was situated and where Alex had grown up. Finally, she halted in front of a small door set into the wall and pressed her hand to the palm pad. The door slid open revealing a narrow, dimly lit corridor. Alex didn't hesitate. Jon stared after her then stepped inside, forcing down the unease that roiled in his stomach. The thick scent of incense permeated the air.

They saw no one about, but Jon could hear low voices coming from somewhere up ahead. Soon, the narrow corridor gave way to a wider one. The light was brighter here, the place luxurious with thick carpets muffling their footfalls and religious art on the walls.

"This place gives me the creeps," Rico muttered from beside him.

Jon agreed. "How are we going to do this?"

"What about good agent, bad agent?"

"Sounds good, as long as I get to be the bad agent."

"Normally, I'd insist, but he already knows you, so it's doubtful he'd believe you're going to be good after he blew up your ship."

"No. Then again—I'm not sure he's going to believe you're good either. You seem a bit on edge."

"I'll be fine."

Alex stopped in front of large silver double doors inlayed with a jeweled cross. She raised her hand to the panel when a sound from behind made Jon whirl around. A door in the wall opposite had opened, and a woman appeared.

He heard Alex's indrawn breath but didn't take his attention from the woman. She was dressed in black, similar to the robes Alex had worn, with a black headdress framing her pale features. Her skin was unlined, but she gave the impression of great age and serenity. Though her eyes had widened at the sight of them, she soon gained control of her reactions. She studied their small group, a frown forming on her face. Her gaze passed over Alex at first but returned to her, her brows drawing together.

"Lady Alexia?" Her tone was full of disbelief and joy. "You're alive. The High Priest reported you were dead."

"Alex?" Rico murmured. "Is this going to be a problem?"

Alex stepped forward. "No." She took the woman's hands in hers and squeezed. "Sister Martha, these are my friends. They've been looking after me."

"But where have you been? And what are you wearing? What have you done with your hair?" She shook her head. "We had no word. The High Priest said you were dead. We started the hunt for a new priestess."

"I'm not dead."

"No." There was a wealth of joy in that one word. She studied Alex then stretched out one hand and touched her lightly on the cheekbone where the faint signs of bruising showed. "But it looks like someone has hurt you." Her sharp eyes peered from Jon to Rico and back to Jon. He tried not to squirm. "Was it these men? Should I call the guards?"

So there were people who *had* cared about her. It made him feel good to know Alex hadn't been entirely without friends. Still, this Sister Martha hardly seemed the cuddly type.

"No," Alex answered. "I told you, they're my friends."

"Alex, we need to move," Rico said. He cast the older woman a cold glance. "Bring her with us."

Alex turned to face him. "You won't hurt her." It was an order not a question. Rico raised one eyebrow but didn't answer.

Alex patted the sister on the arm. "Sister Martha, we need to talk to Hezrai. Would you come with us?"

"Yes, my child."

Jon wanted to tell her that Alex wasn't a child—she was a woman, but he kept his lips shut. Hopefully, the old woman wasn't going to be a problem. He had an idea that Alex might get a little belligerent if they tried to finish the sister off. They'd better make sure it didn't come to that.

Alex dropped her hand and returned to the silver door. She took a deep breath and pressed her palm to the panel. Inside the room, a buzzer sounded and a moment later, the doors glided apart.

The meeting with Sister Martha had knocked her off balance. She'd conveniently forgotten how much the old lady had cared for her. When she was growing up, Sister Martha had been the closest thing Alex had had to a mother. It hadn't been Sister Martha's fault that she'd had no clue how to go about it. That every day of her life, Alex had craved some outward sign she'd cared.

She gave the old lady a long look. Sister Martha seemed as serene as ever and quite unperturbed by the fact that she was flanked by two extremely large, dangerous-looking men. One of whom was positively pulsating with darkness.

Alex had always known Rico hated the Church. Now that hatred felt like a tangible thing she could taste in the air. At least Jon appeared slightly more relaxed; she just hoped he'd be able to keep Rico in control if things went bad.

Hezrai sat behind his huge desk in the tall, carved wooden chair that framed him like a throne. Opposite him, Skylar sat. They both appeared relaxed, though a frown formed on Hezrai's face as he studied the small group in the open doorway.

"Yes, what is it? Can't you see I'm busy?" His tone was impatient as he nodded toward Skylar.

Alex ignored the questions and stepped into the room, Sister Martha beside her, Rico and Jon at her back. She pressed her palm to the panel and the door shut behind them.

Indignation turned Hezrai's face purple. "What the . . . ?" He broke off as his gaze settled on Jon, and his eyes widened. Alex could see him fighting to control the panic that glimmered in his pale eyes.

Jon strode across the room, rested his hands on the desk, and leaned toward the priest. "Remember me?"

Hezrai nodded. His gaze darted around the office, finally settling on Skylar as though she could help him.

"I'm in an important meeting. What do you want? I paid you."

"Yes you did, didn't you? Paid me to hand Alex over, then you blew up my fucking ship. And you know what"—he leaned a little closer—"that pissed me off."

"I don't know what you're talking about."

"Yeah, like you know nothing about the three mercenaries. You handed Alex over to them and would have allowed them to rape and murder her."

Beside her, Sister Martha gasped. "Is this true?"

"Of course it's not true," Hezrai said. "The High Priestess is dead, but it was a terrible accident."

Jon smiled. "Actually, that's not quite true. The bit about the High Priestess being dead, I mean." He straightened and held out his hand to Alex. She stepped forward.

Unlike Sister Martha, Hezrai didn't immediately recognize her. His gaze ran over her, and his frown deepened. Alex reached up, plucked the wig from her head, and tossed it onto the desk between them.

Hezrai gaped at her. "You?"

Funny—he didn't sound particularly pleased to see her. She ran her fingers through her flattened hair and shrugged. "Afraid so."

Alex watched the expressions cross his face. Unlike her, he'd never bothered learning the art of keeping his thoughts to himself. He was too arrogant to bother.

Disbelief, followed by a flash of hatred, and then panic.

He opened his mouth. Swallowed. Closed it. Finally, he managed to get the words out. "Lady Alexia, how . . . wonderful."

Alex almost laughed at the feeble attempt.

He inched toward the edge of the desk, his hands fluttering at his side.

"There's an alarm under the desk," Alex said.

Jon reached across the expanse of gleaming metal, grabbed Hezrai by the throat, and dragged him across the surface. Hezrai was tall, but Jon held him with apparent ease, so the priest's feet dangled inches from the floor. Jon loosened his grip, and Hezrai crumpled to the thick, richly patterned carpet.

His gaze darted around the room, coming to rest on Skylar. She'd swiveled around in her chair to be able to watch the proceedings.

"You can't do anything to me," Hezrai choked out. "You wouldn't dare in front of the Collective."

"Really?" Jon drew back his foot and kicked Hezrai in the ribs.

He rolled onto his side, arms around his middle. Alex waited to feel some sense of justice, but nothing came— just weariness and a need to get this over with. She would have loved to have a go at Hezrai herself, but in a fair fight—not like this. But this wasn't about fighting fair; it was about getting the information they needed.

Sister Martha had started forward, but Rico stopped her with a hand on her arm.

"Let me go, young man."

Rico growled. Skylar must have noticed the sound because she rose to her feet, strode over, and placed a hand on Rico's shoulder. "Are you okay?"

"Of course I'm okay. Why wouldn't I be okay?"

She smiled. "I know you're not keen on the Church. And you seem a little tense."

Rico snorted at the understatement. "I'm fine." He released Sister Martha. "Alex, take her and keep her out of my way."

There was a padded velvet bench running along one wall of the office. Alex led Sister Martha across and sat down beside her. Skylar sank down on her other side.

"Lady Alexia, what's going on?" Sister Martha asked.

Alex bit her lip; she wasn't sure how much to reveal to the sister. But maybe she needed to know the truth.

"Yesterday, I gave myself up to Hezrai. He handed me over to some men and told them he didn't care what they did to me as long as I was dead at the end of it." She touched her finger to her cheek and nodded to where Hezrai still lay on the floor. "He did this before he left. And he broke my ribs. I would have been dead, except Jon came back and saved me."

Sister Martha gazed across at the priest. "I would like to say I don't believe you, but I do. What do your 'friends' plan to do?"

"They need to know why. It's important. They wouldn't hurt him otherwise." Actually, she wasn't sure that was true; Jon had expressed a wish to tear Hezrai limb from limb, but maybe it was best not to share that little piece of information with Sister Martha. "They won't hurt him if he tells them what they need to know." She wasn't sure about that either.

A transformation seemed to come over Rico as he strolled toward where Jon stood over the cowering priest. The tension left him, and he appeared relaxed, a slight smile curving his lips, not quite enough to flash a fang.

"Hey, leave the guy alone," he murmured to Jon. "He's a priest—obviously he hasn't done anything wrong."

Alex wondered if Hezrai could hear the irony in the vampire's voice. Beside her, Skylar snorted. "Oh God, they're doing the good agent, bad agent routine."

"And Rico's the good agent?"

"Yeah, and I bet he's great at it, the smooth bastard. Watch."

Rico crouched down beside Hezrai. "Come on, up you get."

Hezrai was clearly bewildered, but he allowed himself to be helped up and into the chair.

"Let me get you a drink. You've obviously had a shock." Rico glanced around the room, found what he wanted, and headed over to the small bar that held a crystal decanter and a set of glasses. He opened the decanter and sniffed the contents. "Hey, whiskey—a man after my own heart." He poured a glass of the amber liquid and swallowed it in one gulp, poured another, and brought it back to Hezrai.

Hezrai's hands shook as he took the glass. Keeping his gaze fixed on Jon, he sipped the liquid, some of the color seeping back into his skin. He cleared his throat and spoke to Rico. "What is it you want from me?"

Rico perched himself on the edge of the desk. "You had a meeting with Collective member Aiden Ross a while back. We need to know why."

"She's lying," he said, staring at Alex, the old hatred back in his eyes. "Whatever she told you—I never met with Aiden Ross. She's crazy. Always was unstable, making up stories and lies."

A growl rumbled from Jon's throat. He stepped closer,

pushed up his sleeve, and held his arm up in front of Hezrai's face.

"You asked yesterday what I was. Let me show you."

The hand stretched, reshaped before their eyes, elongating, dark brown fur sprouting, razor-sharp claws breaking through the skin.

"That is so cool," Skylar said.

It was. Alex had been trying not to think too much about the whole werewolf thing. It just added another layer of complication. Did werewolves have relationships with humans or did they stick to their own kind? She needed to have a nice cozy chat with Rico. Rico seemed to know everything about everything.

Jon reached out almost gently and ran one claw down Hezrai's cheek. The priest tried to back away, but the chair was pushed up against the desk, locking him in place. Blood beaded up from the cut, he released a small whimper, and his gaze turned to Rico. "Stop him," he pleaded.

"I'll try," Rico said. "But he's a little unstable, like Alex over there. Perhaps you'd better tell him what he wants to know."

"I can't. I didn't meet with anyone."

Rico rolled his eyes. "Shit, I'm bored of being good."

He pushed himself up off the desk and stalked the two steps to the priest. This time, when he smiled, the tips of his white fangs showed. Rico touched one with the tip of his tongue.

Alex wanted to look away. This side of Rico had always terrified her, but her gaze refused to shift away from the tableau. Sister Martha's hand slid into hers and gripped her fingers tight. She was muttering a prayer under her breath.

Rico yanked the priest to his feet, turned him so he held him clamped against his chest, one arm tight across his throat. Hezrai managed a few guttural chokes and went still. His eyes bulged, staring straight ahead. Rico leaned in close to his ear.

"Talk," he whispered.

Hezrai whimpered, but the hand wrapped around his throat prevented him from speaking.

"Oh dear, can't talk. I did warn you."

Rico sank his fangs into the priest's throat. Hezrai's legs kicked but he was held tight in the vampire's embrace. After a minute, Rico raised his head and spat. He pushed the shaking priest back into his seat, but kept one hand on his shoulder.

"Now talk, or I drain you dry." He stepped back and rested against the side of the desk.

"Hey," Jon said. "I was supposed to be the bad one."

"Yeah, well, you need a bit more practice."

"Like a thousand years or so?" Skylar suggested. "I guess you've had a lot of practice."

Rico cast her a lazy smile. "I've had practice at a lot of things, sweetheart. And aren't you glad?" He turned back to Hezrai. "Now, can we get this finished?"

Jon stepped forward again. "Okay, priest, why did you meet with Ross?"

Alex could see that Hezrai was broken, his whole body trembling. She leaned forward to listen.

"Ross came to me, said he wanted a meeting. He wouldn't tell me what it was about over a comm system. We agreed to meet on Trakis Twelve—it's relatively close and almost abandoned."

Jon snorted. "Yeah, wasn't the planet colonized by GMs? And didn't the Church go in and slaughter them all?"

Hezrai shot a quick glance at Jon's arm, which had returned to its human form. "We do God's work," he mumbled.

"Yeah, right—of course you do. So what did Ross want?"

Hezrai licked his lips. "He wanted absolution."

"What?" Jon's tone conveyed total disbelief.

"He wanted to say his confession to a man of God and be given forgiveness for his sins."

"What sins?"

"He wouldn't say. Just that they'd discovered something recently—about Meridian. Ross seemed shocked, scared, almost panicking, but he wouldn't give me any details, only that he wanted a chance of one day gaining entry into Heaven."

"Bullshit," Jon said. "The man was immortal."

"Yeah, he was immortal, yet three months after this, he was dead," Skylar said.

"But why? Who wanted him dead? There's got to be more. This isn't enough to have him killed. Do you know anything about this discovery?"

"Nothing. But Aiden was a member of the inner circle. It's possible they're keeping information from the rest of us, but I've no idea what."

Alex pulled free of Sister Martha's hand and stood up. Instinct told her they were close to understanding, but she still couldn't see the sense of it. She crossed over to where Hezrai huddled on his seat.

"Did you give him absolution?" she asked.

Hezrai's gaze shifted to her, and for a second the old hatred shone in his eyes. "Yes."

And what had Aiden Ross offered in exchange for that absolution? Because there was one thing Alex was certain of, and that was Hezrai never did anything for free. "What did he give you in return?" she asked.

"He offered a possibility of a coalition between the Church and the Collective."

Yes, Hezrai would like that. Anything that might increase the Church's power. But she sensed there was more. "What else?" Alex insisted. "What did he offer *you*?"

His lips tightened.

"Answer her," Rico said, giving him a shake.

"He promised me the Meridian treatment."

Alex stared at him dumbfounded. That had not occurred to her, but maybe it should have. Hezrai was getting old, and he must have a few doubts of his own.

Behind her, Jon laughed, but the sound held no amusement. "Trying to put off your own trip to Heaven, priest. Having a few doubts? Or no longer convinced they'll let a murdering bastard like you in?"

Now it made sense. The Church offered an alternative to immortality. How would it look if their leader took Meridian instead? It would hardly give a good impression. "That's why you wanted me dead, isn't it?" Alex asked. "I reckon your congregation would lose a little faith if anyone learned you were getting the treatment."

"And maybe I just wanted an excuse to finish you off," Hezrai snarled. "But it was Ross who insisted you die. He didn't want anyone knowing of our meeting, and he'd seen you watching us. I didn't believe it was you at that point, not until I got back and found you were missing. You never could mind your own business. Always wanting to change things, make things better." Alex flinched beneath the wealth of contempt in his voice.

"This guy's starting to annoy me again," Rico said. "And I reckon he's given us all we're going to get out of him. And that's fuck-all really. We know why he wanted Alex dead, and we have a connection to the Collective, which we knew anyway, but we still have no clue who wanted Aiden Ross killed or why. That's the information we need to get the Collective off our backs." He sighed. "We'll get back to the ship—see if Janey has had any success breaking those codes." He glanced across at Alex. "What do you want us to do with your friend here?"

Alex started in shock at the question then shook her

head. She didn't know what to say, and she didn't want the responsibility of making the decision. But that was cowardice. Sister Martha met her gaze, but as always the sister gave nothing of her feelings away. Still, she wasn't begging for mercy for Hezrai either.

Alex wouldn't kill him out of revenge for what he had tried to do to her, but Hezrai was evil. How many had he killed in the name of the Church? Left alive, how many more would he go on to kill? And if he were gone, perhaps the Church would have a chance to reshape itself and actually become a force for good.

"Kill him," she said.

Hezrai's eyes widened momentarily, panic flaring, as though he hadn't believed she could do this to him. Rico's fingers tightened on his throat, and his neck snapped with a sharp crack of bone. Alex had thought he would make a meal of it—literally—but it was over so fast.

The body tumbled to the floor, and she stared at it, feeling no remorse but no elation either.

"Do you feel better now?" Jon asked as he came to stand beside her. He appeared genuinely curious, and she shook her head.

"No, I don't feel better."

"Good."

"Okay, we're out of here," Rico said, casting a speculative glance at the sister.

"No," Alex snapped.

He grinned. "Only joking. I take it you're coming with us?"

Alex realized it hadn't even occurred to her that she could stay. But with Hezrai dead, she had no reason not to. She could take up her old position, but now without Hezrai to interfere, she could change things, do things her own way.

The old sense of suffocation enveloped her like she was

drowning in treacle. Jon stood watching her, arms folded over his chest, brows puckered as if he hadn't thought of the possibility of her staying either.

"You'd be safe here," he said, his voice expressionless.

Well, that decided it—she didn't want to be safe. She crossed the room quickly, stooped, hugged Sister Martha, and kissed her on her soft cheek, breathing in the familiar, sweet scent she had known all her life.

"Good-bye," she whispered. "You know, with no high priest and no high priestess—you're in charge now."

A startled expression crossed her face. "That's true. I must sort out the arrangements for the High Priest's funeral. And stop the search for the new priestess now that you're not actually dead and . . ." She broke off and looked at Alex. "Will you return to us one day?"

Alex flashed a glance at Jon; his face was expressionless, but she knew he was waiting for her answer. So she told the truth for him to hear.

"I don't know."

CHAPTER FIFTEEN

Jon stared at the bowl of steaming stew in front of him, but despite the gnawing ache in his belly, he couldn't bring himself to eat.

They were all present in the galley for the evening meal. Well, all except Janey, who was still working on the money transfer codes they'd gotten from Deke. The codes were their only lead now.

And Alex, who had disappeared as soon as they had docked on *El Cazador* and hadn't been seen since. He presumed she was hiding out in her cabin, but from whom or what he wasn't sure. She'd been distant on the way back. But so had he.

Maybe he should take her some food. The thought brought him up short. In pack culture, the offering of food had a deep significance. It symbolized the offering of self, a formalized mating bond. Many wolves paired for life, which was a long time, but always as far as he knew with other wolves, never with humans. He'd never come even close to wanting to share that sort of commitment with any woman, wolf or human. He'd been fond of his wife, but theirs had been a relationship based on friendship more than love.

Now, he couldn't get Alex from his mind. But he was a killer. Sometimes he killed for money and sometimes because he wanted to kill. Either way, he was not a good person, hadn't been for a long time.

He had no right to go after Alex, even if she did still want him, and he was no longer sure that was the case.

Right from the start, she'd been up front about the fact that she wanted his body, not him, and in the past that was the exact sort of arrangement he liked best. Then she'd told him she might be falling in love with him. And he'd tried to pretend the words meant nothing, but they loitered in his mind, waylaying him when he was unwary. Now he was sure she must have decided she'd been wrong, and what she'd really felt was grateful because he'd saved her from Bastion. But since then, he'd saved her from those mercs, so shouldn't she be even more grateful?

Perhaps he should take her some food—after all, he doubted she knew anything of wolf mating rituals—and he could suggest she show her gratitude. Heat pooled in his groin, and he shifted trying to ease the tightness in his pants. Maybe that's what they both needed. A long, hot night of sex to get it out of their systems.

But what if she really was falling in love with him?

Oh God, he wasn't ready for this.

He slammed his spoon down, and everyone stopped talking and looked in his direction.

"What's up?" Daisy asked.

"Nothing." He picked up the spoon and forced himself to eat, though he had no clue what he was eating.

The murmur of voices started back up around him. There was a casual camaraderie among the crew, a relaxed feeling of acceptance that jarred on his nerves. Even Rico, who didn't actually eat, joined them for meals. It reminded him of mealtimes with the pack, when problems were forgotten for a short while.

Occasionally, one of them would glance in his direction and frown. No doubt, he was casting a shadow on their nice, friendly little get-together.

The truth was, he wasn't one of them. He didn't fit in here. Hell, he didn't fit in anywhere.

Christ, he was a maudlin bastard.

He set his spoon down again and pushed his chair back. Rico sat across from him, his face close to Skylar's, and they were whispering and giggling like two adolescents. Revolting. Rico looked up as Jon got to his feet.

For a moment, he thought Rico would speak. Maybe say something that would lead to a fight, but for once Jon didn't even feel like a fight. What the hell was wrong with him?

In the end, Rico held his gaze, raised an eyebrow, then turned back to Skylar.

They were probably glad to see the back of him.

He couldn't believe the thought. Christ, he wasn't only maudlin; he was pathetic.

He turned to stalk out of the room, almost colliding with Janey in the doorway.

She was buzzing with energy; she must have broken the codes. Maybe this was what he needed. Going after the bastard who had got him into this situation in the first place.

If it wasn't for that bastard, he'd still be out there, doing the job he was best at.

But he knew that wasn't true. He'd already decided to get out of the assassination business. For a while, it had suited his mood, but he'd long since grown bored of the killing. Aiden Ross had been his last job.

He'd been going home. The pack lands were gone, but he had enough credits to buy a place big enough to run. Once he'd longed to travel to the stars; now he had a yearning to run through the forests of his homeland. Maybe not forever, but for a while.

He followed Janey back into the room and leaned against the wall, waiting to hear what she'd found. She sat in the chair he'd vacated.

"Well?" Tannis asked. "Did you find out who it leads back to? Do we know who set up the assassination?"

"Not exactly. Gosh, I'm starving. Is there any food left?"

Daisy jumped up and bought her a bowl of stew. Janey took a bite, eating quickly but with impeccable manners.

"Not exactly?" Tannis's tone was grim.

Janey appeared unfazed. She wiped her mouth and put down her spoon. "I haven't got a name, but I've traced the payment back to the initial transfer. I almost lost it—they were clever, they'd double ended the transaction with a circular coding so it kept leading me back to where I'd come from, and there was a trifunctional reference replication sequence—"

"Okay," Tannis interrupted, "drop the techie stuff and give me the good bits."

"I told you—I've tracked the coding back to the computer node that made the initial transfer. But I can't get any more information from the codes. I need to get physical access to the computer."

"And that will give you the name?"

"I think so."

"Think?"

"Ninety-nine percent sure."

"That's good enough for me. Looks like we're going to visit your computer. Where is it?"

For the first time, Janey appeared a little discomforted. "Trakis Five."

"Brilliant," Tannis muttered. "Just freaking brilliant.

Trakis Five—home to just about all the Collective, not to mention the freaking Corps. We're fucked."

Alex lay on the bed in her small cabin. Mogg balanced on her stomach, kneading her with sharp claws. Her stomach rumbled, and the cat leaped off her in alarm. Maybe she should go get some food, but she didn't feel up to company.

She needed some time alone. Everything had changed.

For the first twenty-four years of her existence, she'd lived with her life intricately mapped out for her. Every day meticulously planned. No surprises. And boredom had been a constant companion.

Then she'd spent the last three months wanting to cram as much of life as she could into her time of freedom. While always at the back of her mind was the thought that time was short and freedom was an illusion.

Now, her whole life stretched out before her—filled with limitless possibilities. Well, at least until the Collective caught up with them and blew them up. But she trusted the captain; if anyone could get them out of this, Tannis would.

Alex could go anywhere. Do anything. It was an entirely new feeling, and she wasn't quite sure how to deal with it.

Before, when she'd presumed she was going back, she'd had a lengthy list of things to do. Now that list had dwindled to two items she knew she wanted. To stay on *El Cazador* and to be with Jon. And not just for sex. While she still didn't understand her feelings for him, and she wasn't about to declare undying love or anything, she did know it went way beyond the mere physical. She knew that, because she wanted to make him happy, see him smile, banish the wariness from his expression forever.

He'd told her he liked to do the chasing, so she'd backed off, but the effort was killing her. She had too many years of watching life from a distance. Now, she was fighting the urge to grab hold of what she wanted. Some inner sense screamed that time was short. She just wasn't sure how short. The Collective could catch up with them at any moment.

So, while she was letting Jon take the lead, he was only going to be allowed to run things for a short time. She'd realized today, when he'd been so angry to find her outside the cathedral, that he was scared. Scared of letting himself care. Scared of failing to keep her safe.

Something had happened to make him that way, and she wanted to wipe away the bad memories.

The ship shifted beneath her. Normally, it was hard to feel their movement; *El Cazador* was a smooth ride. They must have turned abruptly.

Were they under attack again? At least this time it wasn't her fault.

When nothing further happened, she headed for the bridge. Daisy was in the pilot's seat; otherwise, the room was empty. She peered over her shoulder as Alex entered and grinned, white teeth gleaming against her jade-green lips.

"Where is everyone and where are we going?" Alex asked.

"Everyone is over in the conference room having a meeting, and we're going to Trakis Five."

Shock punched her in the gut. "Trakis Five? Why would we go anywhere near Trakis Five?"

Jon stared at Alex's mutinous expression as the shuttle door closed between them. She'd wanted to go too and had made it very clear.

In some ways, he understood her desire to cram as much life as she could into every moment. All the same, he was pleased it was Rico who had refused to take her this time.

Rico had quite rightly pointed out that this was not a sight-seeing trip.

They were taking Janey. She would hopefully get the information they needed, and they would be out of there before anyone even noticed their presence.

Of course, Jon had serious doubts things would pan out that way. They were number one on the Collective's most-wanted list and were about to touch down on Trakis Five, administrative center of the Collective and base for the Corps, the Collective's private and extremely effective army. So it was perfect Alex was staying aboard *El Cazador*.

Skylar was coming with them. She was dressed in the uniform of the Corps. It was her job to keep watch and monitor for any Collective activity, maybe manage to run a little interference if they were spotted.

They would take Janey to wherever this computer node was located. Right now, she didn't actually know, just coordinates of a location, but with the way their luck was going, it would be slap bang in the middle of Corps head-quarters. But at least Alex would be safe—or as safe as any of them were at this point.

Slumping down in his seat, he stared at the ceiling. He and Alex had been avoiding each other for the last three days. He'd decided it was best, and she obviously agreed. Until this Collective problem was sorted out, there was no point in making plans. As if he had any intention of ever making plans again.

Darkness was falling as Rico glided the shuttle into the main port area of the city, making no effort at subterfuge. They'd decided their best bet for getting through this was not to draw attention and hope no one noticed them.

They hired two speeders. A large four-seater that held him, Rico, and Janey, while Skylar followed at a distance in the second, smaller vehicle.

Janey sat in the front beside Rico, with a handheld tracking device locked onto the computer node. They headed first into the city, but once in the built-up area she directed them away from the center and into the residential district. The buildings became gradually more luxurious, reminding him of pictures he had seen of old Earth cities.

There was an air of civilized sophistication to Maltrex, the main city on Trakis Five. The walkways beneath them were wide, the air clean. He'd have preferred a few more speeders to blend in with, but as they moved on the traffic thinned even more.

"That building there," Janey said, pointing the device toward the biggest house yet. The building seemed familiar, but Jon was certain he'd never been here before.

On the same principle they had used so far, they went straight to the front gate. Rico pressed his palm to the pad. Nothing happened.

"Looks like no one's home." He turned to Janey. "Can you get us in?"

"No problem, but it will take a couple of minutes."

"Guys?" Jon went instantly still as Skylar's voice sounded in the comm unit in his ear.

"What is it?" Rico asked.

"Do you know whose house you're standing in front of?"

"No, but I presume you're going to tell us."

"Aiden Ross."

"Well, that explains why no one's home."

It also explained why Jon recognized the place. The pictures had been in the files he'd been sent on Ross. He'd never considered a home hit; there was usually too much security, so he'd not bothered to case the place.

"Have you spotted any surveillance?" Rico asked.

"None, and I can't see why they'd bother, as Aiden's dead, but I'd still get in and out of there as fast as you can."

"We're in," Janey said.

The huge metal gates slid open. Rico and Janey climbed back in the speeder, and they headed for the main entrance to the house.

Jon tried to make sense of the information. Had some-one within Ross's own household set up the assassination? He had no family living with him, so it must be a member of the staff. Or had someone infiltrated the house to make the transfer so it would appear as though it came from here? But that didn't make sense. Janey was one of only a very few people who could have traced the transfer back to its origin. Why go to the bother of setting something like that up if the chances were you'd never be found out?

Once inside the house, Jon halted in the wide hallway and stared around him. "Jesus, the guy was a nutter. Look at this stuff."

Pictures covered the walls, all of them depicting reli-gious themes. Most appeared to be scenes of divine retri-bution—a whole load of fire and brimstone.

"Maybe you could take one back for Alex," Rico said. "You know, make her feel at home—get back in her good books."

Jon cast him a quick glance. "Piss off."

"Well, we've all noticed the pair of you aren't talking, and if you aren't talking I doubt you're doing anything else."

Janey giggled.

Christ, they'd obviously been discussing him and Alex. Strangely, the thought didn't bother him, which didn't mean he had any intention of talking about it.

"Which way now?" he asked Janey. "I hope you can get close—this place would take hours to search."

"That way." She pointed to a set of double doors.

The doors led into a large, high-tech office—the de-cor silver and white, the only color in the room a huge crucifixion scene hanging behind the polished silver desk. Janey sat at the console and flipped a switch.

"It's protected," she said. "It'll take me a couple of minutes to get in." She hunched over the console, her brows drawn together. "Do you think you could give me a bit of room here? You're both breathing down my neck."

Jon took a step back but stayed where he could see the screen. Rico leaned against the desk and stared into space while his foot tapped on the floor.

Janey glared at it, and he pushed himself up and paced the room. She turned back to the console and her fingers flew over the keys. Jon had come to respect her over the past few days. They'd spent a lot of time together as they struggled to make sense of the information on Deke's files. And strangely, once he'd stopped trying to flirt with her, she'd revealed herself as a much nicer person, and he'd come to like her as well—something he hadn't expected.

A message flashed up on the screen, and she frowned. "Not right," she muttered under her breath and deleted the entry before Jon could read it.

She tapped again, deleted again, tapped again, and sat back. "That's it," she said. "I thought it was wrong, but it's not. It's coming up with the same answer every time."

"And that is?" Jon said, not bothering to keep the impatience from his voice.

"Aiden Ross."

"What do you mean, Aiden Ross? Aiden Ross what?"

"Aiden Ross made the transfer."

Jon pinched the bridge of his nose. "You're telling me Aiden Ross paid for his own assassination?"

"Yup. Ross not only paid, but he actually set up the transaction."

"You're sure?

She nodded, and Jon spun around and stalked the length of the room.

He'd been counting on this to give them a lead they could use to convince the Collective to back off and get the bounty off their heads. But like everything else since he'd woken up from cryo, this made no sense.

"So Aiden Ross effectively committed suicide," Rico said from behind him. "It would explain how he knew how to take down one of the Collective and make sure they stayed down."

Jon turned to face the vampire. "But why? The man was immortal—why would he kill himself?"

Rico shrugged. "Some people can't handle the whole long-life thing. You must have seen it among your wolves."

It was true—Jon had seen many wolves die and none of them from natural causes. There were ways to commit suicide without actually killing yourself. Just pick a fight with the wrong person.

"He obviously went to great lengths to hide the fact that he committed suicide," Rico said.

"But somebody knows," Jon said.

Rico cast him a sharp look. "Why do you say that?"

"Why else would they try to shut me up? If they thought it was a straight contract killing, why not let me serve my sentence and die in the mines?"

"Then whoever knows must also suspect that you know who paid you to do the job?"

"Or they're getting rid of me because I know how to kill them. Jesus, this is doing my head in. Why would Ross fake his own assassination? And why the hell would anyone care?" He crossed the room to where Janey still sat in front of the console. "You got the proof you need?"

"Of course." Janey sounded offended by the question. "I've transferred the data to *El Cazador*."

"Good. Let's get out of here. We can think it through once we're back on the ship."

Jon headed for the door, but Skylar's voice in his comm unit stopped him in his tracks.

"You have company."

"Who is it?" Rico asked.

"The good part is, it's not Corps. Looks like some sort of local security force. Probably triggered by you going in there."

"And the bad part?"

"There's a whole load of them—twenty at least."

"Okay, thanks, sweetheart."

"You want me in there?"

"Hell, I want you anywhere I can get you, but stay outside for now. Be ready to cause a distraction once we're out of here. I don't want anyone following us back to the *Cazador*."

"Will do. They're heading down the drive now."

Rico turned to Jon. "Keep a watch on the entrance. Yell as soon as anyone gets into the building." He strode across to the desk where Janey still sat at the console. "Can you pull up the plans for the house—find us another way out."

She nodded, and Jon moved away to stand just inside the doorway. From there, the main access to the house was visible. Huge windows lined the front wall, giving a clear view of the approaching men. They wore dark blue uniforms, not the black of the Corps, which was good news.

But even so, these men were alert. Their weapons weren't drawn, but their hands rested on their laser pistols.

"You have about one minute," he said.

Janey's hands flew over the keyboard. They didn't falter as she answered. "I need another thirty seconds. I'm just getting the codes for the rear entrance."

Jon considered closing the doors; it would give them maybe a few more minutes before they were discovered, but it would also block their only exit from the office.

Rico came to stand on the other side of the doorway and

they both drew their pistols. Rico's eyes filled with that familiar dark excitement that Jon knew was reflected in his own.

The front door opened, and the men stood framed in the doorway. They cautiously stepped into the wide hallway, their weapons drawn now.

"Done," Janey said behind them.

Jon turned to tell her to stay down, but too late. She stood up. One of the men in the hallway must have caught the movement; he raised his pistol and aimed it at the doorway.

"Go," Rico said.

Moving as one, Rico and Jon stepped into the open doorway, their lasers already blazing as they moved into position. Two of the men went down, a third got off one shot. Jon countered with a shot from his own laser, and Rico blasted him in the head. The others were falling back but shooting as they went.

Behind them, Janey screamed and crashed to the floor.

CHAPTER SIXTEEN

The men retreated and took cover outside the main entrance. Jon knew they wouldn't stay there for long, though. They only had minutes at most. He turned to glance at Janey. She lay still on the floor, but as he watched, she shifted and rolled on to her knees.

"Stay down," he said.

Janey gritted her teeth. "It's not as though I have a lot of choice."

"How bad are you hit?"

"Not bad. Just a glance." She hissed with pain. "But it got me in the lower leg. I can walk, but I'll slow you down."

They'd be back soon. They must be aware there were only three of them.

It was obvious what he had to do. And maybe it was better this way. At least he'd go out doing some good. He took a step toward Rico, who turned to face him, one eyebrow raised.

Jon nodded toward Janey. "Take her and get out of here. I'll keep you covered."

Rico hesitated.

"There are too many of them," Jon said. "We try and fight our way out, and she's going to end up dead."

Rico glanced from him to Janey and back to Jon. "Let's find out what's happening out there. Skylar?"

"Yes?"

"What's going on?"

"There are more approaching. I suggest you get out of there before you're surrounded."

"Okay. We're coming out the back way." He gave a backward glance to the door and crossed over to where Janey half sat, half lay on the floor. "How you doing?"

"I'm fine. Are we getting out of here?"

"Yeah, we're getting out." He scooped her up with ease, headed to the door, but paused beside Jon. "Don't be a goddamn hero. Give us enough time to clear the building, and then get out of here."

Janey's face was rigid with pain—her mouth a grim line, her eyes closed. Now they fluttered open, and she stared at Jon. "What's happening? We can't leave you here. Alex will kill us."

The idea that Alex might be even slightly upset if he didn't return cheered him a little. Suddenly he wanted to say something. Some message for Alex. But what was the point? Instead, he forced a grin. "I'll be fine—you know I live for this shit. Anyway, I'll be right behind you."

Rico nodded once and turned as Jon stepped into the doorway. Legs braced, Jon fired a continuous stream in the direction of the main entrance. When he peered over his shoulder, Rico hadn't moved. "Go," Jon snapped.

As he watched them disappear, his chest tightened. What had he expected? That Rico would stay and they'd all go down in a blaze of glory? Buddies together? Who the fuck was he kidding? He wasn't anybody's buddy.

He backed into the office as men surged through the door, lasers blazing, cutting off his maudlin thoughts. For a brief second, he considered not responding, letting them kill him and getting it over with fast, but almost at the same time he acknowledged the impossibility of that—it wasn't in his nature to go down without a fight.

He countered their shots almost automatically, until a blast caught him in the arm. The acrid smell of burning cloth seared his nostrils, followed by the sweet smell of roasting flesh. The pain hardly registered, but he realized that their lasers weren't set to kill. They must want to take him alive, which meant there was a chance he could get out of this.

For years, he'd thought himself ready to die, and he'd faced death many times. Now, at the thought of survival, exhilaration raced through him, sending adrenaline surging through his veins. He fought on, countering each blast, getting in a few of his own. Bodies littered the hallway, but there were still plenty more left.

Rico and Janey must be clear by now, but it made no difference. If he moved from the relative safety of the office, they'd be able to attack him from all sides instead of just one. His only hope was that they'd eventually back off again, giving him a chance to run for it.

As a plan, it was downright pathetic, but it was the only one he had. At least there was still hope.

A small black canister rolled toward him, green mist oozing from one end.

Shit.

He held his breath as long as he could, but finally his lungs heaved for air, drawing in the sickly green mist. His belly turned to liquid, nausea rose up in his throat, and a wave of weakness washed over him. The laser pistol dropped from his useless fingers and his legs gave way beneath him. He crashed to the floor.

Alex's gamine face flashed across his mind, and the last thought as darkness took him was he didn't want to die.

He knew it was only a matter of time and pain, however much of each he had left before death took him.

If he could have shifted, he might have had a chance, but they had tied him tight to the seat so he could barely move, let alone shift. There were five men in the room with him. They weren't talking yet, but one thing was clear—they didn't like him. Which was hardly surprising—he'd killed at least eight of their friends.

The burn on his arm from the laser blast throbbed. His stomach still churned from the gas, but he forced down the nausea. He was bound upright, a chain at his throat. If he threw up right now, he'd probably choke on his own vomit. Not a way he'd choose to go.

One of the men with sergeant's stripes on his arm came over to stand in front of him. He had the look of a career soldier, short hair, and perfectly creased pants. Jon just had time to notice them when the man's fist shot out and cracked him in the jaw, and Jon's mouth flooded with blood.

The man smiled at him, an expression that didn't reach his eyes. Smile apart, the guy didn't appear too happy. "Talk."

Jon spat the blood from his mouth. It landed on the sergeant's polished boots, and the man's jaw tightened.

Hey, there was a plan. Maybe he could piss them off enough so they killed him quickly. He'd always been good at pissing people off.

"Talk about what?" Jon asked. "Them perhaps?" He nodded at the row of dead bodies lined along the hallway floor.

The sergeant drew a knife from the sheath at his thigh and studied Jon while he tossed the eight-inch blade from hand to hand. Jon's own hand was splayed out on the arm of the chair. He only had a second to realize what the man meant to do when the knife flashed down and pinned him to the leather.

Shit. That hurt. He focused on the blade handle until he knew he could control the pain, then he smiled up at the sergeant. "Were they your friends? The men I killed? Boyfriends maybe?"

The sergeant reached out and twisted the blade. Red-hot agony shot along Jon's nerves, black dots dancing before his eyes.

"Where are your friends?" he demanded.

Jon shrugged. "I don't have any friends."

It was the truth, but the thought sent a shaft of regret through him. He knew if he'd been a real member of the crew of *El Cazador*, they would never have left him behind to die. Even if it meant dying with him. He remembered how they had behaved with Alex. She had been a danger to the whole ship, and they could have handed her over at any time—even gotten a reward for doing it—but they hadn't because she was one of them, and they would never give up one of their crew.

What would it be like to be part of something like that again?

He was never going to find out now.

A second man came to stand beside them. "Sergeant, we've received a comm. The Collective are on their way. They said to hold him but don't talk to him."

"Screw the bloody Collective." The sergeant loosened his grip on the knife and stepped back. "This piece of shit killed our men; that means he's not getting out of this room alive. We'll get whatever information he knows before we finish him." He looked around. "Has that interrogation kit arrived yet?"

Interrogation kit? Jon didn't like the sound of that. The improvised stuff he could take, but if they started on him with the real professional shit, he probably wouldn't last long. It had nothing to do with how much pain you could take, but the drugs played with your mind. He knew. He'd used them before.

The good thing was there was nothing he could tell them. The only thing would have been the location of *El Cazador*, but he'd given Rico plenty of time to get away. *El Cazador* would be long gone by now.

"Yes, Sergeant. Where do you want it?"

"Where the fuck do you think I want it? Bring it over here."

He placed the black case on the desk close to the chair where Jon was chained and opened it up. Jon tried not to stare at the contents. The sadistic bastard took his time choosing what to use. Jon forced his muscles to relax, but he could feel everything tensing up. The sergeant selected a syringe filled with a pale yellow liquid. He attached the needle, held it in front of Jon's face.

Jon swallowed down the hot bile that rose in his throat. He really wasn't looking forward to this.

"Last chance," the sergeant said. "Where are your friends?"

"I told you—"

He didn't get a chance to finish. Without warning, the needle was stabbed into the muscle of his thigh. Instant agony shot through his body. His muscles tried to convulse, but the chains held him in place. He locked his jaw so he wouldn't scream as the fire raged along his nerve endings as though he burned from the inside.

His head fell back, and he closed his eyes and tried to ride the pain. Finally, it receded until he could think again. He blinked open his eyes as another needle came down, and this time he couldn't prevent the scream that tore from his throat.

Everything went black for a brief moment of respite.

When he came around, his whole body was one big, throbbing mass of hurt.

He'd thought they wouldn't go too far until they were sure he didn't have anything useful to say, but it looked like they wanted payback for their friends more than they wanted the information. And they were in a hurry. The Collective were on their way.

One of the things he hated about dying right now was the fact that he still had no clue what was going on. Had Aiden Ross really committed suicide? And if so, why? And who was trying to stop Jon talking about it?

He was avoiding thinking about the other reason he didn't want to die, but Alex kept insinuating herself in his thoughts. Was it selfish of him to hope that she would be a little bit grieved by the news of his death?

He clung to the thought as another needle arced toward him. Would this be the one to finally finish him off?

Alex stood on the ramp of *El Cazador* and stared at the speeders in disbelief. Rico and Janey were in the first. Janey was slumped in the passenger seat with her eyes closed. Skylar was alone in the second.

No Jon.

Her mind searched for an explanation but came up blank.

She hurried down as Rico got out of the speeder and leaned in to pick up Janey.

"Where is he? Where's Jon?"

Rico's expression remained blank. "We left him behind."

"You what?" The question came out as a shrill scream. Alex didn't care; sheer terror filled her mind. "You left him behind? How could you?"

Janey's eyes flickered open. They were dull with pain. "He offered, Alex. We couldn't stop him, and we wouldn't have gotten out without him."

Alex wanted to scream that she didn't care. They should never have left him.

She had to get out there—find him, save him. He'd saved her twice now. How could she leave him when he needed her?

"We have to go back. We have to go get him."

"Will you shut the fuck up for one second," Rico snarled.

For once, he didn't intimidate her, and she opened her mouth to argue as Tannis appeared at the top of the ramp. She took one look at Janey and hurried down. For the first time, Alex noticed how ill Janey looked. Alex had never seen her less than immaculate; now her hair was mussed, and a sheen of sweat gleamed on her pale skin.

"Is she all right?" Tannis asked.

"She will be, but she needs treatment."

"I'll take her."

"No," Rico said. "We're going to need you. Where's Daisy?"

"On the bridge. Readying for takeoff." She looked around. "Jon's not here?"

"No, he's not. Look, comm Daisy—tell her takeoff is delayed and to meet me in the sick bay."

He disappeared inside the ship with Janey cradled in his arms.

Alex gnawed on her lower lip, trying to cling to the little gleam of hope his words had brought to life. If takeoff was delayed, maybe Rico meant to go back. Alex would go alone if she had to, but she had no illusions that she would succeed without help. She couldn't stand still when Jon could be somewhere hurt or dying—some things you had to do even if you knew from the start they were doomed to failure.

She hurried across to where Skylar and Tannis stood talking in low voices. Skylar glanced up as Alex approached, and a flash of pity showed in her eyes. That look terrified Alex all over again.

"What happened?" she asked. "Is he still alive? Who took him?"

"They got in, got the information, but someone must have been monitoring the place. A squad of the local Guardia turned up. Luckily, it wasn't Corps or we'd probably be dead. Janey was hit, and Rico had to get her out of there. There was no way they could win in a full-frontal attack, so Jon offered to hold them off while Rico took Janey out the back route."

Fear and panic clawed at her mind. She needed to think straight. They didn't know he was dead. "How many were there? Is there any chance he got away?"

Skylar shook her head. "I'm sorry, Alex. There were too many. But I intercepted a call. The Collective are on their way to pick him up. So right now, he's still alive."

"We have to go get him."

"We will." It was Tannis who answered, and some of Alex's panic receded.

"Do we need to move the ship?" Skylar asked. "Do you think he'll break?"

"Jon won't break," Tannis replied. "I've never met a more stubborn bastard."

Alex agreed, but her stomach churned at the thought of what they might be doing to him, and she itched with the need to get moving. She wanted to jump into one of the speeders and head off right now. But she didn't even know the way.

"Come on. We'll go get some more weapons, while we wait for Rico."

Alex followed them up the ramp and across the docking bay to the weapons locker. She waited as Skylar strapped on a second laser pistol. Tannis replaced her weapons belt with a new one that was bigger and bulkier. She slotted a number of round grenades into the pockets at the front, a blaster gun on one hip, and a laser pistol on the other. She was finishing up as Rico appeared.

"You need anything else?" Skylar asked.

He shook his head. "I'm good. Let's go."

Alex stepped forward. "I want another gun."

They swung around to stare at her. No way were they leaving her behind.

"I'm coming," she said.

Rico studied her, his lips pursed. Finally, after what seemed an age, he nodded. "Give her the medical kit. If we do find wolf-boy alive and by some miracle we get him out of there, she can mop his fevered brow." His gaze returned to her face. "But stay out of the line of fire—you're a liability we don't need."

The speeder drew to a halt outside an impressive set of tall gates. They stood open, and Alex could see the imposing house at the end of the drive. At least five vehicles were parked outside, but since none of them were Collective they still might be in time.

She twitched with the need to move, and there was a definite chance that she might throw up if something didn't happen soon. But they had come up with a plan, and they'd be in there in a moment.

"Okay," Skylar said. "Give me a couple of those gas grenades, just in case."

Tannis handed them over, and Skylar slipped them in her pocket. "Alex, you come with me. Bring the medical kit."

Skylar planned to pretend to be an advance from the Collective, here to make sure the prisoner was ready and in a fit state for transfer. Alex was obviously the medic, in case he wasn't in a fit state, but she didn't even want to think about that.

The best-case scenario was they would get Jon out without a fight before the Collective appeared to pick him up, but everyone seemed to think that was unlikely, and no one seemed particularly bothered by the idea of a fight. Excited more like. Alex wished she could feel excitement, but she couldn't see beyond the panic that clawed at her guts. She had been given strict instructions—if Skylar gave her the signal she was to take cover fast. The signal was the word "backup."

As they stepped into the hallway, Alex's mouth dropped open. The walls were lined with the most extremist of religious images. Loads of divine retribution were being dispensed on every side.

The place appeared full of people. They'd all stopped whatever it was they were doing and looked at Skylar as she stepped through the doorway. They took in the black uniform with the violet insignia of the Corps blazoned on her left breast, and their gazes shifted as one to her luminescent violet eyes. And every one of them inched away as though they didn't want to get too close.

Alex gave her a sideways glance. She had come to think of Skylar as her friend, but watching her now, she could understand why they backed off. Skylar appeared taller; her eyes glowed brighter.

A shiver ran through Alex. While maintaining an outward show of support, the inner circles of the Church had always maintained that the Collective were ultimately evil. That Meridian somehow changed the people who took it, tied their souls to their bodies. And looking at Skylar as she assumed the full persona of the Collective, there *was* something inhuman about her.

Alex shook off the feeling. Skylar might be different, but Alex would never believe she was evil.

"Where's the prisoner?" Skylar spoke to the room in general without bothering to introduce herself.

No one seemed to want to take responsibility for answering.

"Someone better speak up. Fast." Even Alex got a chill of fear from Skylar's tone. Finally, as the silence stretched out, one man stepped forward.

"Through there, ma'am." He gestured toward an open doorway.

Alex peered in, but she couldn't see past the small knot of men. She followed Skylar as she strode across the hallway, her boots echoing on the tiled floor. The group parted, and she caught her first sight of the man strapped to the chair.

Oh God.

The world had been reduced to nothing more than pain. Pain that burned, pain that froze, other indescribable pain.

There was a second of respite while his tormentor fiddled with his case of goodies and decided what to try next. They were obviously having fun. At least he was going to die making someone happy.

He hadn't told them anything; though he wasn't sure they cared either way.

Shit, the sergeant had made his decision. The syringe held a lurid pink liquid, and Jon winced. He opened his mouth to make a comment, to prove he wasn't beaten yet, but at that moment, there was a commotion in the doorway, and they all turned to look.

At first, he couldn't see anything as men stood in the way. They parted slightly, and the first thing he saw was a black uniform. The Collective had arrived.

He wasn't sure whether that was a good thing or bad. At least they were likely to finish him off quicker. No dwindling away in the Meridian mines this time.

His gaze was drawn to a figure standing beside the Corps officer. She was small but hard to miss in a bright pink jumpsuit. His vision blurred, and he shook his head.

He must be hallucinating, because he could swear Alex

stood in the doorway, a medical kit clasped tight against her chest. Blinking, he shook his head again to clear the sweat from his eyes. Yes, it was Alex, and he must look even worse than he felt because an expression of total horror was stamped across her face.

He looked again at the Corps officer. Last time his gaze hadn't risen above the violet insignia on her chest. Now he looked into her face.

Skylar.

She frowned at him, and he realized something must be showing on his face. He hoped it wasn't what he was feeling right now, because that would be plain embarrassing.

They'd come for him after all.

They hadn't flown away and left him to rot.

He was actually feeling all warm and fuzzy. It must be the drugs.

He forced his brain to concentrate. They weren't out of here yet. Skylar must have convinced them she was from the Collective, but that would only last as long as it took the real Corps to turn up.

Alex had managed to get her expression under control, though he could still see the shock reflected in her huge eyes.

The sergeant didn't appear suspicious, just pissed off that he'd lost his chance to finish Jon off.

"Release the prisoner, Sergeant." Skylar's tone gave nothing away.

"He's dangerous, ma'am, best keep him tied up until your people get here."

Skylar stepped closer. "Do you think I need 'my people', Sergeant? I said release him."

"Give us a few more minutes, and he'll tell us everything he knows."

The guy was persistent. Or an idiot. It took balls to go up against a Corps officer.

"But we don't want him to tell you anything. Which is why you were specifically ordered *not* to interrogate him."

Her tone was still blank, but even so, she radiated a sense of menace. The sergeant must have finally noticed as well; he was slow but not entirely stupid. He took a step back and nodded once.

Skylar moved toward Jon and stopped. Her eyes narrowed, and she turned to Alex. "Backup is here in thirty."

Panic flared in Alex's eyes, and she clutched the box tighter but nodded. Jon could see her muttering to herself, and he realized she was counting and suddenly knew what was going down.

There wasn't a lot he could do trussed up like he was. But he could get out of the line of fire. He readied himself.

Out in the hallway, all hell broke loose.

The men's attention was drawn to the open doorway. Faster than he could follow, Skylar drew her weapons. She stood in the center of the room, a pistol in both hands. He rocked his chair until it tumbled, finally crashing him to the floor as the lasers flashed over his head. Alex dived toward him and took cover behind the metal desk. All he could see of her was her feet sticking out.

As the men swung around at the sound, Skylar opened fire. Christ, she was good. They didn't stand a chance. They were all down before they could even draw their weapons.

Skylar shot him a quick glance, saw he was still in the land of the living, and ran into the hallway.

Jon lay tied to his chair, staring at Alex's feet. He was alive, and there was a good chance he was getting out of here. It didn't seem possible.

There was a movement to the side, and he turned his head. The sergeant was down but not dead. His pistol was in his hand and aimed straight at Jon.

Just when you thought your luck had changed . . .

Time seemed to slow as he watched the finger tighten on the trigger. Jon wanted to shout to Alex, tell her how he felt, but it was too late for that. Too late for anything.

The man's face erupted, and the laser pistol dropped from his lifeless fingers. He was definitely dead this time, but whoever had shot him was making sure. The laser beam persisted as the body began to smoke, filling the air with the stench of scorched flesh. Finally, the beam stopped.

Jon twisted his head and watched as Alex crept out from behind the desk. She'd dropped the medical kit, but a laser pistol was clamped so tight in her right hand that her knuckles were leached white. The pistol, still aimed at the sergeant, shook visibly.

"He's dead," Jon said.

At the sound of his voice, she swung around and raised the pistol. The shock and panic faded to be replaced by wonder. The pistol fell to the floor.

"You're alive."

"Yes." He nodded at the dead man. "Thanks to you."

She hurried over to where he lay. Outside in the hallway, he could still hear spasmodic shots. He hoped the good guys were winning. The adrenaline was fading from his system, everything hurt, and shivers rippled through his body as Alex crouched down beside him.

"Oh God. Oh God," Alex muttered under her breath, her hands shaking as she tried to unravel the chains from around him. She sounded in a worse state than he was.

"Alex, I'm fine—really, I am. Calm down."

Finally, the chains were undone, and she unwrapped them from around his neck and chest before sitting back on her heels. Her gaze suddenly fixed on his hand, her eyes widening. Looking down, he saw the knife still stuck out of the back of his hand, fixing him to the chair arm. He'd forgotten about it—just one more pain in a big jumbly mass of pains.

"Pull it out," he said through gritted teeth.

She swallowed, bit her lip, and wrapped her hand around the knife hilt. She tugged once, and the blade came out easily, blood pulsing from the wound.

"Don't go anywhere," she said and scrambled to her feet.

"I won't."

He dragged himself half up to lean against the desk. The effort was almost too much, and he closed his eyes as exhaustion threatened to overwhelm him. It was a side effect from the drugs—he was coming down from the high, though high wasn't really the right word.

Alex hunkered down beside him with the medical kit next to her and stared at the contents as though she didn't know what was what—and likely she didn't. In the end, she picked up a bandage and wrapped it around his hand. At least he wouldn't make a mess.

"Painkillers," he said.

Her gaze flashed to his face, and she nodded. "Of course." She pawed among the contents. "I don't know what a painkiller looks like."

"Give it to me."

She slid the kit across the floor, and he studied the contents, located the strongest. "The codinex," he said.

She picked up the syringe and studied it.

"Stick it straight in the muscle on my thigh," he said, but she still looked dubious. "Darling, one more hole in me at this point is not going to add much to my injuries. It's the quickest way, and right now, I'm hurting."

That obviously clinched it for her. She caught her lower lip between her teeth, lifted the syringe, and stabbed it into his right leg. The relief was almost immediate, a delicious numbness spreading through him. For a moment, he sat back and savored the sensation.

"Now a stimulant." He pointed at a second syringe. This

time Alex didn't hesitate, just picked it up, removed the cover, and jabbed him in the left thigh.

Jon took a deep breath and rested his head back against the cool metal of the desk while he waited for everything to work. He could sense Alex watching him.

A few minutes later, Rico's tall figure appeared in the doorway. He took in the bodies on the floor and Jon propped against the desk. "Hey, you look great."

Jon choked back a laugh; he didn't think he could take that amount of movement right now. Instead, he took a deep breath. "Thank you."

Rico grinned. "I bet that hurt more than any amount of torture."

"You don't know how much."

Rico wandered over, his gaze running over Jon, assessing the damage. "Anyway, I didn't come back for you. I came back because Alex would have made my life a misery if I hadn't. Like a yapping little dog."

Jon glanced sideways at Alex. She shrugged.

"Are you okay to get out of here?" Rico asked.

He nodded. "I'll shift as soon as I can stand up."

"Good, because we have about five minutes to get clear before the place is overrun with Skylar's friends."

Skylar and Tannis appeared behind him. "Are we ready to go?" Skylar asked.

"Just about."

Tannis peered down at the headless body of the sergeant, still smoking. "Dayam."

Jon grinned. "Alex did that one."

Alex scrambled to her feet and brushed herself off. She closed the lid of the medical kit and stood fidgeting from one foot to the other. "Are you okay? Do you need anything else?" she asked.

"Don't fuss," Rico said. "He's fine. A bit of bruising, that's all."

Again, Jon would have laughed, but it hurt too much. Checking himself over, he reckoned he could make it to his feet now. With all the drugs inside him, he felt like his body didn't belong to him. That would clear once he shifted. He pushed himself up and balanced with his good hand resting on the desktop while he decided whether he could stand alone.

Everyone was watching him. It wasn't in werewolves' nature to shift in front of people, a hang-up from the old times of total secrecy on Earth. But what the hell, they'd come back for him, he could hardly tell them to get out. Well, he could, but he found he didn't want to.

He stripped off his shirt. Nakedness didn't bother him. Usually. But now he hesitated. Three sets of female eyes watched him, two with curiosity, but Alex just looked worried as though he might crash to the floor at any moment. Tannis caught his gaze and raised an eyebrow.

He looked away, straight at Skylar. Amusement glinted in her eyes as though daring him to continue.

What the hell?

Keeping his gaze locked on Alex, he kicked off his boots, peeled off his pants, and stood naked before them.

Alex winced, and he glanced down. His body was a mass of bruising and burns. They would heal. He searched inside himself, released his wolf, and sensed the rightness as the change flowed through him.

His beautiful body was battered and bruised. They'd hurt him so badly. For a moment, she'd known real hatred and rage. When she'd killed her attacker the other day, she hadn't felt hatred . . . just something that needed to be done for her own survival. This time she had wanted them to die for what they had done.

Alex kept her gaze fixed on Jon, but out of the corner of her eye she could see the smoking corpse of the man she'd killed. He'd been taking aim at Jon and such a fury had built inside her that she'd pointed her laser pistol at him without thinking, just needing to obliterate him. Then she hadn't been able to stop, even when she'd known he was dead.

She still felt light-headed with relief. When she'd first caught sight of Jon, she'd been sure he was dead and such a mixture of emotions had beset her for a minute she hadn't been able to think. When his eyes flickered open, relief had poured through her.

Now she watched him shift, and it was like magic—the change flowing over him, remaking him. When complete, Jon stood on all fours—huge, glossy, dark coat and glowing amber eyes.

"Wow," Skylar murmured.

"Hey, it's only a big shaggy dog," Rico replied. "Now do you think we could get out of here?"

The wolf approached Alex, coming to a halt in front of her. The top of his head reached her shoulder. She stretched out her hand, dug her fingers into the silky fur, and a tingle like magic flowed up through her arm.

In that moment, she knew things were going to be fine, and despite her doubts, she sent up a silent prayer of thanks.

Jon padded beside her as they headed out of the house and back to the speeder. His movements were stiff as though he was still feeling some of the pain that had been so obvious in his human form. He settled into the back seat of the speeder, rested his head on her lap, and closed his eyes.

CHAPTER SEVENTEEN

Alex spent the journey to the ship expecting to hear the sound of pursuit as the Collective came after them, but they got back without incident.

The engines roared to life as soon as they were on board *El Cazador*. They hurried to the bridge and strapped in for takeoff. Daisy shifted from the pilot's seat to copilot, and Rico sat down and started the takeoff procedure. They were off the ground in minutes. Alex could sense the subdued panic, tightly restrained. Even Skylar appeared on edge. She got up as soon as they were in the air and started checking the console readings.

"Nothing behind us yet," she said, flicking through the screens. "But you know, they'll be after us."

"No, I didn't know that," Tannis snapped. "I really thought since we'd gotten away again they might just forget all about us."

Janey appeared in the open doorway, limping slightly, but otherwise she didn't look too bad. Her eyes widened as she took in the huge wolf sprawled at Alex's feet.

"How are you feeling?" Tannis asked.

"Fine, no pain at all. What do you need me to do?"

"Can you extend the normal scanning range? Give us a bit more time to get away if, or rather when, they find us."

"No problem. It will take power, but we're juiced up. The Trog refueled in port." She nudged Skylar out of the way and sat down at the bank of consoles. A moment later, her fingers were flying over the boards. "Nothing yet," she murmured.

"Good," Tannis replied, searching the bridge as if needing something to concentrate on. Her gaze came to rest on Alex and the huge wolf curled up at her feet. He was sleeping now, his breathing even and deep. Occasionally, a slight tremor would ripple through his body.

"Go and get him some clothes," Tannis said, frowning. "You know, we'd better start earning some money soon— I'm betting our boy over there isn't cheap to keep. His clothes bill must be enormous."

A warm feeling stirred inside Alex at the words. Tannis was talking as though Jon was staying with them. Of course, that didn't mean he would, but at least if Tannis had accepted him, there was a chance.

"You might as well go," Rico said. "He'll be out for a while. It's the best thing for him right now. He'll heal and be as good as new when he shifts back. Well, maybe not as good as new—he took a battering, but he'll be okay."

Alex nodded, then took a last look at Jon and hurried away. She found clothes in his room before going to her own cabin, where she showered quickly and put on a fresh jumpsuit. Standing in front of the mirror, she studied her face. The bruising was gone and she didn't look different, but inside she was changed beyond anything she could imagine.

She was in love. Not falling in love, but already there. She'd known it the moment she thought Jon might be dead.

And he had feelings for her, though he was fighting them. He didn't want to feel, and one day she hoped he would tell her why.

Clutching the bundle of clothes, she ran back to the bridge, but Jon was still asleep. She lowered herself to the floor beside him, rested her hand on his head, and closed her eyes.

Something woke her. She'd been in the middle of a great dream, and she kept her eyes closed, hoping to recapture it, until someone nudged her with a boot. Daisy loomed over her, holding out a steaming mug. Alex took it and realized at the same moment that Jon was gone.

She scanned the room and honed in on him immediately. He'd shifted back and was talking quietly with Tannis and Skylar. When he caught her gaze, his expression was wary, lines of strain bracketing his mouth.

He'd dressed in the black leather pants and shirt she'd brought him, but his feet were bare and his hair hung loose to his shoulders, giving him a disheveled appearance.

Alex wanted to go to him, but she forced herself to remain where she was. *Let him do the chasing*, she cautioned herself.

Daisy was back in the pilot's seat, and Rico was nowhere to be seen. He appeared a moment later, waving a silver flask in his hand. Alex watched through narrowed eyes as he crossed to where Jon stood and lifted the flask.

"Hey, dog-boy, you look like you need a drink."

"Yeah."

"Then let's get out of here."

Jon cast her a last quick glance then shrugged and followed the vampire. Alex rose to her feet, meaning to go after them, but Tannis stopped her with a hand on her arm. "Let them go. He needs some time."

Alex took a deep breath and sank down into the chair

behind her, staring at the space where he'd disappeared. "What if we don't have any time?"

Jon followed Rico into the main meeting room, spacious and airy with a number of chairs scattered around. Like the rest of the ship aside from the bridge, there were no portholes and the decor was the standard black and silver.

Rico crossed the room, sat down, and placed the silver flask on the table in front of him. From under the table, he drew out two crystal glasses and placed them next to the flask. When he saw Jon still hovering in the doorway, he gestured to the seat opposite.

Jon had no clue what Rico wanted. Maybe to tell him they'd made a mistake and should have left him to rot on Trakis Five. But he didn't think so.

The metal floor was cool and smooth under his feet as he crossed the room and sank into a chair. Resting his head on the back, he stared at the pattern on the ceiling. He felt eons better, but nowhere near perfect. His stomach still churned with nausea, and he couldn't imagine ever feeling warm again.

"So, how are you feeling?" Rico filled the two glasses and handed one to Jon.

"Like shit." Jon lifted the glass and studied the contents. The liquid was golden, slightly viscous. He sniffed it dubiously but couldn't place the smell. Maybe Rico had decided to poison him after all and hand his body over to the Collective as a sign of good faith. "What is this crap?"

"Whiskey," Rico replied. "It's not poisonous, though it was banned back in the twenty-first century as deleterious to health."

"Perfect." Jon drank the liquid down in one gulp, then sat back as the fire burned right down to his belly. "Jesus." He held out the empty glass, and Rico grinned and refilled it.

Jon sipped the drink this time, the warmth radiating out

from his stomach and warming him from the inside. The shivers that racked his body slowly subsided, and he relaxed against the chair back, closing his eyes.

He remembered Alex's expression as he'd walked out. She would want to talk. Women always wanted to talk. What the hell was he supposed to say to her? What did he want from her? What was he capable of giving in return?

He was bad news and always had been. But maybe he could change. Maybe he'd already changed.

Shit.

He couldn't cope right now.

When he opened his eyes, he saw that his glass was empty and held it out for a refill. Rico raised an eyebrow but emptied the silver flask into the glass. He shook the empty container. "I'll go get a refill."

Jon nodded absently. Why was he worrying about anything? Chances were, the Collective would catch up with them any moment now and that would be the end. They would all die. He wasn't quite as full of self-pity as to claim that was his fault. No one had forced them into breaking him free. But he was glad they had.

Maybe he should have made Alex stay with that Sister Martha woman and go back to the Church. Though actually, thinking about it, she'd probably be better off dead.

Rico came back and placed the flask on the table between them. "Alex wants to know what I've done with you. You know, I don't think that girl trusts me. Actually . . . never has."

Jon sat up straight. "And why's that? What did you do to her?"

"Absolutely nothing. Didn't lay a finger on her. Or a fang. Anyway, I told her to go to bed. You'd see her tomorrow. She looks almost as bad as you do."

"Yeah, it's been a rough few days." He sipped his drink. "Why did you come back for me?"

Rico stretched his booted legs out in front of him, resting them on the table while he considered the question. "Because you're crew."

"Since when?"

Rico shrugged. "Since the captain decided you were. But I'm guessing back on Trakis Two, when you saved Alex from Bastion."

"I didn't save her. I was just first on the scene."

"No, we were too far behind; she would have been dead by the time we got there."

"Maybe. It doesn't matter. It was a reflex thing."

"Yeah. I bet it can be really inconvenient."

"What?"

"That reflex of yours. The need to save everyone."

Jon gritted his teeth. "I don't need to save everyone."

"Come off it—you're an alpha werewolf. Yeah—you've got to be a good fighter, better than the rest, but the real thing that makes an alpha is the need to protect, to look after the pack."

"Well, it turned out I wasn't too good at that."

Rico topped up his glass. "What happened?"

Jon pursed his lips, but maybe Rico had a right to know. This was his ship and Jon was now crew. Apparently. For however short a time they had left. "My pack was slaughtered. I didn't protect them."

"Was it the Church?"

"Indirectly. They didn't actually kill them, but they got the locals riled up into a frenzy of hatred against us. We lived on one of the outer planets. We were fine until the colonists came, and even then, we were okay for a long time—we kept to ourselves. But the humans bred like fucking rabbits. We needed space to run, and they wanted more land."

"Where were you when it happened?"

"Off planet. I was always off planet." He leaned across

and topped off his drink. "You know, me and Alex, we aren't that much different. Both yearning for the stars. Both of us running away from our responsibilities."

"Except Alex didn't choose her responsibilities, whereas I'm presuming you did choose yours."

"Maybe. I did kill the old Alpha."

"Why?"

After all these years, he still experienced the same rush of hatred. "Because he was a fucking bastard, and he deserved to die."

"He was the one who changed you?"

Jon nodded curtly. "He was a bad leader, and there was a lot of infighting in the pack. He encouraged the younger wolves to fight among themselves, and he killed any potential alphas himself. The numbers were dwindling, and they needed new blood. They picked on me, because I was a sheriff, and they thought I might be useful."

"You were a lawman?" Rico sounded incredulous.

"Yeah, so?"

"Well, from sheriff to alpha werewolf to assassin. Quite some career changes you've had there."

"Whatever—he made a mistake picking me. The only way to get rid of an alpha is to kill him. I'd never killed anyone, so it took me a while to work up to it, but I got there in the end."

"So this guy was presumably responsible for the death of your wife."

"Yeah, someone else I failed to protect."

Rico grinned. "*Dios*, you are one miserable, self-pitying bastard."

"It's not self-pity, it's the goddamned truth." Jon shrugged and turned away. "Okay, maybe a little bit of self-pity."

The whiskey was loosening his brain. If he lowered his lids, the room swayed around him. He liked the sensation.

Maybe he would keep drinking, then he wouldn't even know when the Collective turned up and killed them all.

He shook his head and placed his glass on the table. If he was going to die, there were one or two things he wanted to do first. And he didn't want to be unconscious when it happened. He wanted to be with Alex.

Rico was watching him with that same lazy smile, and he realized he felt comfortable with the vampire, as he hadn't done with anyone else in a long, long time.

Jesus. A vampire.

He had no idea why vamps and weres were enemies; it was one of those things entrenched in pack law, probably brought from Earth, and the real reasons lost with the planet. But packs were territorial, they didn't like sharing their land with other predators, while he'd always believed vampires were natural loners who didn't like sharing anything with anyone. Rico was obviously an exception.

"So why the interest?" he asked.

Rico shrugged. "I'm figuring out how much of a liability you're going to be. We need people who can keep a clear head and not rush in the first moment someone looks in need of saving."

"I don't go in for the saving stuff anymore."

"Except with Alex."

"I told you—" He gave up. Who was he kidding? "Yeah, except for Alex."

If he'd ever considered the sort of woman he might fall for, Alex was probably the complete opposite. Always before, he'd gone for strong, athletic types who could take care of themselves and wouldn't be too much of a burden on that overdeveloped protective streak of his. Alex was so small. Even in those ridiculous heels, she only came up to his chest. But while she was small, she wasn't weak. Maybe a little thoughtless occasionally, but he reckoned that came from too many years of having other people do her thinking for her. And her breasts weren't small. They were perfect. He closed his eyes again and pictured her naked. Pale skin and freckles. His mouth pulled into a smile. The sensation was odd. He didn't smile much these days.

"You are in deep shit."

Rico's words interrupted his mental image, and Jon's smile turned into a scowl. Rico leaned forward and filled Jon's glass. "I'm looking at a man who has given up the fight." He pushed the full glass toward him. "You need a drink."

Had he given up the fight? But Rico had no reason to talk. "What about you and Skylar? I hardly see you fighting."

A slow smile spread across the vampire's face. "Yeah, but the difference is—Skylar could protect me, not the other way around. She's one scary woman." Rico seemed far from displeased with the idea, and Jon felt the need to defend Alex.

"Alex has killed two men in the last few days."

"Yeah, she's a hardened killer all right." Rico relaxed back in his chair, closed his eyes, and sipped his drink.

His little hardened killer. But she wasn't *his*. And he had no right to try and make her his. What could a miserable bastard like himself offer her? She was young and still excited about life. If they did somehow manage to survive the Collective, he must do the honorable thing and walk away.

"Dios," Rico muttered. "I can feel the self-pity oozing back from over here."

Jon ignored the comment, and they sat in almost comfortable silence for a while.

Would Alex be in bed now? Naked perhaps. Would she be lying awake, worrying about him? Should he go tell her he was okay? Then tell her why she should forget him?

He swallowed the last of the whiskey and slammed the glass on the table. That's what he had to do. Go see her.

Tell her why he shouldn't be there. He pushed himself to his feet. Swayed a little but balanced himself with a hand to the back of his seat. The room swam.

Rico opened one eye. "Where are you going?"

"To see Alex. I have to tell her all the reasons I'm bad for her."

Amusement glinted in the vampire's face. "Is that wise, right now?"

"Probably not." He let go of the seat to see if he could stay upright. "But a man's got to do what a man's got to do."

"Yeah, but you're a dog."

"Ha-ha. So?"

"Well, the same rules hardly apply."

Jon tried to think that one through, but his brain had turned to treacle. He nodded to the flask. "I like it. We must do this again sometime."

"Next time I save your life," Rico said.

"Or I save yours."

Rico grinned. "Never going to happen."

No, probably not, considering they were all about to die. He took a tentative step and found he could walk after all. Rico spoke again as Jon reached the door. "Good luck."

Jon had never been in Alex's cabin, though he knew where it was. He leaned on the door buzzer, half expecting her to ignore him, but a second later, the door slid open.

He looked around. "Christ, this place is a mess."

Alex sat up in the narrow bed, a scowl on her face. "I like it like this."

A sheet was pulled up to her breasts, her fingers knotted in the material, holding it tightly against her chest. Above it, her slender shoulders were bare. Oh yes, he reckoned she was naked under there.

He lurched into the room, holding onto the wall for support.

Her gaze shot to his face, alarm flashing in her eyes. "Are you all right?"

He shook his head, and the room shifted under his feet. He waited until it stopped moving. "I have been drinking whiskey with a vampire. Lots of whiskey. So I doubt 'all right' describes how I am right now."

Her arched brows drew together and her huge eyes narrowed. They were gorgeous eyes.

"You have the most beautiful eyes," he mumbled.

"What do you want, Jon?"

"I've come to tell you all the reasons we shouldn't be doing this."

"What are we doing?" Her eyes narrowed further. "And why shouldn't we be doing it?"

He shook his head again, taking care to hold onto the wall first. "I cannot remember. But it will come back to me. I just need to lie down for a little while."

After fumbling with the buttons for an age, he finally managed to unfasten his shirt, then shrugged out of it and dropped it on the floor on top of the pink jumpsuit she'd been wearing.

As he stepped closer, he heard a hiss, and a small, black furry animal disappeared beneath the bed. He ignored it; he wasn't interested in anything under the bed. Holding her gaze, he unfastened his pants and kicked them off. For once in her presence, he didn't have a raging hard-on. He gestured at it. "Sorry, it's been a long day."

She didn't speak, just drew back the sheet that covered her and he saw that he'd been right; beneath the thin covering, she was naked. Small and perfectly formed and so sweet. He needed to hold her, so he lowered himself down beside her. The bed was narrow, and he shifted onto his back, put his arms around her, and pulled her tight against his side. She didn't move, but then her arms wrapped around him, held him tight.

With her head resting on his chest, close to his heart, Jon closed his eyes, feeling safe and protected for the first time in as long as he could remember.

"I love you," Alex murmured the words against his skin.

He was asleep, his breathing slow and steady, but at her words, his arms tightened around her. She breathed in, loving his smell, musky and salty, and now with an added sweetness of the whiskey he had drunk.

The heavy weight of one muscular leg lay partly across hers, but she didn't try to move him. She wanted to hold him, keep him safe. Who knew how much time they would have before the Collective found them? While she had great faith in the crew of *El Cazador*, she had no illusions that they could take on the Collective and win. But this would be enough.

Well, maybe she wanted something more. She shifted a little so her nipples rubbed against his hair-roughened chest, and a delicious ripple of sensation quivered through her. He needed to sleep, but soon he would awaken.

When they didn't move the lights dimmed, and they lay in semidarkness. Beneath the bed, she could hear Mogg's deep rumbling purr. She didn't want to sleep, she wanted to savor every moment of closeness, but her eyes eventually drifted closed.

She awoke to a sensation of pure bliss. Jon's mouth was at her breast, his hot, wet tongue lapping at the distended nipple. His lips tugged, his teeth bit down gently so the sensation burned right down through her belly. She was melting from the inside.

The length of his erection pressed hot and hard against her thigh, and he thrust it against her and groaned. Her hips arched against his, and he went still for a second.

He pushed himself up onto his elbows and stared down into her face. "You're awake."

She nodded.

"Good."

"Good?"

"I've been lying here, thinking how to wake you. Sorry."

"Sorry?"

He slipped one of his knees between hers to part her thighs. "I can't wait. Who knows what the hell will interrupt us this time."

She raised one hand and curved it around his face, staring into his golden eyes with their thick, dark lashes, his beautiful, passionate mouth. She needed to tell him she loved him but was unsure how he would take her words right now, and she wanted nothing to spoil this moment. Later, if there was a later, he would have to come to terms with her love. "I don't want you to wait."

He lowered his lids for a breath. When he opened them, his eyes glowed with passion. He kicked off the sheet that covered them both and shifted her so she lay on her back beneath him. One hand slid down between their bodies, stroking the skin of her belly, then ruffling through curls at the base. Alex held her breath as he pushed one finger between the folds of her sex. She was already drenched with desire, and he rubbed the moisture over the sensitive flesh until he found the engorged little bud between her thighs, then slipped lower to push inside her.

He flexed the finger, and her whole body jolted with the shock of pleasure. He shifted her again, widening her thighs, positioning himself between them. "You're small," he murmured.

"And you're not. I know, but I want this, Jon. I've wanted it from the first moment I saw you. Please, don't go noble on me now."

He lowered his mouth and kissed her. She parted her lips for the thrust of his tongue as his shaft nudged at the entrance to her body. Then he was filling her slowly, stretching the tender flesh until he was lodged deep inside.

For this first time, she was content to follow his lead, let him show her the way. There would be time to show him other ways later—she hoped. Pushing the thought aside, she concentrated on the new sensations coursing through her body.

He withdrew, and she shivered at the exquisite drag of his sex against hers.

"More?" he whispered.

She nodded, unable to speak, her throat closed up with emotions building inside her. Jon flexed his hips, filling her again. He leaned in close and kissed her mouth, parting her lips so the languid thrust of his tongue kept time with the glide of his shaft. The world shrank until it was nothing more than the feel of his hard body, the velvet caress of his tongue. The taste of him.

Heat washed through her. She was out of control. Gripping his shoulders, she pulled him harder against her, widening her thighs, needing him closer. He pressed in to her, all the way, then rotated his hips in tantalizing circles against her core, grinding into her, then backing off so she wrapped her legs around him and held him to her. The world shrank further, distilled to that one place between her thighs. The pleasure built to an unbearable crescendo, and she whimpered into his kiss.

He raised his head, held her gaze as he pushed one hand between their bodies, between her legs, gently massaging that mass of swollen nerves, and Alex shattered into a thousand pieces.

CHAPTER EIGHTEEN

He'd been an idealist once, long ago, before a half-crazed werewolf had decided he would be a useful addition to the pack.

Even after the change, he'd known what was right and wrong and had a code of ethics that he'd stuck to in his own way. When he'd killed the old alpha, it was partly because he'd hated him, but also because he was a bad leader, and Jon had thought he could do better.

When he'd gotten back from that trip, found his people slaughtered, their bodies burned on a huge pyre, he'd abandoned those ethics.

He'd reckoned that killing was the one thing he was good for. So he'd devoted himself to it, first for revenge and then for money.

Now he lay beside Alex and knew it was time to make some changes.

The comm unit by the side of the bed blinked. He tightened his arm around her, leaned across with his free hand, and pressed the unit. "What is it?" he asked.

Tannis answered. "I'm alerting everyone. Janey has

picked up the Collective on our tail. They're still a good way off, but closing fast."

"How many?"

"Janey says it looks like all of them. Enough anyway."

"How long?"

"Three hours at the most." Tannis paused. "Is Alex there?"

"She's asleep."

"Let her know. We'll have a meeting in an hour's time. I want us all present."

He rested back against the pillows. While he'd known they were coming, he'd hoped for more time. Alex was still deep asleep, but as his arm tightened around her, she blinked and opened her eyes.

"What's happening?"

He opened his mouth to tell her and shut it again. He needed to think this through. He'd thought he had no options, but maybe he did. Maybe he could do something right for once. "Nothing," he murmured. "Go back to sleep."

She laid her head back on his chest, and her breathing slowed. He held her small body so tightly he could feel the blood pulsing through her veins.

There was no way they could beat the Collective. Rico might get lucky and evade them again, but eventually they would catch up, and they stood no chance in combat. They would all die. His grip tightened.

If it came to a fight, they were done for—Alex included. There had to be some way to convince them to back off. That the others were no threat and didn't know anything that could harm the Collective.

Gently, he picked her up, laid her down on the sheets, and slid out of the bed. He pulled on his pants, picked up his shirt, and headed out.

"Where are you going?"

Alex's sleepy question halted him at the door. Wiping

all expression from his face, he turned to face her. "That stuff of Rico's is lethal. My head's killing me. I'm going down to the sick bay to see if I can't rummage up some medicine."

"You're coming back?"

He nodded and forced a grin. "Get some sleep. You'll need it."

"Okay, but don't be long."

"I won't."

Once outside, he pressed his fingers to his forehead. He hadn't been totally lying to Alex—his head throbbed and the occasional sharp pain spiked the base of his skull.

There was no answer at Skylar's cabin. Jon swore softly—he'd been hoping to speak to her alone. Chances were, she was already up with the captain. Or she might be one other place. He'd try that first.

He came to a halt outside a door and placed his palm to the panel.

"Who the hell is it?" Rico sounded annoyed. "I'm busy!"

Like Jon gave a shit. He pressed the panel again. "It's Jon."

There was a moment of silence, then the door opened. Jon peered inside. Rico's cabin was large compared to Alex's, and decorated in the expected black and silver. Across the room, Rico sat in the huge bed, leaning against the wall, chest bare, black sheets pooled around his hips. A scowl on his face.

Skylar stood beside the bed. She was dressed and strapping on the weapons belt at her waist. Her face was expressionless, but tension filled the air between them.

"We're in the middle of an important argument," Rico said. "So tell me what the fuck you want and get the hell out of here."

"Actually, I want Skylar."

Rico's eyes narrowed. "Well, you can't have her—she's mine." He ran a hand through his hair, muttering under his breath.

Jon shoved his hands into his pockets. Despite the headache still pounding in his temples, he had to stifle the urge to smile. It was good to know the vampire's love life wasn't perfect after all. "So what are you two arguing about?"

"Mind your own business," Skylar snapped.

"It's as much his business as anybody's," Rico said. "Stubborn bitch won't get the hell off my ship. She could go now—they'd take her back."

That was interesting. If Rico was trying to get Skylar to leave the ship, he must believe the situation was grim. But that was only confirming what Jon already knew.

"Never going to happen," Skylar growled, moving to stand beside Jon. "What is it? You know Janey has picked up a Collective ship following us?"

Jon nodded. "That's what I want to talk to you about."

"Can't it wait? Tannis has called a meeting."

"No."

Rico frowned and studied him. "You feeling all right? You know, that whiskey can pack a wallop—you're probably still pissed. Lie down, give it a few hours, and you'll feel much better."

"I already feel fine, and I don't have a few hours. I want to hand myself over to the Collective."

"Why would you want to do that?" Rico asked. "They'll kill you."

"They're going to kill me anyway."

"Ever the optimist." Rico pushed off the sheet and got out of bed. He searched for his clothes, found them on a chair, and got dressed.

"They're also going to kill the rest of you. Maybe I can prevent that."

"*Dios,* you trying to protect us all now?"

Jon considered denying it. Claiming that he was doing this solely for Alex. But the truth was they'd all come back for him earlier. They'd risked their lives to save him. However much he disliked the idea, he owed them.

But this wasn't really payment of a debt. Rather, it was payment of many debts. All those people he should have protected and had failed.

"Yes," he said.

"In which case, you can persuade Skylar to get the hell off my ship and go back to her own people."

"Actually, that's what I wanted to talk to her about."

"You did? Good—I think." He nodded toward where Skylar stood with her legs braced, arms crossed against her chest. "Go ahead, then—be my guest."

"I want you to contact the Collective."

Skylar frowned. "And say what?"

"Tell them I'll give myself up, if they back off."

"They've already said they won't back off. You have information they don't want out in the open, something about Aiden's suicide, I just can't figure out what yet. But whatever it is, it's bad enough that they want you—and anyone you might have told—dead."

This was the problem part of his plan, but he was hoping Skylar would have some suggestions. She was Collective, so she would know how they worked. "There must be a way to convince them that you know nothing." His hands fisted at his side. "I mean to do this. I'll contact them myself if you won't help, but I thought they might listen to you."

Skylar turned away and paced the confines of the room, deep in thought. She was obviously struggling with a decision, and he forced himself to stay silent while she battled it out herself.

Rico was not so restrained. "What are you thinking?"

"That there might be a way."

"If there's a way—why haven't you mentioned it before?"

"Because it would never work without Jon giving himself up, and I believed that wasn't an option." She studied Jon for a moment. "Are you sure you want to go through with this. They will kill you. I can't stop that."

"I know. But hey, when I was captured last time, I expected to spend two years dying in the mines. At least I won't have to go through that."

"Yeah, you're a real lucky bastard," Rico said. "But I still don't see how Jon giving himself up will stop them coming after the rest of us."

"They might—if I go with him."

"You're not giving yourself up with him," Rico said.

Skylar rolled her eyes. "Shit, Rico, you've spent the last half hour persuading me to go back. As you said, they won't hurt me—I'm one of them. I always will be."

Jon frowned. He hadn't planned on taking anyone with him. "You don't need to come. Just set this up."

"Won't work. The reason they want the whole crew dead is they believe you might have passed on anything you know, including how to destroy us. But the truth is we don't know anything, and you haven't told us."

"So tell them that."

She smiled condescendingly. "Would you believe me? I'm one of them, but they don't exactly trust me right now."

"So how will going with me make them believe you?"

For a minute, she seemed undecided, then she shrugged. "You know there's a telepathic link between members of the Collective, right?"

Jon nodded, and she continued. "Well, the link is made up of certain layers. The top layer is usually open—we use it as a way to communicate. The next layer down shows some of our thoughts and feelings, but we can still keep certain information to ourselves. Right down at the bottom, there's a level where all my thoughts are open to them."

"How inconvenient," Rico drawled.

"Exactly, and we normally keep this level shut down tight. If I open that level to them, they'll know I speak the truth. I won't be able to hide anything."

"Interesting," Rico murmured.

"I tell you my innermost thoughts anyway."

"Of course you do."

"So call them up and open it," Jon said.

"No can do. It can only be accessed when physically present. I have to go with you."

It was Rico's turn to pace. "Tannis isn't going to let him go. You know how she is about protecting the crew."

There was that warm fuzzy feeling again. Jesus, what a time to turn sentimental. "So we don't tell Tannis," he said.

"She'll be pissed."

"Well, that's hardly going to be my problem, now is it?"

A smile flickered across Rico's face then was gone. "I might not let you go."

Jon laughed, but the sound held no humor. "You'll let me go because you know we'll all be dead otherwise. There's no way you've survived this long without being a realist. They'll keep coming after us. One day soon, you'll make a mistake, and they'll finish us off. I die either way."

"I still don't like it."

Jon stepped up close. "You don't have to like it. This is my choice. And besides—this way I get to die a hero."

Rico shook his head. "*Dios*, I always said you had a death wish."

"Maybe once. Not anymore. It's ironic really, but strangely I don't want to die." So many times, he had faced death and survived, not really caring whether he lived or died. Now that he did care . . . he wanted to live. Christ, life sucked big-time.

"Well, that's a real tragedy, considering." Rico glanced across at Skylar. "This will work?"

"Maybe."

"Maybe's not good enough."

"It will have to be, Rico. But I think I can make it work."

He studied her for a moment before nodding. "Okay, go ahead."

Jon watched, fascinated, as Skylar closed her purple eyes. She stood relaxed, but behind her lids, he could see the flutter of movement. A minute later, she blinked.

"It's done. They've agreed in principle, but they want *El Cazador* to head back to Trakis Five as a sign of good faith. Once we've done the deep link, you'll be free to go."

Jon didn't like that idea. The whole reason behind doing this was to get the rest of them way beyond the reach of the Collective. He'd be much happier with *El Cazador* heading as fast as she could go in the opposite direction.

"You trust them?" he asked.

"Yes. We're ruthless, but we're not vindictive."

"I like the plan," Rico said. "That way Skylar can rejoin us as soon as you're—" He broke off.

"As soon as I'm dead? Thanks."

"Yeah, as soon as you're dead." Rico held his gaze. Behind the careful facade, Jon could see the frustration. Rico lashed out and slammed his fist into the wall. "*Dios*, I wish I could think of another way out of this."

"But you can't."

"No." Rico turned away, his shoulders tense.

This was going to happen. Now that Jon had succeeded, the enormity of what he was doing was sinking in. This was it. He was going to die. For real this time. Only it didn't seem real. At least it would be over soon.

"I want to see Alex before we leave."

Rico swung around to face him. "Shit—you can't say good-bye. Do you think she'll calmly go back to sleep and let you do this?"

"I won't tell her."

"You do know she's going to make my life hell from now on. This is going to be my fault. *Dios*, I might just come with you. Get it over with fast. Put me out of my goddamned misery." He took a deep breath. "Go on. Go see her. Skylar will get the shuttle ready. I'll go keep Tannis busy. But you need to be off this ship in half an hour, or Tannis will be expecting you at that meeting."

"I'll be there, and thank you."

"What for?" Rico snarled. "Sending you to die?"

Rico stalked from the room. Skylar shrugged and followed him. She paused in the doorway. "I'll see you at the shuttle."

Jon stood in the empty room. This was the right thing to do, the only thing. Glancing down, he noticed his feet were still bare; he must remember to pick up some boots after he saw Alex. That way, at least he'd die with his boots on.

His steps were slow as he made his way back to Alex's cabin. He leaned against the doorway. She was curled up on the bed, but she wasn't asleep—her eyes were open, and she was watching him.

He had no clue what to say.

Rico was right. If Alex got any inkling of his plan, she wouldn't let him go without a fight. So maybe he shouldn't say anything. Maybe he should give her something to remember him by.

Holding her gaze, he stripped his clothes and stalked purposefully toward the bed. Her eyes widened, then her gaze dropped to run over his body in a way that made the blood rush to his groin. He'd been hard from the moment he'd seen her, now his cock throbbed with need.

She opened her mouth to speak, but he gave a slight shake of his head, and she closed it again. He rested one knee on the bed beside her, slid his hands around her narrow waist, and lifted her toward him.

This was no gentle lovemaking. He didn't feel gentle. He kissed her hard, his tongue forcing her mouth open then thrusting inside. For a moment, she went rigid in his arms, but then she melted into him. Her legs wrapped around his waist, her arms around his shoulders, and she kissed him back with her mouth wide open, her small tongue pushing against his.

His hands cupped the globes of her ass, and he straightened and turned, backing her up until she was supported by the smooth metal of the cabin wall. He reached between their bodies and parted the drenched folds of her sex.

Alex groaned into his mouth as he fondled the swollen mass of nerves, then he surged into her in one forceful lunge, filling her completely.

He pinned her against the wall as he thrust into her. She accepted him easily, and for a second, he stayed still, savoring the hot, wet tightness around his shaft, the sense of coming home. She wriggled against him, and he gritted his teeth and withdrew slowly, held himself poised against her as he stared down into her face.

Her eyes flickered open. "Please, I want all of you—I won't break."

He nodded once and shoved into her hard.

He would show her how it could be, the power and passion. With that thought, he released the last hold he had on his control. Then he was slamming into her fast, and she welcomed him. Her head thrashed from side to side, urging him on with muttered pleas. The pleasure was building in his balls and cock, tiny explosions shooting along his nerves, until his whole body hovered on the edge of combustion. She was close too, her fingers biting into his shoulder, her hips bucking against his.

He lowered his head and sucked one swollen nipple into his mouth, biting down as she squirmed against him. He reached between them, rubbed her clit with moist fingers, and she threw back her head and screamed. He held her tight, continuing to thrust as her body spasmed around him until the pleasure was unbearable, and he exploded into her.

She wrapped her arms around his neck and hid her face in the curve of his throat as he pumped his seed into her, and still the waves of pleasure washed over them both.

Finally, she was quiet in his arms.

"That was mind-blowing," she whispered against his skin.

He didn't answer; he was afraid of his words if he started to speak. So instead, he leaned in close and kissed her softly. He carried her back to the bed and lowered her to the sheets, kissed her again. He stared at her for long moments as he imprinted this last image of her into his memory.

But there was something she needed to know. "I love you."

"I'm glad." She slanted him a sweet smile. "I love you too."

He stroked her hair, feeling the tension drain from her. She was asleep within minutes, and this time she didn't wake as he pulled away from her, though he silently willed her to open her eyes so he could look into them one last time. He picked up his clothes and left the cabin, the door closing behind him.

He dressed quickly and headed for his own room, where he pulled on his boots. His weapons belt lay on the table, but he'd hardly need that. Skylar would be waiting for him. He wasn't going to think about what was to come.

She was outside the shuttle having a conversation with

Rico, their heads close together. He paused, not wanting to interrupt them and waited for them to finish. Rico dragged her into his arms and kissed her. It took a considerable amount of time, and Jon was tapping his foot by the time Rico stepped back.

"You come back, you hear. I've given you a ring and that means it's forever."

"I'll be back." Skylar peered over his shoulder at Jon and nodded. "We need to go."

Jon straightened and head past Rico and into the shuttle. Rico put his hand on Jon's arm as he passed.

"I'm sorry it ended this way."

"Yeah, so am I." He hesitated then put out his hand. "Thanks again for coming back for me—it meant a lot."

"As it happens it was a total waste of fucking time." But Rico took his hand and held it for a moment. He let go then pulled the silver flask from his pocket and handed it to Jon. "Here's something to keep you company. Good luck."

Jon gripped the cool silver in his palm. "Yeah, like luck's going to help. Watch out for Alex."

"I will."

He strapped himself into the seat in the shuttle, rested his head against the back, and closed his eyes. He didn't think of what was to come. Instead, he captured that last image of Alex. He hoped she'd get over him fast.

Or maybe he didn't. Maybe he hoped she'd pine just a little.

Finally, he slept as the shuttle carried him back to Trakis Five and certain death.

CHAPTER NINETEEN

Alex slept like a contented baby and woke to the feeling that something was very wrong.

She tried to ignore the feeling. After all, Jon loved her. He'd told her so. She'd never really expected him to get over his fears to that extent, and she should be ecstatically happy.

They would get married, live happily ever after, and have lots of adorable little babies or puppies or whatever it was werewolves produced. If they produced anything.

She sat up in the empty bed, dragging the sheet up over her. Her skin was sensitive, and at the touch of the material, a shiver of remembered pleasure ran through her.

The first time he had made love to her had been sweet and wonderful, but the last time had been beyond anything she could have imagined. Full of raw, primal passion. Jon had made love to her as though she was the only woman in the world, and this would be the only time they had together.

She bit her lip and searched the room for some evidence that he was still around, but his clothes were gone from the floor.

That didn't mean anything. Maybe he was still in pain

and had gone to search out some more medication. Glancing at the clock, she realized she'd only been asleep for an hour. He couldn't be far away.

She showered and dressed quickly, eager to find him and dispel the nagging sense of impending disaster that hovered at the edges of her mind. She'd feel better once she saw him, touched him. At the door, she hesitated, then went back and fastened her weapons belt around her waist.

As she approached the bridge, she heard raised voices.

"Shit, Rico, you shouldn't have let them go," Tannis said, and the words deepened Alex's sense of unease.

"It wasn't my decision to make," Rico's voice was quieter, free of expression.

"That's never bothered you before," Tannis snapped.

Alex peered in through the open doorway, and everyone went quiet.

She quickly searched the room but could see no sign of Jon. Skylar was missing as well, though Janey and Daisy sat at the far side of the room. They both looked away when she tried to catch their attention, and dread twisted inside her.

"Where is he?" Alex forced the words out.

"Why not ask Rico?" Tannis said.

Alex stepped closer. Rico appeared pale beneath his olive skin. She licked her lips. "Where's Jon? What have you done with him?"

"Shit, why does everyone always blame me?" Rico shoved his hands in his pockets but didn't move away. He stood staring down at her, an expression in his eyes she'd never seen before. It took her a moment to identify it.

Pity.

She didn't want his pity. She wanted to know what was going on. A cold, hard lump of fear filled her stomach as she looked from Tannis to Rico.

"Tell her," Tannis said.

Rico shrugged. "He's given himself up to the Collective."

"What?"

"Skylar has taken him back to Trakis Five."

"Why?" Her legs trembled, and she reached behind her, found the edge of a chair, and sank down. "Why would she do that?"

"Because Jon asked her to. It was what he wanted—the only way he could see to save us."

"Save me, you mean, don't you? I don't want to be saved at this price."

"In a big part, yes. But not only you. Jon knew this was the only way any of us would survive."

Alex wanted to rage and scream that she didn't care about the rest of them, she only cared about Jon. But she knew she didn't really mean that. The crew of *El Cazador* had become the family she'd never had. She'd known once they accepted her, they would die for her. That was the way they worked. But she'd thought they had accepted Jon as well, and they'd let him go.

"He wanted you to live—that's why he did this."

"You shouldn't have let him. You should have stopped him."

For a moment, rage flashed across the vampire's face.

Something occurred to her. "What about Skylar?"

"The Collective will release her when this is over."

"You mean when Jon is dead?"

"*Dios*! Yes, when he's dead."

"And would you still have let them go if it meant losing Skylar?"

He gritted his teeth and turned half away from her. "No." The word was quietly spoken, but she heard it.

"I'm going after them," she said, jumping to her feet.

"And how do you plan to get down there?"

Alex bit her lip. She had no clue. All she knew was she couldn't sit here and let them kill Jon. She shifted her hand to the laser pistol at her belt, slid it from the holster, and pointed it at the vampire. He was half facing away, but at her movement, he turned. He looked from the gun in her hand to her face, his own expressionless.

"Take me back," she said.

"Yeah, you're a coldhearted killer, aren't you? You think you can look me in the eyes and pull that trigger?"

Her finger tightened.

"For God's sake, put the pistol away," Tannis snapped. "You can't kill him with that thing anyway. Unless you're planning to kill me, instead."

Despair swamped her at the words, but her hand fell to her side, and the laser crashed to the floor. "Take me back," she pleaded. "Drop me off on the surface and I'll find a way to get there. At least I could be with him. He won't be alone when—"

"What? Maybe they'll let you hold his hand while they blow his head off? Do you think that's what he wants?"

"Shut up, Rico," Tannis said. She turned to Alex. "Ignore him—he's just feeling guilty. He knows he made a mistake, and he can't stand being wrong."

"Yeah, I seem to be getting that a lot lately."

"I have to do something," Alex said. "I'm not being reckless this time, but really, I can't let this happen."

"We won't." Tannis sighed. "We're going in after them."

"And we'll all die," Rico countered, but the words held no conviction. "Just what her boyfriend wanted to avoid."

Tannis shrugged. "Then we die. I don't leave my crew behind. Okay, we need a plan."

Alex sat, hugging her knees to her chest, and let their arguing wash over her.

She wasn't miserable enough to admit that she would rather be dead than live without Jon, though it felt like that right now. But she knew people recovered from broken hearts. What she wouldn't recover from is giving up on him. Accepting his death as a tolerable price to pay for her continued survival.

She would have shot Rico, might even have shot Tannis, if she'd thought it would do some good. But she hadn't wanted to shoot them, and it really wouldn't have helped.

They would get out of this somehow; they had gotten out of bad situations before. But she knew she didn't believe that. Deep down she knew this was a suicide mission, and a flash of guilt shot through her.

If there had been a shuttle left, she would have stolen it and gone alone, but Hezrai had blown up the first one and she presumed Skylar and Jon must have taken the other.

Her head pounded while she searched her mind for a way she could help; she felt so useless. Then an idea occurred to her. Janey was standing with the others, but she came over when Alex beckoned.

"What is it?" Janey asked.

Five minutes later, Alex had explained what she needed from Janey.

Janey thought for a minute and nodded. "I think it will work. Let me sort out the details and I'll let you know before you leave."

There, it was done—for better or worse. Alex just hoped she wouldn't live to regret it. Though things could hardly get worse than they were right now; she had a feeling she was taking them all to their deaths.

Tannis was still talking with Rico, but she looked up, caught Alex's gaze and strolled over. "We're not doing this for you, so you can stop wallowing in self-pity. We'd do it for any member of the crew."

Alex heard the truth in the words, and her despair lifted a little.

"We don't have a shuttle," Tannis said. "So the *Cazador*

will have to take us in. Daisy will stay on board—she can fly her if we don't make it back. And Janey will stay as well—"

"I can help," Janey said.

"No, you can't. You're a crap fighter anyway, and your leg's still giving you trouble. Besides, it takes at least three people to run *El Cazador*. So that's you, Daisy, and—"

"I'm coming with you," Alex said.

"I know you are. I was going to say the Trog. That leaves me, Rico, and you to go in and presumably Skylar will fight on our side."

"She'll fight with us," Rico said.

"Good. Right, this is going to be—what is it you say, Rico—a piece of cake."

"Where is it we're going again? Corps headquarters? Yeah, piece of cake probably covers it." Rico grinned. His earlier temper appeared to have vanished. "Let's go get some really big guns."

"Good idea," Tannis replied. "Blasters. I definitely believe we need blasters for this job."

Alex glanced from one to the other—they were crazy. Rico caught her gaze and raised an eyebrow. "Yeah, I bet Alex's never shot a blaster before. And I reckon we've got a couple of hours before we touch down to teach her."

CHAPTER TWENTY

"I'm sorry I killed your uncle."

Skylar frowned. "What? I was listening . . ." She waved a hand in the general direction of the air, and he realized she must have been tuning in to other Collective members in her head. He wasn't sure he liked the idea.

His pack had shared an almost telepathic bond, and occasionally he'd found it binding. One of the reasons he'd liked to get off planet.

"I said I was sorry I killed your uncle."

"Don't be. Aiden wasn't really my uncle, and he was an asshole."

"Yeah, I know. I had to research him—he was a complete dick. I can't say I felt bad about killing him."

"Did you ever feel bad about killing anyone?"

"Nah. I only accepted jobs killing dicks. Believe me, there are plenty of those around. Enough to keep me in business, anyway."

He'd killed a lot of people, but most of the time he reckoned he'd been doing the world a service. Still, he was probably only getting what he deserved. As far as he was concerned, religion was a load of crap, but he'd always believed there was some form of balance in the universe. You reaped what you sowed, in the end. The thought of religion brought Alex to his mind. He'd been trying his best not to think about her.

Christ, he was in danger of getting maudlin again. He took a gulp from the flask. "So, is there much chatter going on in the internal airwaves?"

Her brows drew together. "No, not a lot. Which probably means they've been ordered to shut down."

"Does that mean they're keeping something from you? Is this going to be a problem?" Rico would curse his dead body if anything happened to Skylar.

"Maybe. I honestly don't know, but I'm pretty sure they won't harm me."

A squadron of Corps had met them as soon as the shuttle touched down. They'd checked him over for weapons but hadn't bothered with Skylar, and she still wore the laser pistol strapped to her waist. Now they'd been left to wait in what appeared to be an interrogation room. But it was large and airy, and he could see the pale blue sky out of the window. Not a bad place to die.

The room held a central table with two metal chairs on either side, and he and Skylar sat together on one side. He was trying to stay cool, but this was taking too long.

He jumped to his feet, too restless to sit any longer, and crossed to the window. It looked out on a concrete courtyard, and the big double set of gates they'd come through earlier. A couple of guards stood to attention, but nothing moved, and he turned back to Skylar. Part of him wished somebody would come and get this over with. But only part of him.

"Where the hell are they?" he asked.

"They'll be here. The colonel wants to do the link with me himself."

"Who is this colonel guy?"

"My commanding officer. Not a big fan of mine at the moment, but he—" She broke off, a frown forming on her face as she listened to the comm unit in her ear. "That was the *Cazador.*"

"Why would they comm you now?" Shock formed a cold lump in his middle as he scrambled for an explanation. "What's gone wrong? Has Alex found out?"

"They're coming for you."

"Who's coming for me?"

"Rico." She bit her lip. "And the captain. Daisy just dropped them off."

His brain whirled with a mass of contradicting thoughts. A rush of hope, followed by a flash of fury. It was a suicide mission. They were right in the middle of Corps headquarters; what did the crazy idiots think they could do?

Skylar was drumming her fingers on the tabletop, but otherwise she didn't appear particularly bothered. In fact . . .

"You look pleased," he accused.

"Rico's doing the right thing. He was going to be guilty as hell over this when he thought it through, and he would have been hell to live with."

"Yeah, and this way he'll be dead, they both will—and you won't be living with him at all."

"Maybe." She shrugged. "Probably."

He threw his hands in the air and stalked away to glare out of the window. Why the hell couldn't the bloody vampire mind his own goddamn business? This was Jon's decision. He'd accepted it. Hell, Rico probably couldn't face the idea of someone getting more of the glory than him. Even if that someone was dead.

He rested his forehead against the cool glass. There was only one good thing about this whole mess. "At least Alex will be safe on *El Cazador,*" he said. "I hope Daisy has orders to get the hell out of here."

"Alex is with them."

At her quietly spoken words, he spun around. She was still seated but watching him warily. His brain refused to make sense of her words.

"What do you mean she's with them?"

"Alex is with Rico and Tannis—she wouldn't stay behind. She wanted to come."

"What the hell has that got to do with anything? They could have tied her up, drugged her . . ." He paced the floor as his panic mounted. "You have to get out of here. Now. Stop them."

"I can't. There's no way I'll be allowed to leave until the link is done."

Jon slammed his fist into the metal table as a wave of hopelessness washed over him. It was going to happen again. He'd be unable to save her, and she would die. They all would. Not if he could help it.

"Jon?"

"What?"

"It's too late anyway. The colonel is here."

It took a moment for her words to make sense. Then he concentrated and heard the sound of booted feet on the corridor outside. Maybe if this was over with fast, Skylar could get away and stop them before they reached the compound.

"Will this colonel be able to pick up that the others are coming?"

"Only if he asks specifically. There's too much going on in a mind, especially down deep. You can't pick up everything."

"Okay. Well, just do this quick."

He sat in the chair and tried to keep his panic from showing too clearly, but sweat was breaking out on his forehead and a tremor shook his hands where they rested on his thighs.

Christ, his life had taken some strange turns, but his

death was turning out to be far stranger. Sitting here, willing them to come along and kill him. Terrified his executioner wouldn't get here fast enough. But beneath the terror was a burgeoning exhilaration. He'd been trying not to think about it—because it only made what he was doing harder—but he'd known they would come after him if they discovered what he'd done. And not just Alex, but Tannis and Janey and Daisy, even the Trog. Because he was one of them. He belonged; he was part of something. He pressed his fingertips to his eyes. Why now, when it was too late?

The door opened, and a man stepped inside. Jon caught a glimpse of two guards taking up position outside the door before it closed behind him. The colonel wore the same uniform as Skylar—a plain black jumpsuit with the insignia of the Corps at his breast. He appeared more boy than man with a pale, unlined face, but when Jon peered into his eyes, he saw the years reflected in their violet depths.

Skylar rose and stood to attention; Jon guessed the action was instinctive. He stayed where he was and kept his lips clamped together to stop anything stupid from escaping, but the colonel ignored him anyway and concentrated on Skylar.

"Lieutenant."

"Sir."

"Are you ready?"

She nodded. The colonel moved to stand in front of her only inches away, his right hand resting on her shoulder. Both of them closed their eyes. It seemed like an age to Jon, but it was probably only a few seconds, when the colonel blinked and took a step back.

He glanced toward Jon. "So Aiden Ross committed suicide?"

"Yes, sir." Skylar replied.

"But you don't know why?"

"No, sir."

He studied her for a moment longer, then nodded toward the door. "You're free to go."

Skylar shook her head. "I'll wait."

Jon wanted to tell her that he didn't need an audience for this. But in fact, the idea that there was a friend present at his death was strangely comforting. For a second he wished Alex were there to hold his hand.

The colonel shrugged and drew his laser pistol. Jon wondered whether he should stand up or remain seated. Was there an etiquette involved with your own execution? He decided to stay seated. It wasn't that his legs wouldn't hold him, but why risk it?

The pistol pointed straight at his chest now. But still the colonel didn't shoot. Jon wasn't afraid to die—not really— but this long, drawn-out process was giving him the jitters. Why couldn't the guy get on with it?

He caught a movement out of the corner of his eye. Skylar's hand moved to rest on her own pistol, her grip tightening.

He shook his head.

For a moment, he thought she would ignore his silent plea, but her hand dropped to her side, and she nodded once.

"Tell them thanks for trying," he said. "Tell them it meant a lot."

Skylar bit her lip, her shoulders tense. "I will."

Jon turned back to the colonel. "For fuck's sake, get on with it," he snarled. "I don't have all day."

Amusement glinted in the colonel's eyes, but instead of getting on with it, he lowered the pistol so it hung at his side. "You're obviously eager to die, but unfortunately, there's been a delay."

Jon had to stifle the urge to grab the laser pistol and shoot himself. The whole situation was turning into a farce.

How hard could it be to get someone to kill you? Even now, Alex might be poised outside, ready to storm the place and go down in a blaze of glory. Goddamn idiot!

"A delay? What sort of delay?"

Some unspoken communication passed between Skylar and the colonel. Her eyes widened, filling with a barely suppressed excitement.

"What's going on, Skylar?"

"Callum Meridian is coming. He wants to talk to you before . . ." She waved in the general direction of the colonel's laser.

"We do not have time for this," he ground out.

"But Callum Meridian . . ." Her tone rang with pure awe.

Actually, he'd be excited himself if it wasn't for the fact that he was on a strict timetable here. Callum Meridian was *the* founding member of the Collective. The one who had started it all. He'd crash-landed on Trakis Seven over five hundred years ago, somehow survived the radiation levels, and discovered Meridian. He was the first. The oldest. He was also a recluse and hadn't been seen in years. Now, he was coming to talk to Jon.

"Well, isn't this turning into a party?" he muttered. "But you know, we *really* don't have time for this."

She shrugged, opened her mouth to answer, when her gaze fixed over his left shoulder. Jon twisted around so he could see out of the window. Out in the courtyard the double gates were opening.

"They're here," Skylar said.

She drew her laser pistol and shot the colonel through the chest.

The speeder came to a halt in front of a set of double metal gates, black with the violet insignia of the Corps stamped on each. Alex wiped her hands down the side of her dress and adjusted the makeshift headdress. She'd lost the original when she'd handed herself over to Hezrai, but Tannis had improvised, ripping up one of Rico's black shirts and making a passable replacement. At least if you didn't look too closely. Her dress was also cut off at the knees where Jon had used it to bandage her cracked ribs, but she reckoned she looked close enough for the part she had to play.

Rico was in the driver's seat with Tannis beside him, and Alex sat in the back, gnawing on her lip while she waited for someone to come. If they failed to get inside the gates, the whole thing would be off. The place was impenetrable.

At last, the gates opened slightly, and two guards walked through. From the color of their eyes, it was obvious they were human not Collective, and she hoped they wouldn't have to kill them.

"Okay, you're on," Rico murmured. When she didn't move, he peered over his shoulder. "You can do this."

Alex wasn't sure about that, but she had to try. She fumbled with the door, managed to release the lock, and almost fell out of the vehicle. She straightened the headdress and forced her face into her best high priestess expression, and addressed the first of the guards.

"I am the Lady Alexia, High Priestess of the Church of Everlasting Life."

"Really?"

The guard examined her, his gaze running over her tattered robes. He didn't appear impressed, and she hurried on. "I apologize for my appearance, but the last few days have been difficult, and there was no time to change. I must see your colonel."

"Identification?"

"I don't have any—it was taken from me, but you can check the database. I've been missing—the Church has been looking for me."

"Step forward."

She moved closer as he flipped on a palm scanner and passed it in front of her face. He read the screen and turned to the other guard. "She's telling the truth. There's a flag attached to the file—missing presumed kidnapped. So why do you need to see the colonel?"

"I have information regarding the assassination of Aiden Ross."

"You do?"

He sounded skeptical, and she nodded. "I think the men who kidnapped me were responsible. These kind people"— she waved a hand at Rico and Tannis, who still sat in the speeder—"saved me from a fate worse than death and brought me here."

The guard looked from her to the vehicle where Rico and Tannis were both doing their best to look like "kind" people. It couldn't have been easy for them.

After what seemed like a lifetime, the guard nodded. "Drive through; wait at the gate while we contact the colonel."

Alex released her breath. They were in. "Thank you."

She climbed back into the speeder, collapsed on the backseat, and gripped her hands together to stop the shaking.

"You did well," Rico said quietly as the gates opened.

They followed the guards into the compound. One of them turned and held up a hand for them to halt, and the speeder pulled up beside him. They were in a large open area, surrounded by two-story buildings built of sandy-colored stone. There was no one else in sight, and she searched the doorways for some sign of Jon or Skylar, willing them to miraculously appear.

"Wait here." The guard headed off across the compound and disappeared inside one of the buildings.

Rico and Tannis climbed out of the speeder. Alex was

halfway out when Rico moved. He flew through the air and crashed into the remaining guard, gripping his throat. A second later and the man collapsed on the ground.

Alex stared at the body then at Rico. It had been so fast.

"Don't look at me like that," Rico snarled. "He's only unconscious. Though now is not the time to be squeamish. I have a feeling there are going to be a few casualties before the day is over."

Alex didn't answer, just stepped down. Tannis had returned to the vehicle and was pulling the weapons belts from under the seat. She handed one to Rico and a second to Alex. She strapped it around her waist, the heavy weight of the blaster dragging her down. Not for the first time, the enormity of what she was doing hit her. While she'd been concentrating on the idea of saving Jon, she hadn't thought about the people who might die achieving her goal. Or more likely not achieving it. Even if they failed, people were going to die.

For as long as she could remember, she'd had doubts about her faith. But she knew what was right and wrong, and she'd always believed that killing was wrong.

But maybe people had to have someone they were willing to die for. And kill for.

Rico dragged the body of the guard behind the speeder and stood, surveying the courtyard. "Come on, let's start looking. This place will be crawling with Corps any second."

But at that moment, Skylar appeared in one of the open doorways. She was alone, and Alex's heart stopped beating. Then Jon's tall figure appeared behind her, and Alex swayed as relief washed over her.

As he stepped out into the open, she ran toward him, skidding to a halt only inches away. For a second, she just stared at him, then she clenched her fist and punched him as hard as she could on the nose. It hurt a lot. Her, at least. Jon didn't even flinch. "What the hell did you think you were doing?" she asked.

"Protecting you."

"I don't want protecting."

"Then you should never have told me you loved me."

"You told me first."

He shook his head. "I wish you hadn't come."

She reached up and stroked his cheek. "It's a two-way deal, this protection thing, and I couldn't let you die without trying to save you."

Jon lowered his head and kissed her fleetingly. "I still wish you hadn't." He stepped back and turned to Rico. "I'd made my decision. You had no right to come here."

Rico shrugged. "It wasn't my choice. And perhaps we could argue about it later. Right now, we need to get out of here."

"Too late," Skylar said. "Get back inside."

Men were spilling out from the door opposite. Men in the black uniforms of the Corps. Jon put his arm around Alex's shoulder and hustled her inside the building and into a large room. Three men lay unconscious on the floor.

"Good to see you've been busy," Rico said.

Jon crossed the room, stooped over one of the bodies, and pulled the laser pistol from the holster. He studied the room, a frown on his face, then crossed to the table and kicked it over so it lay on its side against the wall.

"Get behind that," he said to Alex, "and don't come out."

Alex opened her mouth to argue but bit back the words. She knew enough about him by now to know he would fight much better if he thought she was safe. And he was a far more valuable fighter than she was.

The first shots bounced off the walls as she crouched down behind the table. She drew her blaster but was scared of hitting the others who were ranged in a row in front of her. Focusing on Jon's back, she pushed down her fear and guilt. Why had she let him out of her sight earlier? She should have held on to him. They would likely still have all died, but not like this, in a strange place. She wanted to be back on *El Cazador* so badly it was a pain gnawing at her chest. Out of a window to her left, she could see the courtyard crawling with soldiers, all heading in their direction. This was the end.

In the months since she'd been on the ship, they had come under attack many times, and she'd never experienced fear. Now she was drowning in terror; it coated her mouth and throat, froze her mind, and turned her arms and legs to useless slabs of stone.

She didn't know how long the fight went on—time lost meaning as the world was reduced to chaos. Jon stood shoulder to shoulder with Tannis, Rico beside Skylar. They were shooting steadily, deflecting the incoming blasts with ease, and shooting down the soldiers as they appeared in the narrow entrance. But every time a man went down, another took his place.

"Brace yourselves," Tannis shouted. She plucked a gas grenade from her belt and rolled it out through the doorway. Alex gripped onto one of the table legs and a second later, the shock wave washed over her. There was a moment of respite, as the men retreated from the dense cloud of sickly green gas.

Jon turned to her.

"You okay?"

She nodded, though it was a lie.

"I love you," he said.

"I—" There was no chance to finish the words. The window exploded, raining shards of glass into the room.

She shook her head, clearing her vision, as a shot from behind spun the weapon out of Jon's hand. A figure stood framed in the window, pistol outstretched, aimed at Jon's exposed back. Alex didn't think, just acted on impulse, pushing herself up then diving forward.

The world seemed to slow. From the corner of her eye, she could see Jon twist around, screaming at her.

"No!"

His urgent cry sounded in her ears but too late. Her momentum carried her onward. She raised her blaster, knowing there was no time. An arc of bright light blinded her as an agonizing pain blossomed in her chest. Strong arms wrapped around her as she fell. And then darkness.

Jon collapsed to his knees, Alex's limp body held tight against his chest. Frantic, he searched her face; her eyes were closed, but a slight pulse fluttered beneath the pale skin of her throat. The blast had hit her in the side, and the scent of scorched flesh rose from her body. But she wasn't dead.

Yet.

A tortured howl rose up inside him as his wolf awoke and screamed in denial. Jon had done everything he could, given himself up, and this time he thought he'd succeeded, that he'd saved her.

But even as the doubts flashed through his mind, he forced them aside. He'd been ready to die, but his friends hadn't been ready to let him—Alex hadn't been ready to let him. They believed in him, and that changed everything.

Maybe they would all die here, but it wouldn't be because he had given up.

The gas from the stun grenade was dispersing and through the thinning cloud, he could see the soldiers massing outside. Tannis shot a brief glance in his direction, her expression worried as she took in Alex's small figure clasped in his arms. "They're coming back."

Jon nodded. He lowered Alex gently to the floor and tucked her behind the relative safety of the metal table, her back against the wall. Working quickly, he tugged the scorched material away from the wound, and his gut clenched up tight.

He knew then that she was beyond any medical help. There was only one thing that might save her now. His mind veered away from the option, but inside his wolf growled in approval.

Alex's eyes blinked open, dull with pain. "I'm sorry," she whispered.

"There's nothing to be sorry for," he said, his tone fierce. "We're getting out of here. All of us. Just don't give up."

A brief smile flickered across her lips. "My hero. You'll save me, you always do. But whatever happens, I'm glad we came for you."

He opened his mouth to answer, but Tannis called out a warning from behind, and he pivoted at the urgency in her voice.

"Shit."

Where was his gun?

He'd lost his pistol just before Alex was hit, and he searched the floor as the first laser shots blazed through into the room. Rico, Skylar, and Tannis stood in a row, returning fire, but there were too many crowding into the open doorway. This time, as soon as one was cut down, two more took his place.

One man took aim at Jon, and without thinking, he hurled himself across the room, his arm shifting as he flew. The man went down beneath the force of the impact, and Jon ripped his clawed hand across his neck, slicing open the jugular vein. Crimson splashed the walls behind them, and the heavy scent of blood mixed with the smell of charred flesh.

He grabbed the man's pistol from his limp fingers and whirled around as two more came at him from the side. He kicked one in the groin, slashing the second's throat out in one fluid move. They both collapsed at his feet, and he blasted them in the heads to make sure they wouldn't be getting up anytime soon. Adrenaline roared through his veins as he stared around, searching for more enemies.

"Get back, Jon."

Tannis spoke from behind him, and for a moment, the words made no sense. Then they filtered through the killing rage that gripped his mind. Shaking his head, he dived for cover as Tannis rolled another grenade out beyond the open doorway.

The blast shook the room and the thick gas drove their attackers back. They had some respite but he knew it would be fleeting.

"That's the last of the grenades," Tannis said, coughing, and holding her hand over her nose as the gas drifted into the room. She cast a glance at Alex, who lay where he'd left her, her hand gripped to her side, face pale, eyes closed. "How is she?"

He shook his head. Alex was dying, but he wasn't about to let that happen. Inside, his wolf clawed at his brain, howling to be free; he'd recognized Alex as his mate and would fight to the death to protect her. But they couldn't fight their way out of this; they were up against too many—next time they would be overrun, and that would be the end.

Somehow, he needed to convince their attackers that killing them wasn't a good idea.

This whole thing had been set in motion, at least partly, because the Collective believed Jon had information they didn't want released into the world. Could he use that information to save them now?

Positioning himself to the side of the window, he peered out. He had an idea, but unless he could make them listen, he wasn't going to get anywhere. Out in the courtyard, a mass of armed men filled the area, but his gaze settled on a tall, cloaked figure, standing perfectly still and alone in the shadows of the building opposite.

Callum Meridian.

"Skylar?"

"What?" She looked up from where Rico was examining a blaster burn on her left arm.

"Callum Meridian is here."

"I know."

"Can you get him to talk to us?"

"Why?"

"I want to make him an offer."

"Ballsy," Rico said. "I like it. What are you going to offer him?"

"I haven't worked that out yet. But get him here."

"I'll try." Skylar closed her eyes for a second, and across the courtyard the cloaked figure glanced up to the window, then headed in their direction, the men parting around him.

Jon crouched down beside Alex and touched her lightly on the cheek. "Just hold on a little while longer."

Her eyes fluttered open. "Jon, there's something I need to tell you. Something I did."

"Later, there will be time later."

"But I . . . oh." Her gazed fixed over his shoulder, and he straightened and turned. Callum Meridian stood in the doorway, easily recognizable with his lean face and short, dark hair. He was tall, though his body looked strangely bulky beneath the long, dark cloak. As he stepped over the bodies into the room, no words were spoken, but the soldiers at his back melted away. The door closed behind him, and the air crackled and thrummed with power.

His gaze swept the room, his lips pursed as he scrutinized each of them in turn. "Can someone tell me"—he spoke softly, his tone almost gentle—"how the hell does one shipload of fucking misfits give me so much goddamn trouble?"

Jon started at the words. They weren't what he'd been expecting, though he had no real clue what that was; some pompous denouncement for killing Ross, perhaps? It threw him off balance, and he struggled to pull his thoughts together.

"Hey," Rico said, "I'd watch who you were calling a misfit if I were you."

Callum ignored the comment. "Today, I've had to sit through an extremely boring meeting where you lot"—he waved around the room, encompassing them all—"were the main topic of conversation. My council wants you dead, and to be honest, I think they've got a point. I've had enough of you all."

"Well, feel free to piss off," Rico drawled. " After all, this whole pile of crap is hardly our fault."

"Maybe not, but it is hers." Callum waved a hand in Skylar's direction.

She'd hunkered down beside Alex, now she shot upright. "Sir?"

"You were given a simple job—hire a crew, break Aiden's killer out of prison, and allow us to shoot him in the process."

Skylar's lips tightened, her hands went to her hips. "Yeah well, it might have worked out that way if someone had informed me about that last bit." She sounded pissed.

"Any other ship and crew, and the mission would have gone as planned. Why choose this one?"

"They looked . . . interesting." Now she sounded defensive.

"Interesting?" Callum repeated the word as though he didn't quite believe it. He shook his head and turned his attention to Jon. "This has gone on long enough. You were never even supposed to get as far as prison. You were to die at the site of the assassination. Another fuckup. Well, it's over." He turned to Skylar. "You're free

to leave or stay but I'm giving the order to finish this now."

"I wouldn't do that if I were you," Jon said.

Callum swung back to face him. "Why?"

Jon stared into those glowing violet eyes and a shiver ran through him. No one really knew how Meridian worked. How it changed the human body, rendering it virtually indestructible. At least, if the Collective knew, they weren't telling. They had always claimed the change was a minor one, a mere matter of chemistry, but now, staring at the first and oldest of their kind, Jon sensed that the changes went far deeper.

He took a deep breath. How he did this would decide whether they all lived or all died. "I assassinated Aiden Ross, one of the 'indestructible' Collective. Except you're not indestructible, are you? And I'm the one person who knows how to kill you."

Callum raised one eyebrow. "But luckily for me, you don't have the means to do it right here."

"Maybe not. But if we don't all leave here safely, a comm will go out to the entire civilized universe telling them exactly how you can be killed. And I'm betting a man in your position has made a few enemies who would love that information."

Callum seemed unimpressed by the threat. He stepped closer, pulling the cloak tighter around him, and Jon had to fight the urge to back away. The intense violet eyes seemed to suck him in.

"You're lying," Callum murmured. "You have no comm set up. The information will die with you."

The words held such certainty that Jon knew it was over. How Callum was so sure, he didn't know. Maybe the man could read his thoughts. Whatever the reason—it was finished.

He moved closer to where Alex lay. Now he just wanted to go to her, hold her at the end.

As though she sensed his stare, she opened her eyes. "No, it won't."

For a moment, her words made no sense, and it took him a second to realize she was talking to Callum.

His gaze narrowed on her. "The Lady Alexia, I presume."

"Yes. And Jon might be lying, but I'm not." Alex's voice was thready with pain but filled with conviction. She licked her dry lips and this time she spoke to Jon. "If we don't get back, Janey will send out the information on an open wave."

"You told her?" Skylar's tone was incredulous as she turned to stare at Jon.

He felt a wild resurgence of hope inside him. When he'd given the disc to Alex, he'd thought it might one day help if the Church came after her again. After all, information was power, and it had been the only thing he'd had to offer her back then. Now, he crouched down beside her, and his hand cupped her cheek. "Did you know I love you?"

She turned her head slightly so she could kiss his palm. "Yes."

Callum studied them both. "How about I just blow your ship out of the sky and the information with it?"

Alex gave a weak smile. "Janey's not stupid. She said to tell you she's uploaded the file to an external link. Without a code sent from *El Cazador* every hour, the information *will* be released."

Callum shook his head. "This day just gets better and better."

As he turned away and paced the room, Jon's gaze ran down over his tall figure; there was something very wrong with the man; beneath the cloak he appeared misshapen, almost deformed.

Finally, he stopped in front of them. "I'm going to get shit from my council for this, but I'm guessing while they want you dead, they want this information released to the public even less." He glared at Skylar. "Did I mention this was all your fault?" He threw up his hands in disgust. "Just call your ship and get your misfit friends the hell out of my face."

Skylar opened her mouth to argue, obviously thought better of it, and opened her comm link instead. "Janey, come and get us."

Jon wouldn't allow himself to believe, not until they were safe on *El Cazador*. Impatience gnawed at him. He needed to get out of here. Somewhere he could shift. Now he'd accepted what he must do, he wanted it over with, but the enormity of what he planned struck him, and terror warred with hope. His palm rested over Alex's heart. She was clinging tenaciously to life, despite the horrific wounds, but she would need some strength if she were to survive. "How long?" he asked Skylar.

"Five minutes."

Too long. He bent down and picked Alex up in his arms, holding her close to his chest while he stared up at the sky out of the broken window, willing *El Cazador* to appear.

As he tried to curb his impatience, he realized there was still something he needed to know to make sense of all this. "Why did Ross commit suicide?" he asked.

At his question, everyone turned to look at Callum. For a moment, he remained silent, as if considering whether to answer. Then he shrugged. "Why not tell you? Soon it will be common knowledge. Ross came to the council a year ago, said he'd had enough, and wanted to die. We told him to get a grip and sent him away. I guess he decided to take things into his own hands, but at least he retained enough sense to make it look like an assassination rather than suicide."

The answer told Jon nothing. "But why? Why had he had enough? What had changed?"

Callum pursed his lips. "Aiden was a fool. He was also a coward—he couldn't come to terms with what we were becoming, so he chose the easy way out."

Skylar took a step toward him, her brows drawn together. "And just what are we becoming?"

A small smile curved the corners of his lips. His hand went to the fastening of the cloak, and it fell to the floor.

"Holy freaking moly," Tannis muttered.

"Madre de dios." Rico sounded equally awestruck.

Half of Jon's attention had been on the night sky beyond the window, now he turned back, and his mouth dropped open.

A huge set of wings sprouted from Callum Meridian's back. Black, leathery, the tips almost touching the walls on either side of him. He flexed them, and a sound like the wind filled the room.

"Jesus," Rico said and let out a short laugh. "Did you know you're the spitting image of the devil? Was Aiden Ross the same? I bet that scared the shit out of him."

A spark of answering amusement flashed in Callum's eyes. "He had them amputated, but each time, they grew right back."

"So where did they come from?"

Callum hesitated then shrugged again. "We might not have been entirely truthful about the nature of Meridian."

"And?" Rico prompted, the impatience clear in his voice.

"And it seems it's not an element after all but a living organism—one we had never seen before."

"Fuck me," Rico said. "You're a goddamn alien. You're turning into a real, honest-to-God, goddamn alien."

"Maybe. In part."

"Hmm, and I guess that makes you abominations, doesn't it?" Rico grinned. "Aiden Ross—staunch supporter of the Church—an abomination. Brilliant." He glanced toward Skylar. "Hey, are you going to grow a pair of those? That would be so damn hot."

Skylar appeared slightly alarmed at the idea. "Am I?"

"Probably," Callum replied. "In a few hundred years."

Jon turned back to the window, as a blaze of lights trailed across the night sky. "The *Cazador*'s here," he said, tightening his grip on Alex before heading for the door.

Rico followed him but paused as he passed Callum "You know, you don't seem particularly concerned about us leaving—why are you really letting us go?"

Callum shrugged. "While you might be a bunch of misfits, you've successfully managed to evade my entire army for over a week. Soon we'll reveal this"—he gestured to the huge wings, now folded neatly against his back—"to the world. And it occurred to me that at some point in the future, I might find it useful to have some friends in . . . low places."

"Well, feel free to call—our rates are very reasonable," Rico drawled.

"I will. Now piss off, before I change my mind."

"Good idea. Right, we're out of here. Tannis!"

Jon glanced back. Tannis stood rooted to the spot, gazing at Callum Meridian—her cold yellow eyes filled with wonder.

"Tannis, move. This is no time to get a crush." Rico grabbed her shoulder and hustled her through the door.

Outside in the courtyard, Jon gazed up at the star-filled sky as a shadow passed overhead. A minute later, *El Cazador* touched down gently.

"Hold on," he whispered to Alex.

Her eyes fluttered open. "I want to go home."

"I'm taking you home." He carried her up the ramp onto *El Cazador* and through the docking bay.

"Get her to the sick bay," Tannis said.

"It's too late for that." Instead, he headed toward the heart of the ship, and into the large conference room.

"You know what you have to do," Rico said.

"I know," he growled.

Many years ago, he'd been attacked by a werewolf and changed by force. That day, he'd sworn he would never do the same to another. Now, for the first time, he was about to try, and the thought terrified him. If only it wasn't Alex. But then it was only for Alex that he would do this. "I've never—"

"You'd rather I try and change her?" Rico asked.

Horror flashed through him. "God, no!"

"What are you two talking about?" Tannis asked.

"Nothing," Rico replied. "Come on, let's leave them."

"Why? What's going on? We need to try and save Alex."

"Jon will save her."

Jon heard the conviction in the vampire's voice, and his fear left him. He could do this.

"Go," he said. "And lock the doors."

He was only dimly aware of them leaving as he laid Alex gently on the floor.

After stripping off his clothes, he willed the change to come over him, shivering as energy enveloped him. A minute later, he stood on all fours. The scent of scorched flesh was much stronger now, and beneath that, he sensed the closeness of death. He padded toward her, his claws clicking on the metal floor. He leaned in close, then nuzzled the soft skin where her shoulder met her neck, licked her face.

Her small hands fluttered in the fur at his nape, and he drew back. Her eyes were open, filled with loss. "I don't want to leave you."

At her whispered words, the last of his doubts vanished.

He drew back his head and lunged, his teeth sinking into the warm flesh of her throat.

EPILOGUE

A month later . . .

They ran, weaving between the gnarled trunks of ancient trees, their feet making no sound on the soft forest floor. All her senses acute, her ears catching the small animals that scurried from their path, her nostrils scenting their warm flesh. Then they were out in the open, racing under a fat yellow moon, and she drew ahead, reveling in the stretch of muscle and sinew.

A sense of freedom filled her to overflowing, and she came to an abrupt halt, threw back her head, and howled to the heavens. Beside her, the huge dark wolf sat on his haunches, amber eyes laughing in the dim light. He nipped her on the shoulder then looked up at the skies. She followed his gaze, and high up, amid the stars, the lights of an approaching spaceship blazed a trail toward them.

Loss mixed with anticipation as she turned and loped after the dark wolf heading back to the clearing where they had left their clothes. Normally, they would shift back and make love out in the open air and afterward she would lie in Jon's arms, stare up at the stars, and wonder about all those places she had never been.

Tonight, she shifted back and pulled on her clothes.

El Cazador had dropped them off on Jon's home planet and told them they would be back in a month. The time had been magical, the happiest of her entire life, and if Jon wanted to stay, she would stay with him. They hadn't talked about the future, just lived in the present, but she knew he'd found peace here, had at last come to terms with his past. He'd even told her of his pack and she understood his fears. But she also knew that peace came from within, and some part of her would always yearn for the stars.

"What are you thinking?" he asked.

She fastened her weapons belt, crossed the clearing, and kissed his mouth. The now familiar heat welled up in her body, and she melted into him.

"That I love you and I'm just wondering if we've got time for a quickie."

He laughed and pulled her tight against him as the clearing lit up around them.

"Looks like that's a no," he murmured against her hair. He kissed her again, and for a minute, she forgot about the future.

"*Dios*, I hope you two have been using protection," a voice drawled from behind her, "because I'm not having my spaceship overrun with goddamn puppies."

Alex drew away and turned slowly to face the shuttle that had landed. Rico lounged in the open hatchway. Tannis appeared behind him and sauntered over. "The honeymoon's over," she said. "We've got a job, and we're on a schedule."

Alex looked at her closely. Beneath her deadpan exterior, Tannis was buzzing with excitement.

"What's the job?" Jon asked. "Legit?"

Rico grinned. "Hell no. At least I hope not."

"Dangerous?"

"Well, we've been employed to protect the most powerful man in the whole universe. I'm guessing there's danger involved."

"Callum Meridian?" Jon asked. "Protect him from what?"

"We don't know, and Tannis doesn't care. She's got a crush."

Tannis elbowed him in the gut.

"Hey, it's true, and she's in a hurry to get to him. So get on board before she flies away without you."

Alex waited for Jon to speak. To say it was too dangerous and they were staying. She held her breath.

Finally, he wrapped his arm around her shoulder. "Come on, let's go home." And he led her toward the waiting shuttle.

Alex hugged him tightly to her side as joy filled her soul. They were alive, Jon loved her, and they were heading back to *El Cazador* and the stars.

Maybe God didn't hate her after all.

ACKNOWLEDGMENTS

Thank you to Entangled Publishing for taking me on, and for my fabulous covers, which I love! And especially to my editor Liz for her wonderful enthusiasm, which always cheers my day, and her fantastic edits—always so easy (her words not mine!).

GIRLS' TRIP OUT

They surrounded her like a guard detail and Alex supposed that's what they were—bodyguards. Though what they were protecting her from, she wasn't sure. Rico maybe. In case he decided she was too much trouble after all. Except Rico was off hunting a vampire.

She peered around Daisy, who was taking point, hoping for a glimpse of Jon, but they met no one on the way to the docking bay. Skylar was already there, leaning against a speeder. Dressed in her usual black jumpsuit, she'd also pinched Rico's long leather coat and looked supercool. A brief glimpse underneath showed the coat had a practical use—Skylar was armed to the teeth. As well as her usual laser pistol, she also had a blaster tied down at her thigh.

She gave Alex a comprehensive stare as they came to a halt and then a quick nod of what Alex hoped was approval. "You'll do." Reaching out, she straightened the wig on her head. "Let's go."

Daisy jumped into the driver's seat. Alex climbed in beside her as Skylar and Janey got in the back. The speeder lifted into the air, hovered for a second, and then they were away.

Her dark depression was lifting. She was alive and she hadn't expected to be. Everyone might hate her now, though she didn't really believe that. It was probably more truthful to say they considered her a pain in the ass. She just had to make sure that she reined in her pain-in-the-ass tendencies in future.

And she was going shopping.

She'd never been shopping, not in her entire twenty-four years. Then something occurred to her. Something bad. "I don't have any money."

"I do," Skylar said from the seat behind her. "Tannis gave me your wages for the last three months."

Wages? She actually got paid? She'd sort of presumed she'd been working for her keep.

She was also on her way to Pleasure City, and that had been close to the top of her to-do list. She could already see the lights in the distance. The sun never rose on this side of Trakis Two, but the place was never truly dark because the city never slept. The Church considered Pleasure City as the seat of all evil and there had often been proposals to clear the place out—so far nothing had come of them.

She wanted to see everything—this might be her only chance. "Can we go to a brothel?"

Daisy cast her a sideways glance. "You want to get laid?"

"No!"

They all laughed at her emphatic answer.

"I'm guessing she'd like to get laid," Janey said. "But she's not hankering after anything she'll find in a brothel in Pleasure City."

"Shut up," she muttered and they laughed again. She was obviously totally transparent, and she'd thought she was such a good actress. "I just want to see everything."

"We'll see what we can," Skylar said. "But first we need to get you clothes. Any preferences?"

"Anything but black." She guessed she'd be back in black soon enough, but until then she would live it up.

They were coming into the city now, and passing other vehicles. She resisted the urge to sink into her seat, to hide herself from the danger of recognition.

Skylar leaned forward and touched her shoulder. "Any sign of trouble and you run."

"There won't be any trouble," Daisy said, patting her knee. "We'll look after you."

Skylar snorted. "I remember the last time I went out with you two. Daisy nearly gutted some poor guy—"

"Hey, he called me an abomination."

"And Janey got arrested for murder. So today, let's try and keep a low profile."

Soon there was so much to see that the worry faded to nothing; her senses were assaulted from every side. They'd slowed to a crawl as the volume of traffic increased, and Daisy was weaving between buildings now, buildings that flashed with neon lights. Music throbbed in the air, spilling from the open doorways of bars and clubs, and the scent of food, spicy and sweet, filled her nostrils.

"You can get every type of fast food ever invented in Pleasure City," Daisy said.

But Alex wasn't hungry. She was too excited to even think about food, almost bouncing in her seat.

Finally, they entered a narrow alley. Daisy lowered the speeder to the ground and switched off the engine. "Right, where first?"

They all climbed out. Up ahead, Alex could see the bright lights of the main thoroughfare. She blinked a couple of times and shook her head. It was so loud.

"This way," Skylar said. "Remember, any trouble and you run. We'll see you back here. If you can't make it back, find somewhere to hide and comm us." She reached into her pocket and pulled out a comm unit. "Arm."

She held out her wrist and Skylar strapped the unit in place. Then she headed off toward the bright lights and Alex followed. Daisy and Janey were behind her, no doubt watching for trouble, and she relaxed a little.

They passed windows where men and women lounged in various stages of undress. She stopped at one where a young man, around her age, relaxed back on scarlet cushions wearing nothing but a pair of black leather pants. He was pretty. And he smiled when he saw her watching.

"You sure you don't want to get laid?" Janey whispered in her ear, her voice laced with amusement.

But she shook her head and hurried on after Skylar. Daisy handed her some sort of food she didn't recognize. "Here, you can't not try this—it's the specialty—supposed to be an aphrodisiac."

She suspected the last thing she needed was an aphrodisiac, but she took the cone and nibbled as they walked. It was sort of sweet and sharp and melted in her mouth.

Finally Skylar stopped at a doorway and ushered them all in. The shop was small and crammed with clothes of every color. A man hurried over to serve them straight away.

"Can I help you?"

"Alex?" Skylar prompted.

She stepped forward; she had a good idea what she wanted. "Jumpsuits," she said. "Like hers." She waved a hand at Skylar. "But not black. I want pink and orange, maybe yellow and red. Anything but black. And boots with heels. High heels." She wanted to be taller.

Half an hour later, she stared at herself in the full-length mirror. "Holy shit."

"Quite right," Janey said. "You look hot."

She wore a pink—hot pink the sales assistant had called it—jumpsuit that was skintight. She still looked small, but perfectly proportioned. Turning to the side, she admired the thrust of her full breasts, then fiddled with the fastener, lowering it to reveal more than a hint of cleavage.

The boots made her legs look long though she wasn't sure how successful she was going to be if she had to do that running.

At least there was no way anyone was going to identify her as a priestess in this outfit. She looked absolutely nothing like a priestess. A grin tugged at her mouth. How could Jon resist her?

Janey carried an armful of bags containing the rest of their purchases.

"Okay," Skylar said, "we have time for one quick sightseeing trip."

"Let's go get Alex a pinkie."

She knew that pinkies were the recreational drugs available in all the bars throughout the system. And trying pinkies was on her list along with visiting a bar. She would get to cross off two things in one go. She nodded.

They kept in a tight-knit group as they made their way along the main street, Alex doing her best to take in all the sights around her. Suddenly, she came to an abrupt halt. Daisy banged into her from behind, but Alex was too busy staring up at the wall head. It took up the whole of one side of a three-story building.

Her.

Well, Alexia, the High Priestess of the Church of Everlasting Life. In her long black robes, her face pale against the black, her expression serene. REWARD. The word flashed up beneath the picture and she gasped at the amount. Hezrai really wanted her back. She hadn't thought he cared.

Ahead, Skylar had stopped. She peered over her shoulder, then followed the line of Alex's gaze and stared up at the wall. Her lips pursed, then she grinned. "You sure don't look like a priestess, kid."

Alex dragged her gaze away and peered down at herself.

The blond hair curled against the pink of her jumpsuit. No, there was nothing of the priestess.

At that moment, a door to her left was flung open from inside, disgorging a group of men. They stumbled onto the street, one of them barging into Alex, and she stumbled. He grabbed her, holding her upright, then smiled into her face. "Hey, gorgeous, don't I know you?"

"No." But without conscious thought, her eyes flicked to the poster, then away again. Skylar gave a little shake of her head. *Keep cool. Don't panic.* She took a deep breath and tried to pull away.

The man's grip tightened, his fingers digging into her arm, and she felt the first stirrings of panic.

"How about I get to know you?" His gaze dropped, lingering on her breasts.

"Let her go, asshole." Daisy spoke from behind them and he glanced around.

"Well, if it isn't an abomination?" he sneered.

Daisy went rigid. Janey came up beside her, her eyes narrowed. "Who the fuck are you calling an abomination, dick-brain?"

"Mind your own business, bitch."

"Are you calling my friend a bitch?" Daisy stepped forward and threw a punch at his nose. It crunched, he squealed, and the grip on Alex's arm loosened, so she could pull free.

"Shit," Skylar muttered. "Here we go again." She swept back the coat, revealing the firepower beneath, and for a second, the street went still. "Time to leave."

"Spoilsport," Daisy mumbled.

As Alex turned to go, someone grabbed her by the hair. For a second the grip held her immobile, then the wig slid free and she staggered forward. Her accoster stood, the blond wig dangling from his fingers, an expression of horror on his face. A hysterical giggle rose up inside her.

He looked from her, then slowly raised his head to stare at the poster behind her, and the urge to giggle vanished.

Skylar grabbed her arm, and she was running, weaving between the crowds, Janey and Daisy in front of them. They didn't stop until they reached the speeder, and Alex was breathing heavily. Skylar drew the blaster and stared into the alley behind them, but there was no one following.

"Well, that was fun," Janey said, tossing the shopping bags into the vehicle.

"Yeah," Skylar replied dryly. "It's always fun with you guys. Look, maybe we don't mention this back at the ship. Or you lot will be grounded for eternity."

"What they don't know can't hurt them." Janey agreed. "Captain's got enough on her mind."

Alex settled into the seat as the speeder lifted into the air. Her first shopping trip. And it was official. She was no longer Al the cabin boy. She was gorgeous!

FIRST SHIFT

"I now pronounce you man and wife." Tannis turned around to the audience. "Does this shit actually mean anything?"

"Back on Earth, it was legal for couples to be married by a ship's captain," Rico said. "That's you."

She shrugged. "I guess so. I can't see that it makes a difference, but congratulations."

"And you may kiss the bride," Rico added.

Jon lowered his head and kissed her gently, as though she were some fragile little thing that might shatter if he was too rough. He hadn't done any more than kiss her gently since she'd come around, and he'd told her just what he'd done to save her life.

It was six days since they'd fled from Trakis Five. Six days since Jon had sunk his teeth into her throat. She'd lived and she was getting stronger, though she still felt weak. Jon had said that once she shifted, she'd be fully recovered. But so far she hadn't managed to drum up the courage. He'd said it would be different once they were out in the forest. Apparently, spaceships messed with werewolves' heads.

She was a werewolf. It didn't seem real.

No one had followed them from Trakis Five, and the captain reckoned they were safe for now, though Tannis had hardly been herself since they'd escaped. She seemed distracted. But Skylar, as security officer, had stated that they were going to lay low for a while after they had dropped her and Jon off. And after they'd gone through this weird little ceremony which Jon had come up with after talking with Rico. Who'd have expected a vampire to be an expert on weddings?

Anyway, they were now in orbit around Jon's old planet.

Daisy came forward and hugged her . . . gently, then Janey. "You make a beautiful bride." Rico had suggested she wear white—it was traditional, but that was almost as bad as black. So she was in a scarlet dress, which Janey had somehow altered to fit her. It left her shoulders bare, skimmed her body and the ground, and clashed beautifully with her hair.

Jon was in black though, but he looked good in it. With his dark hair pulled back into a ponytail and a smile on his gorgeous lips, he actually looked . . . happy.

"Look after him," Rico said as he kissed her cheek.

"I will."

He poured drinks and she leaned against Jon's side, sipping whiskey as Daisy took the ship down. In the docking bay, Jon hefted a rucksack with a few supplies and a change of clothing onto his back and they headed down the ramp. Jon wrapped her smaller hand in his and pulled her close.

"Aw, isn't that sweet," Rico said.

"Fuck off," Jon growled. But he sounded positively mellow.

"We'll see you in a month," Tannis said. "Don't do anything I wouldn't do."

They watched as the ship took off, staring up into the sky until she disappeared, merging with the stars. Then Alex looked around her. They were in a clearing in a forest, huge trees all around them. It was nighttime, a sickle moon hung in the sky, and stars twinkled over the vastness of space. A light wind rustled the leaves and she lifted her head and breathed in deeply. The air was heavy with the scent of growing things and something alien stirred to life inside her. Waking and stretching.

Jon turned to her as though he sensed the change. "You ready?"

Was she? She was a goddamn werewolf. What would the Church think of their priestess now? What did God think of her? Though really why should she care? God hadn't saved her back there on Trakis Five. Jon had.

She nodded.

"Good." Reaching out, he loosened the ties at the shoulders of her dress, and it dropped to the ground, pooling around her feet like blood. Though the air was warm, she shivered as Jon stepped back and stripped off his own clothes. Her breath caught at the sight of him and she trembled. He wasn't aroused, but as she stared, his cock twitched and pulsed.

"Later," he murmured.

"Promise."

"I promise."

The thing inside her growled and raked a claw down her insides. "Ouch."

"It's time," he said.

Her skin prickled with energy, tremors rippled up her spine, and fear flickered inside her. Her skin was burning, shooting pains jabbed at her muscles.

"Relax," Jon said. "It only hurts if you fight it. Trust me."

And she did. Suddenly the night throbbed with magic.

Alex relaxed, and the fear receded as she gave herself up to the enchantment, and the change flowed over her.

The world was altered. Twisting her head, she stared at the rich dark red fur that covered her back. She lifted each paw in turn, placing it down with exaggerated care, digging her sharp claws into the soft earth.

The weakness that had afflicted her had vanished. She felt vital, alive, everything sharply defined. Her ears swiveled to pick up the sound of the wind in the treetops above her, and somewhere far off a bird hooted. She opened her mouth and tasted the damp air on her tongue. The scents of the night filled her nostrils, the rich soil, leaf mold, the musky aroma of wolf.

Jon!

He stood close by, watching her from his dark wolf's eyes, his plumed tail waving. He stepped toward her, his muzzle touched hers lightly, then he yipped once, whirled around, and headed into the trees.

She ran through the dark forest, the pads of her paws making no sound on the soft, leaf-littered floor. Effortlessly, she weaved her way between the trees, following where he led. As the trees thinned, she picked up speed, running ever faster, until she was aware of nothing but the wind flowing past her. All her tension, the weakness that had plagued her for so long, fell away beneath the relentless stretch and release of muscle and sinew. A wild exhilaration filled her.

She ran until she was exhausted and then stood, head hanging down, breathing deeply, feeling each breath, the hot blood flowing through her veins. She sensed Jon come up beside her. He nudged her with his nose, and she followed him to a small overhang. Collapsing to the sandy ground, she rested her head on his soft silky fur and closed her eyes.

When she awoke, she was back in human form, lying on the cool sand with Jon's hot body wrapped around her. She could feel the hardness of his erection pressing against her ass and she wriggled.

He had promised.

She pressed back against him, wriggled again just to make her intentions clear.

One big hand cupped her breast as the other slid between her thighs. He kissed the sensitive skin at the back of her neck and she shivered.

"Are you okay?" he asked.

"Yes." She was better than okay, but she couldn't find the words to tell him, so she rolled over, took his face between her hands and placed her lips to his, putting everything she felt into the kiss.

"Just in case I forget to tell you . . ."

He nuzzled her neck, then pressed her down onto her back and came up over her. "Hmm?" he asked. "Tell me what?"

Then he filled her with one hard lunge of his hips and her breath left her on a sigh. She lay for a moment, as her body adjusted to the size of him, the fullness, then she bucked her hips to show she was ready for more.

"That I love being a werewolf," she said.